THE QUEST BEGINS

A woman stood before him, a faint glitter of blue light around her sad face. She extended a hand and he saw that there were tiny webs at the base of the fingers and that the nails were long and clawlike. Then she fixed him with an unwinking gaze.

"Now I will tell you a tale, Dylan d'Avebury. You know of the great swords?"

"I know of the Fire Sword."

That is one, yes. There are others. The one you seek is quite different. Go to Franconia and find the Sword of Earth. Bring it forth from darkness, and the maiden who holds it. Find your life, Dylan."

THE CRYSTAL SWORD

ADRIENNE MARTINE-BARNES

AVON
PUBLISHERS OF BARD, CAMELOT, DISCUS AND FLARE BOOKS

THE CRYSTAL SWORD is an original publication of Avon Books. This work has never before appeared in book form. This work is a novel. Any similarity to actual persons or events is purely coincidental.

AVON BOOKS
A division of
The Hearst Corporation
105 Madison Avenue
New York, New York 10016

Copyright © 1988 by Adrienne Martine-Barnes
Front cover illustration by Romas
Published by arrangement with the author
Library of Congress Catalog Card Number: 87-91622
ISBN: 0-380-75454-1

First Avon Books Printing: January 1988

Printed in the U.S.A.

K-R 10 9 8 7 6 5 4 3 2 1

This one, finally, is for Larry

ACKNOWLEDGMENTS

Some works are easy to write, others difficult. This was one of the latter, and I could not have managed the task without the help of several people. My extremely able and patient amanuensis, Linda VonBraskat-Crowe, who not only types my words from crabbed hand to professional manuscript but puts up with the frustration of waiting days and weeks between chapters while my hapless characters dangle in awkward and uncomfortable situations, is a jewel—a large amethyst, perhaps—among women.

The helpful and thoughtful suggestions of the Every Other Thursday Writing and Dinner Club—Dorothy Heydt and Jennifer Tifft—made the work go easier. They gobbled up the pages with appropriate greed and laughed in all the right places. And, as always, I cannot overstate the aid and comfort of my husband, Larry, who puts up with a marriage that is always a work in progress.

ORPHIANA AND THE SMITH

In the time before time, when earth abided, yet man and God had not yet come to their terms of mutual entanglement, she who girdled the world with her sinuous and unending body, that ineffable elemental whom some call Orphiana, the Earth Serpent, had a lover who rejoiced in the making of objects. He was cunning, this early artificier, proud of his long, strong hands and sharp mind. And, as the gods began to arise from the bosom of the Creative, he conceived the notion of an object which seemed a perfect mirror of his own inner perfection, a great sword to echo that which hung between his limbs. Too, he had become envious of Orphiana's power; that she had no hands and was content, that she made nothing and yet ruled everything. And he saw that if he sharpened the edges of the thing he had in mind, it would cut through flesh and bone, even that of his mistress.

Long he labored over his forges, whispering words and making incantations over white-hot metal as his hammer fell, for he had learned much of his lady; sweating and struggling until at last he brought forward that which he had but glimpsed in his mind's eye. It was long and straight, beautiful with the spells he had woven into the very metal of it, filled with the power of the very fire he had forged it in. He stroked it, loving it as a man loves a woman, adoring the product of his mind as a man adores a god, and he brought it to his mistress, eager to gather her praises of his efforts. Orphiana looked at the sword, shifted her great body so that a small island chain in a yet un-named ocean exploded and sank under the waves, and scorned the thing for what it was: a poor, pitiful imitation of the life a man could give. He was wroth that she should abuse his great effort, and he swung the blade about his head and cut off her huge head so the skull flew through the air, and for a moment the whole earth stilled, so no bird sang, no insect hummed, no river ran. Then the skin of her long body sloughed away and rose up, wrapping itself around the bloody blade as her head returned to its accus-tomed place. The sword lay powerless in the smith's great hands and she said, "No man shall wield that *thing* with-out my leave," and returned to her task, so a new set of islands emerged from the green sea, the birds sang more loudly, the insects raced about their many errands, and the rivers rushed in their courses. Thus the Fire Sword came into the world of things.

Chagrined at his failure to overcome or even cow his mistress, the smith returned to his forges to ponder if the shape of the sword was to blame, and after a time he made another, not long and straight, but short and broad and flat as a great leaf. He bound it with spells of strength and brought it again to Orphiana. She glanced contemptuously at it with her glittering eyes and said nothing, until the silence reached into the void and even the stars paused in their endless song a moment. The smith clove the serpent's head in two with a single blow and her great body writhed. Mountains which almost touched the heavens vanished forever and cold seas boiled and bubbled. The varicolored skin of Orphiana fluttered in the still air and swallowed the leaf-shaped sword, and the broken skull was whole again. "Fool," she said. "You cannot slay me with myself, and you may not wield that without my will." And so the Crystal Sword passed into the world of being.

For eons the smith pondered these words, filled now

with no desire but to have mastery over his mistress, until he bethought to fashion a sword of light itself, shapeless, edgeless, and yet powerful. Long he labored over it, and this sword he did not present to Orphiana for her inspection, but crept up, while she meditated upon the patterns of the cosmos, and severed head from body, grasping the flat skull in one hand so it could not rejoin the rest. Winds rose and scoured the land, making deserts where none had been before. The head twisted in his hand and the great fangs sank into his wrist. The soft, pink mouth swallowed the unseen sword, until he found himself empty-handed, with Orphiana restored to herself entire, and the blade he had made now visible, a shimmery, wavy-edged object, like heat rising across the sands of a desert. And she said no words but swallowed the sword again, so it emerged wrapped in her gaudy hide halfway across the yet unpeopled globe. All the colors of the rainbow danced in its blade and across the great yellow diamond in its hilt.

The smith retreated, unbelieving yet that she could not be conquered by his art, for he had that fatal pride which afflicts all who make yet do not truly create, and set again to work. This blade was lightly curved like the bow on the newly-born moon upon the halcyon sea, and he filled it with the ebb and flow of the waters of the world. Its hilt he made of a great white stone snatched from the bosom of the oceans as they reflected the bright moon in her yet unsullied glory. Of all the objects he had made, this was the most beautiful, and he sang over it, drawing the light of the moon into it until her fair face was scarred and dark from his thievings.

Orphiana waited, watching the arising of the great and petty godlings who would claim her works for their own, touching a mountain here, a seacoast there, as an artist touches the almost completed canvas with light strokes, breathing at last the moment of life into still pigments. Soon those half-wild creatures called men would set their unshod feet upon her breast and time would begin. Like the smith, they would be tool makers, and they would hack her body with plows and spill their red blood into her with devices made in imitation of their forms. Like the smith, she regarded their activities as a source of amusement, something the Creative had made to while away the boredom of her task. She had awaited their coming and the beginning of time with the detachment of her kind, knowing that even as they destroyed her, so would they restore her again, and that until time ceased again, some would always raise their voices to praise the wonder of earth.

The smith came, cloaked in night, in that moment when Orphiana rested and drank from the mingled waters of the world, and he lifted the bright, curved blade and cut her in half. An ocean floor far across the globe plummeted down, down, down, sending startled fishes into inky darkness. The serpent turned her head slowly, gracefully, the sweet waters of her spring falling from her triangular head like drops of molten argent, and seemed to smile. The sword turned in his hands, arced, and descended upon his upturned face, splitting him in two. The mouth of his mistress gaped and swallowed him, then brought him forth as twins, one dark, one fair. The two faced each other, rivals, hating one another yet longing again to be one.

The spirit of the smith was not in either of his two halves who glared so sullenly at each other. It hovered in the sweet air of earth, fretting and gibbering, until even the endless patience of the Great Serpent was tried beyond endurance. Her huge eyes glittered and her tongue flickered in and out.

"So, you would have a sword still, my love," she crooned. She breathed and her lover's spirit was made flesh once more, unhumbled by his defeats. He sulked. "Let us see if we can forge that thing you are so proud of into something more substantial," she said calmly, and he watched in horror as unseen hammers struck his body, battering him into smoothness, warming his sinews in Orphiana's fire, smashing the new mind and body into a great sword. The smith screamed when at last the work was done, for now a great sword of wood hung between his limbs, the hilt standing out from his back, so he was impaled on his own vision.

Orphiana was not yet done in her work, for she had loved the smith with all her heart, and she had known betrayal at his hands. She sent him far to the north, where chill winds howled and the ice lay thick upon the ground from season to unnamed season. There, out of her great heart, grew a tree, an ash some say, with roots that reached to the core of the world. She hung the smith by his hair and drove the shaft of his ambition into the grey-green wood of the world tree, and left him there, between heaven and earth, to contemplate his deeds as his twin selves began their never-ending chase and rivalry.

Time began, and the smith finally saw the folly of his makings. He could not master himself and was condemned to always be the serpent's child, ever in her dominion, to pursue himself from pole to pole, until the end of all things.

I

Aenor hurried blindly along the twisted corridors, her sandaled toes stubbing themselves on small pebbles or smashing into unseen cavern walls. It was cool in the winding tunnels, but her body was warm from both her fear and her haste. Moisture covered her high brow and she could feel fine tendrils of her pale hair curling across it. She brushed a long, embroidered sleeve across her face and felt the metal in it make fine scratches on her skin.

The floor beneath her feet dipped downward, and she paused and frowned. She wanted to go up, up and out, into the warm light of day. Into the sun. She rolled the word in her mind for several seconds, savoring it, because it had cost her months to remember it, years perhaps. There was no time here in the caverns of the White Folk, just endless song and fair jewels that emerged from the cave walls, and the constant tinkle of tiny crystal bells which hung around their throats or lay upon their chests on baldrics. There was light, of a sort, where the Queen sang, a strange colored light that flickered from the walls and beamed from huge crystal lanterns hung from the ceiling, a strange pinkish light unlike the sun or even that other, silver light whose name she could not quite recall.

Aenor felt a hard knot of fury blossom in her bosom at her inability to remember. She balled her hand into a fist for a moment, then raised it to the huge jewel that hung around her throat. They had stolen her memories, made her helpless as a newborn, robbed her of speech for many years, but they had not been able to remove the gem from her neck. Several had perished trying. She felt a certain savage satisfaction in that. They had simply shriveled up and turned almost to dust.

Although she could not see it in the darkness, Aenor knew the smooth faces of the stone as well as the planes of her own visage. It was green as the eye of a salamander, green as the nameless things that grew beneath the golden sun of her memory. Her mind scrabbled vainly for words which seemed to hover just out of reach, and she kicked a wall in frustration, then bit back a howl of pain that would have brought discovery. They would find her eventually— they always did—but for the moment she preferred her blindness to the terrible light of their faces under the rosy gleam of crystal lamps. This corridor did not lead to escape, but she noticed an interesting smell, a spicy scent that meant one of the Rock Folk, the salamanders, had passed by not long before, and something else she could not identify. She liked the salamanders, particularly Fejool the Fool, who often crept into her bedchamber and thrust his soft nose against her hand. For a long time she had thought him a dumb brute, but now she heard his mind when she touched him. It was a curious mind, full of memory of the ways of rock, of long gone, terrible White Folk, famous spell singers and great web weavers, of strange wars in the endless dark or the pale light of the Queen's court, the ruddy forge-lit glow of the King's court. Fejool was her friend, her only friend in this miserable place, unless she counted the misshapen dwarf Letis who hung her gowns and smoothed her long hair. But Letis spoke only a sort of brutish gabble and lived in terror of the White Folk, while Fejool made strange jokes and played with words like bright baubles.

She began to follow the salamander scent and the other smell down the tunnel, groping carefully with outstretched hands and taking small steps lest she tumble into some invisible chasm. The jewel around her throat seemed to throb with heat and she paused to touch its usually cool surface. Surely it was warm, warmer than her skin.

The corridor ended in a smooth wall and she could smell the tantalizing unknown odor almost seeping from the rock. Aenor ran her fingers across the stone, seeking an opening, and finally found a faint crack, a straight line no wider than her smallest finger. She followed it up as far as she could reach, then found another crack descending two arm lengths across the rock.

Aenor traced the shape with her fingers and tried to think what it reminded her of. It was something almost familiar, like so much in her mind, and clouded by the chanting of the White Folk. Her mind seemed to be endless dark corridors with the song of her captors at every turn. If only she could find the right words! If only she could sing a clear tone and command the rock to open, like Margold Amethyst Singer.

Aenor almost laughed at the thought. Of all the White Folk, the spell singers were the greatest, greater even than the forge masters of the King's dark court, and she was nothing like them, a poor captive nobody who barely recalled the glowing orb of the sun and could not even name the wonderous green things which grew beneath it. Somehow she was not even sure such a light existed. It might be only a phantom of her dreams, like the fair but sad-faced lady garbed in green who often seemed about to speak but never did, or the big, dark man with hair around his mouth and one hand like silver.

She pressed her body against the smooth rock, her arms outstretched, and breathed the strange smell. It was tempting, like some delicious food, like those funny brown steaming lumps she sometimes dreamt of, rocky crust on the outside, grainy soft within. She could almost remember the flavor, and her mouth watered. The White Folk ate nothing like it.

One of the dark places of her mind was suddenly bright. She saw a wide open space all covered in square-cut stones. In the center was a rounded structure beneath small overlapping scaly things. A fat woman in a long brown dress padded across the space holding a flat object against one broad hip. She touched a bit of metal on one side of the structure and it swung outward. A cloud of steam billowed out as the woman wrapped a white cloth around her hand and reached within. She pulled out a rounded lump and put it on the flat tray. A thin wisp of vapor coiled up from it.

Words crowded into Aenor's mind, meaningless noises like Letis' babble. She clutched at the smooth rock and tried desperately to sort the sounds into sense. It was like grasping air. She moaned and muttered aloud.

"Bread, yard, oven, door. Door. Door!"

Aenor's breath was short and ragged as she repeated the word. She drew back from the rock and found that she could see just a little. The jewel around her throat cast a dim glow, and she could just make out the narrow cracks that ran from the floor to a point well above her head then down again. She peered at it, seeking a thing to open this door with.

A curious gem was set into the rock, flat against the smooth surface. She touched it lightly and a tingle ran up her arm. Within her mind she could "hear" the song which locked the door, an ancient song like one of the old lays the White Folk sometimes chanted to recall long-gone heroes or great singers of their past. It was a strong spell, and not as fair as most, as if it had a different purpose than others she had heard. Six notes—no, seven—chimed within her.

Aenor felt her jewel throb, as if it too heard the spell, and she found her hands were wet with moisture, her brow dripping. She wiped her face hastily and rubbed her palms against suddenly trembling thighs. She swallowed because her mouth was dry, and licked her lips uneasily.

In all her wanderings she had never found another door within the realm of the White Folk, and she knew that no fragrant bread-filled oven lay behind this one. Perhaps it held some fearsome monster. The chants spoke of several such: the dreadful worm which now roamed the broken paths of the abandoned Crystal City; the fire beast which had consumed King Alfgar the Witch, the only male spell singer in their history; and the monstrous stone bear that had ravished Queen Koriel and gotten upon her a fearsome brood. The White Folk bore no offspring from couplings with their own kind, yet mated fertilely with other races, or so they said. At least they claimed her as distant kin from some ancient lord who lay with a mortal woman. The salamander Fejool claimed it was the very same Alfgar who was eaten by the fire beast, but he had told her so many things she could hardly believe, that she was not sure if it was true.

Her gem seemed to hum, to press against her throat as if to compell her to voice the spell which held the smooth door closed. She wondered if the door might lead to the dreamed of world of sun or the courtyard where the bread was baked, where she might remember that other name she had once been called and walk upon the soft, green stuff that grew between the stones. A longing filled her, so her heart seemed to ache in her chest, and she croaked a single note from a dry throat, then shook her head.

For an instant she "saw" the spell like lines of gold in the darkness. They swam before her eyes, then plunged into the great green jewel around her throat and into the very flesh of her body. The ancient song rang in her bones, her blood; coursed along her muscles like a sudden fever. Aenor rolled the notes out of her mouth as if she had chanted them a thousand times before, like a dream made manifest.

The door swung open soundlessly, and she was both surprised and calm, as if she had simply relearned some long-forgotten skill. The curious smell which had so tantalized her swirled up into her nostrils, not bread or anything like it, but a cold, dead smell which carried memory with it. She saw a boy, an awkward, rawboned fellow with reddish hair and too much nose. He carried a long metal thing in his two hands and he swung it back and forth as he moved across a sunlit yard. Someone shouted, a deep-voiced man, and then he strode into view. He was big and square, fair haired and greying, scarred and rough.

"Arthur, you damn fool! That is no fairy wand you hold. It's a sword! Your sister could have killed you half a dozen times. I do not care if it is a practice weapon—behave as if it is real and your life depended on it." The big man bellowed the words and the boy grimaced as if he had heard it all before.

Aenor knew he had, and as the vision faded she looked around into the dimness and saw piles of swords and strange helms, battered shields and worn scabbards. The smell of rusting iron and rotting leather wafted past her as a red-eyed rat skittered across the fading emblazon of some long dead warrior.

Bitter disappointment filled her heart for a long moment. It was just an old armory full of discarded weapons of some ancient war of the White Folk. She picked up a helm idly, and realized how small it was. Surely it had never graced the noble head of any of the King's court or the Queen's guard. Nor would it have fit upon the huge heads of their dwarf slaves. Besides, the guardmen carried only long spears tipped with glassy barbs. Had some mortal men invaded the realm of the White Folk? If so, they sang no songs of it. With a start she realized she had never seen a sword during her endless days in the Queen's court. Tiny knifes sung out of jewels, yes, but nothing like these weapons nor anything fashioned of iron or leather.

The gem around her throat seemed to tug her into the armory. Aenor stepped past broken swords, their jagged edges catching the hem of her long, pleated gown. Something gleamed faintly in a heap of crumbling leather chest pieces, a bit of coppery metal like a tiny plate with two bands of color twisting beneath it. She reached for it and drew out a strangely formed blade.

It was barely as long as her arm, and its edges curved out from the point before they narrowed below the hand-grip. The metal seemed green in the pale light of her gem, and was unmarred by rust or decay. It was light in her hand, and she moved it back and forth, feeling her muscles recall old, forgotten motions as fragments of memory floated in her mind. She had handled other swords, heavier ones, and she could remember the feel of smooth stones beneath booted feet and the smell of fat-smeared ring mail mixed with sweat, the scent of animal droppings in a great house of beasts. They had soft noses and warm breaths, and hard bony feet. Their name eluded her.

There were other beasts too, things with swordlike bones growing from their foreheads; and once she had called them and they had come from the green places to bear her on their narrow backs. Aenor remembered how the air streamed across her face as she rode. Her eyes filled with moisture, then dried. The Queen had banished her tears along with hunger and thirst. She longed for release, but the spell was too strong.

Aenor studied the handgrip, examining the glassy inter-twining of blue and green across the metal. Like serpents, she decided, as she looked at the flat plate that ended the hilt. Four bits of metal stuck up like fangs and she thought there was something graven on the surface. She peered closely, and the gem around her throat flared. Her hands moved against their will, bringing the hilt end against the jewel.

She fumbled the braided cord which held the jewel over her head, and placed the stone into the barbs around the plate. It fit exactly, and she knew somehow that the two belonged together. The jewel filled the cavern with green light, and she lifted the sword to test the balance anew. Her fingers curled around the enamelled serpents; it felt like an extension of her arm. Her mind filled with a terrible light, and power seemed to surge into her. And, far away, someone's scream echoed through the caves and caverns.

II

The large blue fly buzzed and hummed and made another sortie on Dylan d'Avebury's broad brow. Dylan wrinkled his nose and made deep furrows on his forehead, but the fly refused to leave. It walked towards one of his heavy, dark eyebrows and he shook his head to dislodge it. The great cathedral was so crammed with the nobility of Albion come to see their wild Prince Geoffrey safely tied up in marriage bonds that he could not use his hands without jostling someone. They were squeezed together like grapes in a wine press.

His head throbbed at the sudden movement. There had been altogether too much wine the previous night, good, flinty Somerset wine, as he and Prince Geoffrey and several of their cronies had attempted to drown the Prince's sorrow over his approaching nuptials to the plump and pale Isabeau of Flanders. He could see the bride and groom kneeling before the Archbishop, and from the bent of Geoffrey's head, he too was suffering from a monstrous headache. Dylan should have asked his mother for some willow bark tea before the service.

As if she had heard his thought, Eleanor d'Avebury turned her head and looked at him. Her grey eyes crinkled a little at the corners, and her lips moved silently. The fly promptly departed as Dylan contained his shock. He was quite used to his mother's small magics—like the way she lit the hearth with a touch of her hand—but it seemed almost indecent somehow for her to use them in a church.

The cathedral was stifling in a sudden warm spell that covered the land in late April, as if nature herself rejoiced in Prince Geoffrey's wedding. Dylan knew Geoffrey well, since King Arthur had made Eleanor godmother to his firstborn, and they shared a natal day. Geoffrey was younger by two years, and seemed to have been born with a gift for mischief. He had spent many summers at Avebury, learning woodcraft and swordwork from Dylan's father, Doyle, and manners from Eleanor. He had also seduced, or tried to, every pretty maid in the district, and had fathered his first bastard at the tender age of fifteen, when his beard was still something a cat might lick off. He had even tried to tumble Dylan's three sisters, though not very hard. Dylan suspected that his sister Rowena might have been willing, if she had not known perfectly well that Geoffrey was notoriously inconstant. The royal wedding now being performed promised to be a perfectly miserable marriage, for the Prince had taken a great dislike to his bride-to-be, and only Arthur's pigheaded determination to have his son wed into a house that was both regal and advantageous had forced the situation. The Flems alone on the Continent were free of the terrible plague of Darkness that Arthur had driven out of Albion, and they were merchant partners as well. A Franconian Princess would have been better, but communication between the two nations was sparse and irregular. The Albionese ambassador, Giles de Cambridge, wrote nothing but letters begging for funds and filled with dreadful news concerning the state of Franconia. Dylan knew him vaguely from his tedious term as a page in Arthur's court, and considered him something of a fool. He felt glad that he was rather a nobody and that he would never have to deal with the alliances of nobles and Kings.

Dylan sighed. He was twenty, and his life stretched before him as unbroken tedium. Albion prospered under

Arthur, and he secretly longed for some adventure such as his mother had undertaken before his birth. The Fire Sword she had once wielded to save Albion from the Darkness hung from the King's slender waist. Soon he would be forced into marriage with some boring female like the squinty-eyed daughter of Trent who stood beside him now, thrust there by her ever-smiling mother with a loathsome smirk. He would hunt deer in the forest, a pursuit which gave him little pleasure for he admired the beautiful creatures, attend the occasional joust which Arthur permitted to keep his restive chivalry from too much mischief, father a brood of squinty-eyed brats, and die without regret.

He glanced at his mother's straight back in front of him, then at Rowena, his eldest sister, who stood on his left, her face expressionless as she watched the ceremony. He suspected his sister was fonder of the Prince than she showed. Dylan wanted to hug her and tickle the solemn expression off her handsome face but that would have been too shocking in church. She turned her head slightly and arched her eyebrows elegantly in silent query, her grey eyes twinkling a little. She was very like Eleanor, a bit taller and her hair not quite so dark, but with the same stern features which turned to beauty when she smiled.

That was the problem, he decided. He was spoiled for women by his mother and sisters. Perhaps it was some quality she had brought with her, for Eleanor d'Avebury had come from another time and place, a far future where men drove horseless carts and flew through the very air, or, perhaps, that she commanded magics great and small. She was a scholar, and wherever she travelled in Albion she pestered folk for strange tales and wrote them down in a fair hand, until she had volumes of them at Avebury. Now she was trying to persuade the King to let her endow a chair at the university at Oxford to preserve and study these stories. He tried to imagine Amelia of Trent telling tales round the hearth and almost laughed aloud. He wanted a quick-witted woman, and not some simpering female who thought of nothing but gowns and babes. *I shall molder into a crabby old bachelor,* he thought glumly, *and be an uncle to my sisters' brats. If they ever marry, either.* He could not imagine Rowena or Beatrice or little Eleanor tied down to some beef-faced squire who cared for nought but his horses and his dinner. Dylan felt one of his black moods begin to settle on him like an inky cloak. It was not fair. To be the son of a famous father and even more famous mother was almost too much to bear. Why, minstrels even sang songs about them. *I could drink the Thames dry and they would not sing of me!* His crossness began to fade as he tried to decide where one might start such a task. On London Bridge at high noon seemed plausible, and he decided he was not quite sober yet.

The real problem, he admitted to himself, was that his mother did not wish him to go adventuring. Two years before, Arthur had mounted an expedition against the bands of Reavers, the terrible changeling folk who still terrorized the mountains of the north, and though he was a belted knight, Eleanor had forbidden him to accompany the King. If he sneezed she forced foul-tasting brews upon him. Dylan heartily wished some willful god or goddess would snatch him from his bed and set him down in a strange land to slay a monster or two at least, as St. Bridget had done to his mother. Sometimes he almost choked on her constant fussing.

He pushed these unhappy thoughts aside. They were not proper in this house of the Almighty, and those other deities his mother told so many stories of were damned elusive, even Saille, the Lady of the Willows, who resided in Silbury Hill near Avebury.

Dylan remembered a day when he had been hunting rabbits amongst the willow trees around the foot of Silbury Hill. He had been about ten, and the day had been charged with a golden light that was so splendid, so different from any he had ever seen that he had sat down by the winding stream to feel it. There was a little pool, almost still, which reflected the willows in their spring glory, and he felt himself in a waking dream. He studied his face in the mirrorlike surface of the pool and wondered when he would have a beard like his father. After a moment he saw another face reflected in the silvery water, a white face with great grey eyes and dark red lips. It did not surprise him overly much to find his mother wandering here, for such was often her custom, until he remembered that when she had departed that morning Eleanor had been about to set out for a visit to St. Bridget's Priory, some thirty miles away.

"Hullo, Mother. Did you decide not to go?" Dylan looked up at the face and went chill in the warmth of the day. This was most certainly not his mother, though they had a striking similarity. The face was a bit more oval, the eyes wider set, the mouth less generous.

"I . . . beg your pardon, my lady. I mistook you for another."

"Nay, child. There is no sweeter word you can call me than mother, nor any soul I hold more dear than dear Eleanor's." The lips curved in a smile and Dylan saw sharp white teeth. "I will not bite you, I promise." She paused. "Do you like my pool?"

The words were like honey, and he found he wished to run away and could not move.

"Yes, it is very nice, but . . ."

"But?"

"Well, this land is part of our holding, so the pool is my mother's. And my father's," he added hastily, although he knew perfectly well that against all custom Avebury Hall was his mother's property, not his father's. The King himself had given it to Eleanor for her service to the crown.

"It was mine before it was hers. Shall we call it 'ours,' then?"

Dylan decided that this woman was gently mad and ought to be humored. "As you wish, my lady."

"Do I look like a lady?"

He considered her question seriously. She wore a plain blue gown without a scrap of decoration, her hair unbound into midnight billows, and her feet were bare. She did not look exactly like anyone he had ever seen before, not like Queen Marguerite, who always wore a necklace of amethysts, nor like any of the elegant women he had met in London the year before, Countess Brent and Duchess Amelie. He couldn't imagine them barefoot in any woods. They must have been born shod and hosed. But there was something very grand about this strange woman, something more regal than any duchess or Queen he had ever seen.

"Yes and no." He recalled an evening a few days before when his mother had been absent from the hall until well after nightfall and his father had paced before the fireplace like a sullen bear. She had finally come in, cheeks a little rosy from the chilly air, eyes alight with some special pleasure.

"Where have you been?" Doyle had growled.

"Out watching the stars with the Lady of the Willows, love, as you perfectly well know."

"I sometimes think I would prefer it if you were putting horns on me with one of the shepherds."

"Oh, Doyle, stop acting like an Irishman. You know I love each of you, just differently."

Dylan had watched them embrace and crept back to his bed aware that he had eavesdropped when he was supposed to be asleep. He recalled other times when Eleanor had been absent—once for several days—while his father terrified the servants and spoke in monosyllables to his children. Dylan struggled to comprehend what ruffled the usually loving relationship of the two people he loved most in the world and dropped off into uneasy sleep.

"Yes and no," the woman repeated.

"Not 'my lady,' I think, but *the Lady*. I do not think my father likes you."

"No, he doesn't. He's not one to wear the willow." She chuckled over her own joke and Dylan found himself smiling too.

"Then you are the one she comes to see—at night."

"Your mother has a loving heart, and a loyal one as well. It is a shame she has to love a pair of bitter spirits like me and Doyle."

Dylan didn't understand that. "Why do you disturb them? My father never did you any harm."

"No, he has not. But it is not my choice. It is your mother who draws me to her, not the other way around. And your father knows it. Well, I am a little selfish too. I was so lonely before Eleanor came into the world. She gave me her love so freely, and I had almost forgotten how precious a thing love was."

Dylan felt her pain and loneliness. It was such a great thing that it seemed to fill every part of this young body. It was an endless ache, an unheeded hurt, and he knew that if his mother had ever felt it, she would not rest until she had attempted to cure the pain.

Heedless of his boots, Dylan walked across the pool and flung his arms around her neck. "Poor willow woman. Do not be so sad. I will be your friend too, and then you will not feel so alone." He planted a wet kiss on one smooth cheek, and felt a warm, bitter tear touch his lips.

She hugged him back, laughing and crying at the same time. "I suppose it is all right. Eleanor thinks of me as her mother, so that makes you my grandson, doesn't it?"

Dylan, who had long been conscious of the absence of any grandparents in his life—or uncles, aunts, or cousins—and had felt somewhat forlorn at the want, nodded. "I do have a grandmother somewhere in Hibernia, but I have never met her." The strange woman's embrace was comforting and he leaned against her shoulder. She smelled faintly of earth and the bitter scent of broken willow leaves and not like a person at all, but it did not matter.

"Your father isn't going to like this, I think." She ruffled his hair. "He will probably accuse me of stealing your affections as I did Eleanor's."

Dylan was torn between his love for his magnificent father and the desire to sit in this woman's lap forever.

"Then I will not tell him," he said finally.

He never had, even when he grew older and learned the marvelous tale of his mother's exploits, and that his Hibernian grandmother was a great serpent (a part of the story he did not quite believe) an how the Fire Sword became a treasure of the House of Plantagenet. He knew now that the grave Lady of the Willows was old, older than he could imagine, a goddess from an earlier time, but she remained only a treasured friend and a secret. It did not trouble him to speak to a goddess, for like most of the country people of Albion he worshipped the One God on Sundays and did not bother about him the rest of the week. The Church wisely did not trouble itself over peasants dancing around pagan fires a few times a year, as long as they made their tithes and brought their infants to the ritual of baptism.

He had not conversed with her, except in strange dreams, for over a year. The dreams troubled him, and he wished he could consult with his mother about them. Unfortunately, he was fairly certain she would fly into a proper Hibernian fury, for the goddess seemed to be trying to send him upon a journey to the east, where the wide continent of Europe lay in Shadow. If Eleanor d'Avebury would not let him go hunting Reavers, she would certainly prevent him crossing the Channel to Franconia. And perhaps the dream was only a wish, a desire for adventure, and not a message from the lady at all. Dylan bit his lip and decided to speak to his father. They were not close, for Doyle was somewhat distant with him, but he had found his father's advice upon the bedding of women and the drinking of wine to be useful in the past.

Relieved by this decision, Dylan returned his attention to the Mass as the Archbishop ended the ceremony and Prince Geoffrey planted a tepid kiss on his bride's cheek. Isabeau smirked like a placid ewe, and Dylan had a wicked vision of her sheep-rich father's carnal relations with his flocks. He was tempted to share the jest with Rowena, but thought she might find it too ribald. *Such thoughts in church,* he chided himself, and knew that the One God seemed too abstract and distant to him for true reverence. Saille was real, but poor Jesus was just a device for getting money out of peasants and fools.

Prince Geoffrey attempted to abandon his bride at the altar, signalling Dylan over the heads of the crowd, for both were very tall, but two grim-faced equerries urged him back into line as the doors of the cathedral opened and the procession began to exit. The King followed his son, looking thoughtful, and Dylan bowed as he passed.

"Was it not lovely, Dylan?" murmured Amelia of Trent, turning her face up to him adoringly, and fluttering her eyelids provocatively. It was an unfortunate gesture, for her eyes were slightly crossed. "It makes me long for my own wedding day." She sighed deeply and exhaled an herby breath that barely disguised her rotting teeth.

"A pretty ceremony, I suppose, if one cares to spend a fine April day in a packed cathedral. Hot, isn't it?"

Eleanor turned at the sound of Dylan's voice and smiled. She was past forty, and her dark hair was slashed at the temples by two streaks of silver, but her skin was smooth as a girl's and her teeth unblemished. She looked more like a sister to her daughters than a mother. Doyle regarded his wife with undisguised affection, and slipped a large hand around her curving hips. Eleanor gave the hand a playful slap, softened by a blush upon her fair cheeks.

"Not in church, Doyle!"

"Why not? We are married, after all. God won't mind."

He brushed her forehead with a kiss, and Eleanor bent her head against his great chest for a second, then slipped away.

She reached up and pushed the black curls on Dylan's brow aside with cool fingers. "Did you comb it?" she asked.

"Perhaps. I cannot recall. I woke rather late, and this new tunic that Rowena made me seems a little small in the shoulders. Very difficult to reach my head, you see," he added, lifting his arms.

Rowena, who was proud of her needlework, eyed it critically. "You have filled out some more since I finished it. Yes, your shoulders and neck are bigger." She shook her head. "Are you *ever* going to stop growing? You are half a head taller than father now."

"I think I have stopped going up and am spreading sidewise, instead," he answered.

"It is all that swordwork he does," Eleanor added, frowning a little. "I wish you had more talent for books and less for chivalry."

"Mother, I would be a wretched cleric and a worse lawyer. I leave the books to you and Beatrice."

"You are so much like your father." She sighed.

"And who else should he be like, my pretty?" Doyle answered, planting a smart slap on his wife's bottom and so scandalizing Amelia of Trent that she took herself off in search of her formidable mother. "That young woman has her eye on you, my son, and if she catches you, I hope you will not bring her to visit often at Avebury. I cannot abide a woman who will not look me in the eye."

"She cannot help that, Doyle," Eleanor replied, "but I must admit she is not a woman I want in the family."

"And who would you have me wed, Mother?" Dylan asked.

"At the moment, I cannot think of one, though that red-headed child of Count de Wyvern seems bright and spirited enough for you."

"Mother! She's barely twelve!" *And hipless and breastless as a boy,* he added mentally.

"Your father is much older than I am."

Dylan shifted from foot to foot, uneasy as always at the mention of those qualities of legend that gave minstrels stuff to sing about. Doyle counted his years upon the earth more than four hundred, if Dylan believed the stories. But it was too like the serpentine grandmother, difficult to swallow. He was never absolutely certain that portions of the tale were not pure invention. His father never spoke of it at all, except to say his life had begun when he first looked in Eleanor's grey eyes. Dylan wondered if he would ever meet a woman who would make him feel that way. Certainly it was no Amelia of Trent or Jacqueline de Wyvern.

The crowd had left the cathedral, except for a few little pages, their heads bent together in some plot or game, and two priests clearing the altar. A faint breeze stirred the incense-ripe air, carrying the faint smell of water and willows as well. Dylan sniffed it curiously and looked around for the source.

There was a small chapel on one side of the cathedral, one of several, dedicated to the Virgin of Sorrows. The altar within it pulsed with pale green light, coalesced into the shimmering figure of a woman.

"Saille," said Eleanor and Dylan with one voice. His mother looked at him with narrowed eyes, though whether it was jealousy or fear or both he could not guess, and Rowena gave a little cry of delight and smiled.

Doyle bowed gravely at the vision. "So, we finally meet after all these years."

"You have been avoiding me, Daughter, and I am greatly displeased. And inconvenienced—to have to seek you *here*. It is time for Dylan to begin his work, to find his life without you!"

Eleanor d'Avebury was pale as the white of her shift,

except for two burning spots on her cheeks. "No! I will not have it. He is only a boy!"

"He is a man, no matter how you pretend. And he must go to Franconia."

"No! It is not fair. I did enough, more than enough. Find someone else to do your dirty work, and leave my family alone!" Eleanor trembled with rage and her rich voice was full of anguish.

"And what of me, good Grandmother?" asked Rowena, as if her mother had not spoken.

"Not yet, child, not yet. Patience. You still have much to learn."

"You!" Eleanor rounded upon her oldest daughter, seeking a target for her fury. "What have you to do with Sal?"

"I am not some miser's treasure to be held in one heart only, Daughter," admonished the Lady of the Willows. "Long have I known each of your children, and loved them. Little Eleanor gave me all her dolls when she felt herself too old for them, and Beatrice has wiled away many afternoons with grave philosophizing. Dylan used to sweeten my days with boyish kisses, and Rowena has shared the secrets of her heart, as you once did."

"What must I do?" Dylan interrupted, ignoring his mother's further protests until she boxed him soundly on one ear. He caught both her wrists easily in his large hand, then thrust her at his father. Doyle accepted a kicking Eleanor and swung her up over one shoulder like a bag of grain, so her fists fell harmlessly on his broad back.

He planted a resounding smack on her bottom as the two priests and the pages gawked. "Stop yowling, woman, or I'll give you a proper beating!"

"I'll never forgive you for this," she almost screamed.

"Of course you will, *macushla*. You are very kind-hearted. Oof!" One of Eleanor's knees caught him in the chest.

"Go to Franconia and find the Sword of Earth. Bring it forth from darkness, and the maiden who holds it. Find

your life, Dylan.'' The Lady of Willows began to fade,
and for a moment another woman appeared, a fair-haired
female who seemed almost familiar. A green gem hung at
her throat, and a sword dangled from it between firm
breasts. Her hands moved slowly, and her eyes sparkled
almost angrily.

The chapel returned to its accustomed dimness and Doyle
held a sobbing Eleanor against his chest.

"I cannot bear it! No, no, no. Oh, Doyle, why? Why? I
did enough."

"Shh, shh, beloved," Doyle answered, stroking her
netted hair. He raised his eyes and met Dylan's with a hint
of a smile. "Everything will be all right."

"Nothing will ever be right again," she answered as
Dylan turned and left the cathedral, free and purposeful
and heartsick at the same time. The sun seemed blinding
as he walked across the cobblestones, pacing back and
forth nervously, until his family rejoined him, and his
stomach announced that Franconia would have to wait
until after the wedding feast was eaten. Perhaps a bit
longer, if the sullen expression on his mother's face was
any omen. It occurred to him she might use her influence
with the King to prevent his adventure, and unless he
turned into a fish and swam the sea, Franconia might as
well be the moon.

Doyle clamped a hand on his shoulder. "Let me handle
your mother, son."

"Gladly. I only wish it did not hurt her so much."

"You are her favorite, and she has always wanted to
keep you from harm. Do not bother your head overmuch.
Women are more sensible than men, in the end. Otherwise
the race would have perished long ago."

Dylan was elated and depressed simultaneously. He was
favored by the goddess with a task, not condemned to a
humdrum existence, and he wondered if he were able
enough. His mother's endless store of tales was not without its share of tragedies and failed quests. And who was

the fair maid who wore a sword between her breasts? He tried to banish the memory of his mother's face in the church, the fury and despair combined, and he wondered if perhaps she knew his future, knew that he might perish in some distant place. It seemed unlikely in the warm sunlight. Then he shrugged the disturbing thoughts aside and followed his family to the wedding feast where Prince Geoffrey sulked over his beef and his plump bride consumed an astonishing amount, and drowned his doubts in wine that seemed to have lost its savor.

III

Aenor heard the jingling bells of her pursuers before they came into view. Above it, she could hear the steady chant of several light tenor voices, and by the song she could identify them as the Sapphire Guard, the Queen's own men. Out of the Queen's presence they always chorused this particular song. She bit her lip a moment, feeling frustrated, then looped the braided cord back around her neck, so the jewel hung once more against her throat, though somewhat lower because of the weight of the sword; the weapon lay against her body, the hilt between her small breasts. There was no place to go, for the armory cavern was a dead end, and she had gained nothing by her adventure except the memory of bread and ovens.

"Aenor-child," said a hesitant voice she recognized as Hamar, the chief of the guard.

"Do not call me *that*. I am a woman, not a child, and I should have had a fat babe or two at my breast by now!" Her words surprised her, and she realized she had remembered more than swords and bread. It was all muddled, like the weapons around her, but she knew that she was different from what she had been a short time before. The White Folk never spoke of children, except those curious bastard breedings with mortals or monsters.

Hamar entered the cavern and cringed. He was tall and slender, pale haired and light eyed, and he shivered in his

29

bright blue tunic and moved his sandaled feet uneasily. "Come away from this dreadful place. How did you get in?"

Aenor felt a smile tremble on her lips as she remembered her sudden command of the ancient spell that had sealed the chamber—or her jewel's command, she reminded herself, raising a hand to touch its well-known facets. "The door opened," she said.

"Opened? Impossible! The spell . . ." Hamar trailed off, frowning. "I must tell the Queen. Come along, girl. There is nothing here for you."

"No, there isn't. I found what I came for, I think." She had not turned when he entered, so she stood in profile to him, and he could not see the sword which lay upon her flat belly. "But I rather like the smell. It makes me remember much I had forgotten."

"Remember? What?"

"Oh, just words, like iron and leather and bread and ovens, things I knew once. And will know again."

One of the guards behind Hamar hissed.

"Nonsense," Hamar replied stoutly. "Those are but phantasms. You remember nothing except what the Queen wills."

Aenor bent forward and scooped up a long strip of leather, then turned to face him, amused by his consternation and the expressions of horror on the faces of those behind him. "This is a belt, and once it graced the body of a cow, an animal which makes both milk and meat. A very stupid beast but useful, more useful than you are." She wished she could remember the name of the other beast, the one that ran so swiftly, but it remained just out of her mind's grasp.

"Where did you get *that?*" Hamar answered, pointing at the sword and ignoring her lecture on cows and her insults as well.

"This sword? I found it here."

The guards clutched their long spears with white knuckles and muttered to one another.

"She is coming unbound."

"The spells are not holding."

"The Queen's power weakens."

"Silence, you babbling fools!" roared Hamar, his voice cracking. "Elpha is as strong as ever. Or do you want to go to the King's forges and carry coals like a dwarf?"

"You are a fool, Hamar. We all know how this door was sealed, and if those spells are fading, what hope have we? Elpha's desire to reclaim the . . ."

"Silence! Sing, and speak no treason."

The six guards exchanged glances that boded no affection for their captain, shrugged, and took up the "Sapphire Way." The light within the cavern increased as they chanted, casting great shadows on the walls and the piles of discarded arms. Hamar, grim faced, gestured her to follow him.

Aenor did, accustomed as she was to obeying their commands and bemused by a sudden insight which had always eluded her previously: Song and illumination were intertwined like the green and blue enamelled serpents that graced the hilt between her breasts. When she had sung the tones which opened the cavern, she had become less blind. And her jewel—which she had clung to with sheer stubborness despite the entreaties, threats, and promises of the White Folk, had a song in it. She could "hear" fragments of it, but she could not grasp the whole. Aenor paced along behind Hamar, the guards following her, and found their chant drowned out the music that thrummed within her. She could not think straight.

Aenor reached for her jewel, stumbled over a pebble, and caught the blade of the sword instead. The cool metal bit into the soft flesh between her thumb and forefinger, and she lifted her hand to her mouth and tasted warm, salty blood for a moment before the cut healed itself. For an instant she knew who she was, and more, and then it

was gone in the ceaseless chorus of the guard. She would
have commanded them to silence except she knew they
would not heed it, and for a second she felt she might turn
and slay them with the sword, just to still the cursed chant.
Then the power was gone again, and she followed Hamar
numbly through the unending corridors.

The Queen's court was aglow with Elpha's light as the
second singers, the Lapis Choir, toned out the "Pure
Crystal Chant," counterpointed by the beat of several
glass drums with Rock Folk skin heads, and the lesser
stone harps playing a descant. The music crawled across
her skin like biting insects, and Aenor struggled to retain
her hard-won memories. The huge lamps which hung from
the ceiling of the chamber shifted colors—now rose, now a
pale blue, then golden, until she felt battered and dull.

Elpha, seated upon a throne of rosy quartz, lifted a
hand, and the chant diminished, shifted, altered, and became something else. The Queen smiled graciously, then
saw the sword on Aenor's chest. A faint frown creased the
smooth brow, and her silvery eyes widened a little. Her
major spell singers—Margold of the Amethysts, her sister
Angold of Opals, and Garnet Alilian—moved restlessly
beside her, their pleated draperies fluttered around their
crystal-shod feet, and the glassy bells across their breasts
jangling discordantly. The web weavers, who alone of the
White Folk showed any hint of age, thrust long fingers
into their spidery cloaks and mouthed silently.

"Why did you leave us, Aenor-child. You know how it
distresses me to have you out of my sight. You are dear to
me and—"

"I could not bear your wretched crowing," Aenor answered, her mind somewhat clearer. "You sound like a
. . . croaking of frogs." She wasn't quite sure what a frog
was, but the words came easily. The spell singers glared at
her.

"We know you cannot comprehend true beauty, child,
but that is no reason to be ill-mannered," the Queen

admonished gently. "We have treated you kindly, and you pay us back with insults."

"Kindly!" Aenor narrowed her eyes and felt her heart jump with anger. "You took my memory, my mind, my will—and call it kind. Your heart is as hard as the silly jewels you make. What a poor exchange you made—gems for children—until you get so hungry for life within your loins you will lie with any comely mortal, or even the Rock Folk. Cave rats squeak fairer than your song, Oh Great Queen of Nothing!"

Elpha gave a single tone from her slender throat, and Aenor's tongue felt leaden and useless. "Such foolishness. We have kept you ageless here, and ask nothing but the return of our jewel which you wear about your throat. Come, give it to me. It is too great a burden for you. Feel how it hangs against your chest like stone. Give it over, and you will walk our storied halls in joy and serenity."

Aenor could barely breathe. It felt as if the braided cord of hair around her throat was strangling her. Her flesh felt lifeless. With a great effort she moved her hand and cut her fingers on the blade of the sword. It burned like flame, and she flicked the welling blood in a spatter across the Queen's feet as she remembered scuffed elbows and knee-caps from long gone sun-drenched days. The pain gave her power, a fragment of her jewel's song even against the faint, constant choir of the Lapis Singers. It almost faded before she could capture it, so she stubbed her toes against the cold floor of the chamber.

"Come and take it. I shall like to watch you turn to dust."

Elpha leaned back against her throne, pale and fragile. Angold reached a hand out and touched the Queen's arm. "Your Majesty, we cannot have her here any longer. She begins to *know*."

"I can see that!" the Queen answered angrily, pushing aside the comforting hand. "Her blood burns. How could the gods be so unjust, so cruel to the fairest folk they ever made? How could they favor these Clay People, these mortals who know nothing of beauty, nothing but sweaty lust and endless wars? Why do they have the trees?'' It was a cry of anguish.

Aenor barely heard in her excitement. Trees. The word opened mental vistas and a tumble of names for objects and creatures. Nuts and squirrels danced in her mind; she was not sure which was which, but was glad to possess even this much memory. Her jewel flared, flashing green against the rose of the lanterns.

''Bind her again,'' urged Margold.

''I do not know if I can, now the stone is rejoined with that . . . that *thing*. How did she get it? It was spell hidden—well, I thought—and yet she wears it. All I wished was to restore our former glory, to walk again under the chiming crystal towers. Who would have thought a miserable mortal could be so difficult?''

''We cannot keep her here any longer. She will learn things; she has already. I warned you not—''

''Rebuke me not, Amethyst Singer. It is long past time for that.''

''Send her to the King's court. They sing not, there, so she will not learn our secrets, and a few seasonless years in his realm should make her eager to surrender the jewel.'' Alilian spoke calmly. ''She, like all her kind, fears the darkness. The cave rats will gnaw her toes and chew away at her face, and she will beg to come back. You never should have let her stay in the court to begin with, Your Majesty. You know her bloodlines.'' The Garnet Singer gave Aenor a spiteful glance as she started to hum.

Aenor was terrified and angry. Her dwarf servant, Letis, had told her nightmare tales of the endless forge-lit night of the King's court, the ceaseless clatter of hammers on anvils and the stink of constant burning. She struggled against the spell the singers were creating, groping blindly for the bit of song within her jewel. Her mouth and throat seemed parched and frozen.

She stamped her feet and felt the jolt rattle her spine. Aenor touched her jewel and ached to release the words that lay upon a dry and lifeless tongue. Green light pulsed against her sweating palms, and she lifted her hands around a glowing orb of energy. A hot tear ran down her cheek, burning like molten silver.

The globe of light flickered, then flared, and she felt the song well from her heart, sweet and almost wild, until she was a vessel for it. It swelled and bubbled in her throat, then flowed into her mouth like all the waters of the world unleashed:

> "Weep, O Queen
> Broken thy song
> Fracted thy jewels
> Dust at thy feet
> Dust in thy hands
> In silence, go!"

The lesser harp of stone gave a moan like a dying creature; its silver strings snapped; and its jeweled and carven upright exploded, sending fragments of rock across the chamber. Elpha gave a terrible cry as the Lapis Choir and the Sapphire Chorus added their voices to the spell singers, muffling Aenor's tiny, weak song. She lifted a hand to touch the tears she cried and knew nothing except the binding of her mind once more.

IV

Dylan d'Avebury turned his back towards Albion. The white cliffs glittered in the morning sun, and he was certain there was no more magnificent natural feature in all the world. He could almost hear his mother's chuckle in his mind. "Don't be provincial, son," she would have said. "You have not seen the Grand Canyon or the Muir Woods." He had never been quite certain which of his mother's tales were real and which were not. She said there was a continent far to the west beyond Hibernia, where the folk had skin of bronze and lived in skin houses, where there were trees taller than the tallest yew, and a great ditch over a mile deep, running over the length of several counties. But she also spoke of a great wolf named Fenris and frost giants and other wonders.

This was his first experience with the sea, for he had never left Albion before. The pitch of the little Flemish sailing vessel made him feel slightly queasy, and he was aware of a faint tension in his body not unlike the first time he had ever jousted with a living man. It was both fear and pleasure, and he liked it in a restless kind of way. The sea was a splendid greenish blue, fluffed with curls of white as the prow cut through the waves; and the sun shone clear and golden. The breeze had a clean smell like nothing he had known before. By the time the west wind reached Avebury from the sea, its scent was always heavy with the green smells of earth, and the odor of the Thames in London was full of human waste.

Dylan left the place amidship where he had been standing and worked his way forward to the prow, clinging awkwardly to the railing and avoiding coils of rope and other stumbling blocks. The crew, a dour lot of silent Flems, ignored him.

Dylan grasped the prow and leaned into the point of it. The wind ruffled his black hair and he felt a strange thrill as he stared into the waters of the Channel, white cliffs and Albion forgotten. A sleek head emerged from the waters, and a dark eye regarded him thoughtfully. It gave a strange bark, then vanished below the waves to reappear a moment later in an upward leap that revealed a long body and great flippers that clapped and waved at him. Other heads appeared, and the boat was surrounded by a herd of laughing, honking creatures, arcing in and out of the water like leaping trout.

A shout from one of the crew made him turn. The Flems were grinning to split their faces. One, a bit younger than the rest, came up to him.

"Fortune smiles on you, my lord."

"Does it?" Dylan had trouble understanding the man's thick accent.

"Aye. These is dolphins, the good beasts of the Virgin."

"Ah, dolphins. They seem to be having a party." He could also hear his mother's voice. "The dolphin is sacred to the god Apollo, and to the goddess Aphrodite. It is not a fish but a warm-blooded beast which nurses its young as I nursed you. They are very intelligent, smarter than some humans, though we do not speak their tongue—yet. Well, Doyle might. You were born to the sea, my son, though you have never seen it. Your father and I spent a godawful bit of time dashing about in it before you were born. Like Jonah, you have been some time in the belly of a whale." Eleanor had smiled and held her husband's hand tightly, as if the memory both pleased and disturbed her.

"Always a party for them, my lord. And when they play, a sailor has naught to fear." The crewman looked to the east, towards Franconia, where the sunshine seemed less bright somehow, and shook his head. "Better you should stay here than go where you are going."

"What is it like?"

"Dark, my lord, as is all places of the Shadow. There's foul things abroad in the land, and if the captain did not owe his soul to the moneylenders, we would not be taking you to the other side."

Dylan nodded. It had taken weeks, for his mother had refused her consent and put every obstacle in his way she could manage. She had gone to the King and used her enormous influence to prevent Dylan's quest, and she would have succeeded had Arthur's awe of the goddess not been greater than his respect for Eleanor. There had been a rather heated scene that he was glad to have missed, for Dylan found he had little taste for the vociferous brangles the rest of the family seemed to revel in.

Once the King had determined that Dylan might indeed leave Albion for Franconia, there was the difficulty of finding a ship, for the Flems avoided the Franconian coast whenever possible, and Arthur had stepped in to help, an act which Dylan resented as much as anything. Then he found he must carry letters of introduction to the Albionese ambassador, Giles de Cambridge, and to the King of Franconia, whoever he might be presently, so that spring faded and summer was well begun before the parchments were completed in a fine chancery hand, sealed and rubricked to the satisfaction of all but himself. Dylan had no intention of going to Paris, though he had no clear idea what he would do instead. He had been confessed and vigiled and blessed until his head throbbed, and clung to by his anxious mother until his temper was frayed to bits.

The days had passed in endless conferences, the nights in dreams of Sal pointing a white finger to the darkling east, and of the fair woman with the sparkling eyes. Now

he wore a good sword, heavy with clerical beatitudes—
half the Bishops of Albion had laid their hands upon
it—and a breastful of the terrors of those who loved him.
The sword was by far the lighter burden.

The light seemed to fade as he remembered his parting
from his parents. Eleanor had been dry-eyed, though sus-
piciously reddened around the lids, quiet and bearing a
calm that Dylan was sure was a stillness between two
storms. She had kissed him and whispered, "Be safe,
beloved," before she turned away.

Doyle had embraced him in a great bear hug. "There
were so many things I meant to tell you."

"Please . . . any more advice and I will go mad."

The great black beard had split with a grin. "Go mad!
Why, boy, you're Irish. We are born mad. Just be careful
of folk who will not look you in the eye, and do not
believe everything you hear."

"And don't get my feet wet, or go to sleep without
saying my prayers and—"

"Pah! Since that meddling willow witch has sent you on
this venture, prayers will not avail thee. And she quite
glories in the occasional wet foot. Just be the good, true
man I know you can be, and all will be right."

Dylan was roused from his reverie by a spatter of cold
sea water. A great dolphin leapt up almost in his face,
squeaking noisily. Dylan reached out a hand and brushed
the sleek hide. It cried one last unintelligible greeting, then
arched away into the waves.

"Farewell," he called, as the herd sped north upon its
business. "Good fishing." A glimpse of the sharp teeth in
the dolphin's mouth had left him in no doubt that this beast
was a predator.

The sunlight dimmed, and the crew seemed to hunch
down to their tasks. After a few minutes, he could see a
dark line at the horizon. It grew and became land, a rocky
shore. The crew lowered a tiny boat and tossed his gear
into it, as if eager to be done with the job.

Dylan entered the boat gingerly, his sword an awkward impediment, and a huge muscled crewman joined him, plying the oars like a devil. After a time, they beached the boat, and unloaded his packs. The crewman pushed the boat away from shore and was gone without comment, leaving Dylan alone on a sandy shore, the waves gunneling between his boots.

"So much for keeping my feet dry," he told the uncaring sea, and shouldered his burdens.

Dylan walked along the shore, heading north, for a while reluctant to leave the mysterious waters which lapped beside him, recalling his mother's tales without trying to decide which were fact and which were fable. But finally he turned inland, his feet squishing damply across the strand.

It was a warm day, but the sky was grey and the sun seemed a distant, watery blob. He had never known Albion when it dwelt under the Shadow, for by the time he was ten, Arthur had scoured the land free of that dark curse, and the sun shone clear and golden. Still, Eleanor had described the leaden sky of her early journeyings to him often enough that he knew why the sky was no longer blue. It depressed him vaguely, and he hummed a tune under his breath as he crossed the rocky boundary where the kingdom of the sea ceased and the domain of the true land began.

There were trees now, dispirited things with droopy leaves. An ancient apple stood knee-deep in half-rotten fruit. He shook his head and walked on. A coney darted out of a bush, escaping some unseen enemy, and vanished into another.

After an hour, he passed the first farmhouse, a low building falling into wrack and ruin. Its roof had tumbled down and its heavy door stood ajar like a gaping mouth. A large rat sauntered out and eyed him insolently.

The land had sparse stands of trees, and from time to time he crossed what he recognized as fields, their dividing hedges untrimmed and the weeds rank in the shallow furrows. He passed two more deserted houses, one lightning struck, and finally came upon the remains of a village. Only the stone church was fairly intact. The rest of the structures were burnt and twisted.

Dylan stepped into the church. It was dark and quiet, and the faint smell of incense seemed to linger even after many years. The dust upon the flagstones was thick and it curled up under his feet like mist. The altar was empty of tabernacle and candlesticks, but a side niche revealed a Lady altar. The little statue of the Virgin smiled benignly into the dimness, one hand clasping the stylized heart across her breast, the other lifted in benediction. She seemed to smile at him, and he smiled back. Her unbound hair was dark beneath a circlet of silver with the crescent moon in its center, and she reminded him of his mother and the Lady of the Willows. He knelt in the dust for several minutes, trying to form a prayer, but none came to him.

He retreated from the church into the leaden light of late afternoon. He was tired and his shoulders ached from the two packs he was carrying. Dylan wondered if he should spend the night inside the abandoned church, but decided to go on instead. He decided a night in a fallow field was preferable to a night in a ghost-ridden village.

An hour's march later he heard voices and crashing from a copse of trees beside the remains of the road he had followed out of the nameless hamlet. There were angry shouts and a scream. Then a great animal leapt through the trees, pursued by a motley gaggle of half-starved men and women. For a second he thought it was a horse. Then he saw the wicked horn which coiled out of the beast's brow, and knew it for a licorne.

It spun on its hooves to face its attackers, rearing and plunging. The mob, armed with sticks, scattered and regrouped, leaving one fallen beneath the flailing legs and another clutching a gash that ran from chest to shoulder where the horn had rent tattered cloth and flesh with equal ease. The wounded man screamed terribly, and his body seemed to shimmer with a strange blue light.

The licorne paused for a moment. It was black as night, with a silver tail and a short stiff ruff of the same pale hair along the ridge of the great neck. It was more stag than horse, and it was cut along both flanks by sticks and stones. It gazed at the howling folk, then looked at Dylan. Its eyes were pale, almost argent, and it shivered all across its skin. Then it gave a cry, a bellow of challenge, and charged the mob.

Dylan dropped his two packs with a thump and pulled out his sword. Without consideration of the chivalry involved, he hacked down a white-faced man as he brought a stick down on the licorne's right flank. As if finally aware of his presence, three of the mob turned to face him. They gabbled unintelligible words, and he cut off a hand as a stone missed his head by inches. He cursed himself for not wearing his helm, and cleaved a hapless peasant through the shoulder. Oddly, no blood spurted out. The fellow just collapsed and tripped the man beside him.

The licorne gutted a woman and trampled a man, and it was over. The beast gave a trump of triumph and stepped daintily away from his victims. Dylan watched in horror as the bodies of the slain flared briefly with blue light, then began to decompose before his eyes. A charnel stench filled the air and he gagged and backed away hastily. He had seen his first Shadow Folk and they were much more terrible than he had ever imagined. His mother's stories had never given him a true sense of how dreadful the soulless folk of the Dark were.

A soft nose nudged him between the shoulder blades, and he turned to face the beast. It stared at him with silver eyes and blew a greeting or a thanks from its mouth, displaying large, dangerous teeth. Something sticky dripped from its horn and a thin line of blood rilled down across the left shoulder, but it seemed serenely beyond the concerns of mere flesh.

Dylan felt awed. It was the most magnificent beast he had ever seen. Slowly, tentatively, he lifted a hand to stroke the great neck. The licorne suffered his touch graciously. It was more than sixteen hands high, bigger than most horses, and he saw that its head was more like a stag than an equine. The horn in its forehead was a spiral of black and white, and it recurved slightly at the end. It was a creature fit for moonlight and starlight, not for the grim, grey day of Shadowed Franconia.

Dylan tore some dry grass from the ground and wiped his sword, then put it in its scabbard. He tossed the stuff aside, and took a fresh handful. Reaching up his full height, he daubed at the stuff on the horn. The beast lowered its head and made a warm, low noise. Dylan wiped away as much of the mess as he could.

"We should go find a pool or stream to wash off in, you know."

The licorne blew its lips and turned and trotted a few steps away. It looked back at Dylan and tossed its head. With a shrug, he picked up his packs and prepared to follow the animal. "My mother met a wolf once," he told it conversationally, "but you are much prettier. I had heard there were licornes in the forests of Franconia, but I am afraid I did not believe the tales. They tell me my grandmother is a snake, and I do not really believe that either." The beast gave a soft grunt and led him away.

As he walked beside the licorne, Dylan's thoughts ran to his parent's tale, caught first in bits and pieces as conversation, and intermixed, inextricably interwoven with his mother's unceasing ocean of stories. How many times had she sat nursing one of his sisters and told him of Heracles and Arthur—not the King he knew, but an earlier one, a legendary man whom many in Albion believe had returned in their monarch—and Charlemagne and Paul Bunyan. He recalled the first time he had heard the *Lay of Eleanor and*

Doyle, the King himself singing the words he had written for her years before, accompanying himself on a small harp, not the magic harp which rested on the altar at Westminster, but an ordinary instrument. He had heard his father's death on the tusks of a great boar while the man sat beside him, grave and untouched by his own demise. Dylan had never been sure how much to believe. Perhaps belief was unnecessary. Certainly beside this great, strange beast it seemed needless.

They entered a proper forest, the earth deep in the rotting mulch of seasons of leaves. Here was oak and birch and wild apple, all familiar and yet different. It was a still, silent place, with no birdcall or squirrel chatter, but only the rustle of boot and hoof amongst the debris. He felt he was alone at the start of time, the only man alive pursuing a dream woman. If only he were in one of those tales with the talking beasts, he might ask his companion where they were going. It was hard, he discovered, to follow blindly into the unknown with only the white finger of the Lady of the Willows to guide him. His mother's bravery in similar circumstances seemed an astonishing thing, but she had had a magic sword and a cloak, gifts of the capricious and impatient goddess Bridget.

Dylan chuckled to himself. He had, he realized, marched into his adventure with some unnoticed expectations that it would be both more exciting and tidier somehow. Slashing up Shadowbound peasants and getting his feet wet had not come into his calculations somehow, and he wondered if such minor discomforts and disappointments were somehow swept aside by the storyteller's art. Probably they were, for only great events were of any interest to the listener.

The woods grew thicker and he followed close to the licorne's great flanks, smelling the blood and warmth of them. If the forest had a heart, he thought they must be close to it. A sudden opening in the trees almost startled him.

It was a pool, perhaps tens ells across, smooth as a mirror. The licorne bent its head to drink, and Dylan caught the wavery reflection of its horn as the muzzle made circular ripples in the water. Dylan knelt and drank and laved his face. Then he undid the napkin from around a sweet loaf which Rowena had given him, and wet the napkin with cool water and washed the licorne's cuts. The beast suffered these ministrations stolidly, without any equinelike pleasure in the attentions it was receiving.

"Here. Let me get that stuff off your horn," Doyle said.

The licorne snorted, but bowed its great head so Dylan could reach the spiral of black and white. The bone was hard and cool beneath his chill fingers, and he washed away the dried blood and nameless bits of tissue that clung to the turnings. He gazed into the silver eyes for a long moment when he was done, seeing there a sort of intelligence that was neither human nor bestial, then rinsed out the fine linen, wrung it out and tucked it into his belt to dry. *One day on the road and already I am a clothes line,* he thought, grinning.

The licorne headed away around the pool and he grabbed his bundles and followed it. He wished he could have brought a couple of horses and a squire with him, but the captain of the little ship had refused him passage for his steed, and no squire could be found who would dare the dangers of Shadow-hidden Franconia. Prince Geoffrey would have come, but his father had forbidden it, of course, and Isabeau of Flanders would have looked unkindly upon such an adventure.

The trees seemed greater beyond the pool, silent giants of deadly yew and spreading oak. Night stole into the darkness of the forest as if it were an intruder into the dim world beneath the branches. So busy was Dylan avoiding fallen branches that he barely noticed when a path opened between the trees. Only when he was well into an avenue of stately yews, two columns of silent sentinels, did he realize that he had passed out of the world of nature and back into the world of men.

Ahead, a dark outline against the sky, Dylan could make out a structure. A keep by the shape of it. The licorne lengthened its stride a little, free of obstacles, and he had to trot to keep up with it. He was panting and sweaty by the time they reached the yawning gates.

There was a courtyard beyond the gates, empty of all but leaves and a well with a broken cover. Beyond it the door of the tower stood ajar. Dylan paused a moment, sniffing the air like a hound. There was only the faint sound of the breeze, the clop of the licorne's hooves on the cobblestones, and the smell of dust and leaves. Still, he put one hand on the hilt of his sword as he walked towards the entrance.

The great hall was dim and empty, though the light of his own spirit, his aura, cast enough of a glow to reveal the grosser features. The reeds strewn upon the floor were dry and brittle, and the trestle table was bare except for a couple of gleaming trenchers, two goblets, and a flagon. It had the look of a place just vacated, and he puzzled that anyone would leave behind silver trenchers. The two great fireplaces were filled with logs, and he walked towards one, wishing he had his mother's gift of making fire with her will alone. Bridget's Fire, she called it, and said it was a gift of the goddess, but his father insisted it was something which might be learned, like riding a horse, in time. Magics, Doyle claimed, were nothing more than natural abilities coupled with hard work. Dylan had long before realized he had no natural affinity for fire, and carried flint and steel with him instead.

He knelt before the cavernous fireplace and opened his belt pouch. It held a whetstone for his sword and his flints. He peered under the logs but there appeared to be no kindling, so he thrust some of the dessicated floor reeds under one log and started striking.

So intent was he upon his task that he did not hear the

faint slither of something being dragged across the reed-strewn floor until it was almost beside him. He whirled to his feet, sword drawn, eyes wide, his mind making pictures of dragons and great, deadly worms.

A woman stood before him, a faint glitter of blue light around a sad-faced female of indeterminate age. She was pretty in an odd sort of way, her face too long and narrow for real beauty, her eyes wide and unblinking. The woman's hair, if it was hair—the dim light made it difficult to be certain—seemed to have been cut in tiny half circles, like fish scales, and seemed a color which was neither blue nor green. She smiled, displaying what seemed like a great many teeth, and Dylan felt the hair on the back of his neck bristle.

His mother had always told him to try being courteous first and draw his blade second, so Dylan forced a smile onto his face and bowed from the waist.

"Good evening, milady."

"Is it? I suppose it must be, if you say so. Still, I never was one for putting qualities on time, you see. If it were raining, would you say 'bad evening'? Still and all, a fire would be nice. Well, not nice, precisely. Fire isn't anything but hot and hotter. Except *her* fire, of course, but you and I have no feeling for that element, do we?"

The lady moved a little closer to him as she babbled, and the long train of her gown moved oddly, as if she had some beast concealed beneath it. She extended a hand towards him in a friendly manner, and he saw that there were tiny webs at the base of her fingers and that her nails were long and clawlike. Her gown rippled like water below her long waist.

Dylan swallowed in a very dry throat. He felt the sweat break out under his arms and he had an urge to either pull out his sword or run. Instead, he said, "No, my mother is very good with fire, *her* fire, as you put it, but I am not."

"Yes, yes. You do take after your father more, as your sisters are like your mother. Are you surprised? I see you are. That is one of the things denied me—surprise. It seems a great gift, that ability to know what is ahead. Let me tell you, it gets quite tiresome always knowing what is going to happen. By the time it finally does, you are bored to eternity with the whole thing." She gave a great sigh and smiled again.

Dylan suspected it was meant to be reassuring, but he still felt uneasy. She had such sharp teeth. At the same time, he felt he ought to know who she was, that his mother's capacious store of tales should offer him some clue to her identity. His mind felt like cold oatmeal, so he turned back to the fireplace and got a small blaze working.

He rose, dusting ash and reed from his palms and knees, and found her still standing patiently behind him.

"It must be very lonely for you here," he said quietly.

"Yes. Once this place was the gayest keep in all the land, full of music and dance. I miss the dance the most, I think, and the intrigues of the court. Still, all things pass away in time. Well, most things. I do not, unfortunately. I endure, like some old song that everyone has almost forgotten. Come, let us drink a glass to time." She gestured towards the board.

Dylan, remembering his manners, offered her his arm, and she laid a webbed and clawed hand lightly along his forearm, so they made a stately progress across the crackling reeds. Her hand was cool through the cloth of his tunic. He held a chair while she arranged her body into it, and saw a glimpse of something like a serpent's tail before it was hidden again by the folds of her gown.

The lady poured wine from a crystal flagon, a sharp, flinty white that had a tang of sunshine in its nose. "I seem to have lost my talent for putting mortals at ease."

"I beg your pardon, my lady. You are a rare puzzle and—"

"And like all mortals you must have an answer to it. Curiosity is another odd feature of your kind." She sipped daintily from her goblet, then fixed him with an unwinking gaze. "I am not your foe, Dylan d'Avebury."

"No, I suppose not, but one may be neither a friend nor a foe."

"Ah, the endless alliances of men, with their accompanying betrayals. I am beyond such matters. I am old and endless, and I was once foolish enough to love one such as yourself. He is dust, long since, and I am alone. The halls of memory grow very dreary when all is said and done."

"If you say so. You are not, by any chance, a relation of my grandmother?"

She laughed. "Goodness, no. Though I can see how you might make that mistake. Oh, perhaps in the beginning of time we were, but I am from the line of Draconis, which is somewhat different than Orphiana's. We are of the waters, not the earth."

Dylan felt a jiggle of memory, a tale of a dragon-woman who had married some ruler of Franconia. What was her name? She had made her husband promise that he would never try to see her upon Saturday, and when he had violated his vow, she turned into a dragon and flew away forever, leaving behind several children, one of whom was a supposed ancestor of Arthur Plantagenet. Melinda? Melissa? Not quite. "Melusine," he said suddenly.

"I have been called that, yes. I have drifted into legend, but I still remain, trapped between the worlds. I cannot die, but neither can I really live. It is quite tedious." She sounded very matter-of-fact about it. "Sometimes I am almost tempted to put on my aspects and fly around terrifying the peasants, just to relieve the boredom." The train of her gown rustled and the cloth slid back revealing a strong tail with sharp barbs at the end. "But the few souls who live nearby are already so frightened of the dreadful place that Franconia has become that I am not sure they would even notice me. And besides, I never found much good in frightening folk. It makes them angry, and they dash about with torches and make a dreadful mess."

Dylan laughed. She sounded like a harried housewife. Peasants, it appeared, were the same everywhere, patient, hardworking, and eager to destroy anything that seemed unreal or unusual. "Yes, and they always track in mud," he said.

Melusine grinned, a frightening sight, and he wondered how that ancient King had fallen in love with such a smile. Perhaps she appeared differently then. "It is good to hear laughter. I miss it so much sometimes. And now I will tell you a tale. You need more wine. You know of the great swords, the Swords of Power, which were made by Orphiana's lover just before time started?"

"I know of the Fire Sword, which my mother and my father once bore, and which now belongs to Albion's King."

"That is one, yes. There are others. The one you seek is quite a different weapon. When it was made, the smith set a great, green gem into the hilt. Many ages passed— always—and when the time of man began, the White Folk made their bargain with the gods for everlasting life, the fools. That was before my time, but they should have known better. They took this sword away with them into the caverns—at great cost—and wrested the stone from the hilt and set it to be the sun of their spired city of crystals. This was done by great magics such as the world will never know again, and many of them perished."

"Wait, please. I thought you just said they were immortal?"

"I told you it was a poor bargain. Death is undeniable. Everything perishes eventually. Even Orphiana will pass one day, and the earth with her. These folk were already long-lived, but when they saw the advent of mankind, short-lived but fecund, they thought only to outlast them. They disdained the Clay Folk, as they called you, sure that man would destroy himself in his haste, his impatience, and his curiosity, and then they would again hold sway. They are a proud race, a haughty folk who wish only to rule. They thought it was their right as elders, and they could not understand that time was passing them by. So, they petitioned the Lord of the Living, first asking that he negate his new creation, and failing that, that he grant them the boon of everlasting life.''

Melusine paused and her strange eyes seemed to darken. Dylan refilled her goblet, fascinated, and she drank. ''It is not wise to attract the notice of the gods. He made them a cruel bargain. They would not grow old, he said, but neither would they bear offspring except from the loins of other races. And they must relinquish their forests and glades for the bowels of earth, and see the sun no more.'' She sighed. ''It was no bargain. It was an edict. They cried out against it, but it was too late. They had angered him by asking that he destroy man, and he took a slow, terrible vengeance upon them.'' She heaved a great sigh, and her tail stirred across the dried rushes on the floor. ''The Lord of the Living is just but not kind. Never kind.''

Dylan knew she spoke of herself, not the strange folk of her story now, and he thought he had never heard such sorrow in a voice before. It must be dreadful to be alone as she was, solitary and friendless. Unthinkingly, he reached out a hand and patted hers gently.

Melusine roused, as if she had been musing, and gave him a faint smile. ''But, I digress. The beryl was made into a false sun and the elves made the best they could of a poor bargain. They sang their songs and danced their dances and risked the light of night—for they avoid the sun like death itself—to ensnare the occasional mortal deemed fair enough to be an object of their love.'' She hesitated. ''I think it was need of story stuff that drove them, for they have no love for Clay Men, in truth; but for a folk of song there must be a source, and forbidden love is perhaps the greatest well-pool of minstrel lays to be found. And they loved, I suppose, in their way, the mortals who became the objects of their interest. A strange sort of love but love nonetheless. And even that was betrayed.

"There was a great prince of elvish kind who developed a terrible passion for a human female who was quite beautiful but also monstrously stupid." Melusine chuckled. "She could not come up with the same sum twice counting her own toes. But she was beautiful, and the White Folk have always been great ones for seeing no more than the surface. They did not see, when they looked at man, the spirit which burns within him, that soul which sets him apart from all previous creations, but only saw his dim eyes and hairy cheeks and great, tearing teeth. She was pretty, and she demanded great boons of this Alfgar before she would submit to his lust. Not, you see, that she was terribly virtuous, but she was shrewd and full of low cunning. And once, in jest, she demanded the sun for a bride-gift.

"Alfgar was quite maddened with desire, and he was fairly young as the White Folk go, and not very wise. But cunning, like the woman. They were well matched. At this time there was war amongst the elves, for having been denied sunlight and offspring they had fallen to fighting amongst themselves, as children will do on a rainy day when they have too little to occupy them. And Alfgar stole the beryl in such a fashion that each side supposed the other to have done the deed, and the Crystal City was destroyed and the White Ones much diminished by their strife. Alfgar ran away to his silly ladylove and offered her the beryl. She took it and spread her legs for him—once. It was enough. Nine moons later she bore a daughter, and when that daughter grew to womanhood, she received the hilt-stone of the sword as well. And, so it has gone for untold generations—each mother gifting daughter or granddaughter with the accursed thing and the White Ones bending every effort to recover it—forgetting what price they paid to use it in the first place. Long life does not always mean wisdom." She drained her cup, weary and tired looking now. Her face seemed less and less human as the night advanced, but there was a sort of splendor about it, a courage he admired.

Dylan found his hand still lay over hers, and he could feel the delicate webbing between her fingers. He refilled her goblet again. "A strange tale, milady, and one even my mother did not know. I hope I shall tell it to her one day, for she will like it. She has told me many stories of elves, but none such as these White Folk."

"You seek the Sword of Earth and she who holds it. She is captive in the caverns of the White Folk, frozen in time, unaging, even as I am. Sometimes I would cry out at my fate, would scream at this wretched existence, and so I am touched by her plight. Or perhaps I meddle out of ennui. If any deity offers you eternal life, young Dylan, refuse it. Forever is too long to be friendless and alone."

Melusine drank deeply, and he thought her eyes were bright with unshed tears. Dylan tried to think of something comforting to say, but failed. "You must have loved him very much."

"I did, I did. I made myself fair to his eyes, eschewing my natural form except for the one day, and now I am neither one thing or the other, neither truly a woman nor yet a dragon. It is a punishment for trying to deny my nature, I suppose." She cast him a piercing look. "There is much you do not know yet about your own."

"Does any man know himself?"

"If you do not learn your soul's secrets, they will destroy you. But you must seek the sheath of the sword before you seek the sword itself, Dylan."

"Another hunk of my grandmother's hide, I suppose," he answered, thinking of the gaudy scabbard of the Fire Sword. "Sal did not mention that."

"Goddesses! They are all the same! Cryptic. I believe they fear to lose their mystery if they speak plainly. Or perhaps they cannot. Your Sal is good enough as her kind go, but that is not saying a great deal."

"Tell me, if you will be so kind, of this sheath."

"When the smith made the swords, he drew from the elements such essence—pah, no human tongue possesses the right words—such essence that the world itself was imperiled by its existence. And Orphiana gave of herself, of her body and spirit, to restore the balance. A sword must always have its sheath, as a man must have his mate. It lies somewhere near Paris, but more than that I cannot tell you."

"I thank you, gracious Melusine, and only regret I have no way to repay your hospitality," Dylan answered, somewhat chagrined to find himself going to Paris despite his intention to avoid it.

"Ah, Dylan of the gentle heart, you have gifted me most nobly by your sweetness and your touch upon my hand. The sound of your voice has healed my weary heart, for oftimes, I should have died of loneliness in this living tomb. Were I as wicked as legend makes me, I would dare the wrath of your formidable mentor and keep you for myself. But I will not. If I but had the power, I should bring this hall alight with tapers and brighten it with lyres and tympanum, and we should dance away the rest of the brief night."

"But . . . did you not have two children who went with you . . . I mean . . ."

"They hated me for what they were and what I was, and abandoned me long ago. As if I could help my nature." The bitterness lay in every syllable of her words.

Dylan could almost hear his mother saying, "Life is not fair. We just have to make the best of it."

"Then let us dance, milady. We need no musicians. I am a fair whistler, and I know all the dances of the court of Arthur of Albion."

Melusine looked at him, great jewels of tears hovering in her dragon eyes. They rose together and stepped away from the great table. Up and down the hall they trod stately measures of dances old and new; she hummed, he whistled, and they laughed like children at their occasional awkwardnesses. Her tail and train left pathways in the crumbling reeds, and his boots made a ruin of the rest.

"The dawn comes, dear friend, and I must go. Sleep before the fire. None will disturb you. And go upon your journey with a good heart."

Dylan leaned forward and kissed the sharp cheek of the dragon-woman, his lips feeling the slight scaliness of her skin without revulsion. She gave a sigh, a sound like the wind moaning through poplar trees, and rested her proud head against his shoulder for a long moment, one arm caught around his slender waist, the other across his chest, the delicate fingers brushing his throat.

Then she was gone, and only the tracks amongst the rushes and the presence of two goblets and a flagon assured Dylan he had not dreamt the whole encounter.

V

Aenor rubbed her forehead, then shrugged her shoulders to ease the constant ache. The continuous clamor of hammer upon anvil within the great galleries of the King's court left her numb, and she had a ceaseless headache. The air was sere and filled with flying smuts from the forge fires, and she was as filthy as the poor misshapen dwarves who scurried from anvil to anvil, bearing baskets of coals or refilling the great stone basins of greasy water used for tempering. Her lungs seemed to hurt from the dry air.

At first she had sat on the floor of the little cavern they had led her to, coiled in a wretched dwarf blanket which barely covered half her body, heedless of her surroundings. She slept and dreamt but remembered nothing. The King spoke to her sometimes, but she only stared at him in mute incomprehension.

Then, a few sleeps ago, she had cried out in her dream, and when she opened her eyes, a flood of memory had swept her mind. Her voice returned, and with it hunger and thirst and a sullen fury. She had left her chamber and walked out into the nearest forge gallery, sat on a convenient rock, and stared at the work of the King's court. Now she knew the names of the various masters and the objects they labored over, and each moment brought her fresh knowledge. The spell singer's work was failing.

The green gem rested against her throat, the sword

depending awkwardly from it, the weight making her shoulders ache; with a start she realized there was another way to carry the burden. The strange braid of silvery hair which held the stone was not long enough for her purpose, but some pieces of her meagre blanket would serve. She bit at the rough and filthy cloth and tore off two ragged strips, lifted the jewel and sword over her head, then tied the cloth to the short sword, knotting them tightly, then bound the pieces around her slender waist. That was much better, she decided, as she shifted her weight back and forth to accustom herself to the feel of the sword on her left hip. The blade tore at the remnants of her pleated gown along her thigh. Her movements upon the uneven floor of her chamber made her remember the rough cobbles of the practice yard, all gold and warm with sunlight, and she gave a little cry of pleasure.

Aenor unknotted the waist tie and grasped the hilt of the sword. She moved it through the air, slowly at first, then more rapidly, her arm muscles protesting a little at her sudden abuse. Her faint shadow on the chamber wall echoed her motions, and she heard a gruff voice in memory admonishing her to do this or that. Breathless and sweat sheened she finally ceased her exercise, wiping her face with a grimy sleeve. Her head ached less now, and a slow smile lifted her lips as she retied the sword to her waist at a slightly different angle. She curled her left fingers over the green gem and felt a tiny thrill of power run along her muscles and bones. It was almost like a song.

Pondering that, Aenor walked out into the first gallery and took her now accustomed seat. The forge masters did not notice her any longer, but several of the dwarves looked up from their tasks, and one gave her a wide grin before he scurried off for more coal.

The King, Alphonze, was making his progress up one side of the gallery, checking the work of the masters. He seemed unaware of the occasional glances they cast at his

back, sullen looks of envy or even anger. He was tall and
well-made, his black hair circled with a crystal band of
shifting rainbow hues, his black tunic crossed with an
argentine baldric bearing dark glass bells, almost invisible
in the flickering red light of the court. No crystal lamps
hung from the cavern ceilings here, and no stone harps
resonated in the walls. There was nothing but great forges
and the river of molten rock that split the chamber in two,
emitting a constant ruddy glow.

Like hot blood, she thought, and puzzled over that.
Each waking now brought memory and strange ideas, and
Aenor struggled to sort them out, so that sometimes she
fought against sleep lest she be overwhelmed. She let the
thought pass and watched the steady rise and fall of strong
but slender arms above hammers great and small, the
scurry of dwarves and the shifting patterns of the molten
river.

Alphonze gazed at her and arched his brows. A flicker
of doubt seemed to flash in his pale eyes. They made her
remember another pair of eyes, grey-blue eyes beneath a
tumble of curling black hair, a flattish nose and a grin
which split a wide beard. Eyes like the stormy sea. But that
was just a dream, a memory of some long dead person, no
doubt.

"Greetings, Aenor-child."

"Greetings, O King of Rackets," she answered, sur-
prising herself as well as Alphonze, for she had not previously answered his occasional questions. "No wonder
the Queen keeps your court so distant. It is dreadfully
noisy—and most inharmonious." Her tongue seemed compelled to exercise after long disuse.

The King scowled, and several forge masters paused to
look at them. "The Queen does not keep me here."

Aenor smiled because she knew it was a lie. The forge
masters and the King were excluded from the Queen's
court out of the Queen's distaste for artifice. That which
could not be made from song was displeasing to her and to

her court, while the King's men held in contempt anything that had not come from their skillful hands.

"Then I must suppose you enjoy the stink of forges and the light of your fires. It is surely a shame you cannot sing, but only croak like . . . like frogs."

The King flushed an ugly red. It was a very sore point amongst the White Folk that the females could make beauty by their voices alone but the males must labor with their hands. The guards and male courtiers could do neither, and were regarded with contempt by all except themselves.

"You know nothing, stupid clay girl."

Defiance rose in her throat like a sweet draught of clear water, and she curled her palm over the beryl. "I know you rule by Elpha's grace—and that you cannot even make a circlet for your brow but must beg it from her."

"That is not true!" At his bellow of rage the hammers fell silent and the forge masters almost smirked. The dwarves cringed and shuffled hurriedly towards the shadows about the walls.

"So why do you wear that thing instead of a crown of gold or silver?"

"It is a mark of honor."

"Like the collars of the dwarves?" Aenor felt her heart pound with excitement.

Alphonze turned on his heel and marched over to the closest forge, wrested the hammer from the master there, then plunged his hand into the molten river and drew out a huge mass of living rock. Globules of it dripped down and spattered on the cavern floor, glowing redly for a moment before dulling to grey.

The King slammed the mass onto the forge, shouted for coal and a bellows worker as the forge masters watched avidly, and began to ply his hammer. A dwarf was shoved out of the huddle of tiny bodies in the shadows by his terrified fellows, and he trudged forward reluctantly. He worked the bellows without energy until the King kicked him into obedience.

The hall rang with the furious blows of the single hammer while the forge masters clustered a good distance back from the King. They hissed between them at this folly, for it was an open rebellion for the King to try to crown himself. No one had done that since Alfgar the Accursed, he who stole the green jewel from the Crystal City and brought the exile of the White Folk artificers. He who was the ancestor of the troublesome female who now provoked Alphonze to madness. They eyed her with both loathing and speculation, wondering if any amongst them were powerful enough to rescue the gem from her grasp and restore the supremacy of the artificers over the singers, and more immediately, which of them would take the King's place if the Queen discovered what had occurred. They cast uneasy glances at one another, wondering which of them would perish in the inevitable war that would follow. They were ancient and could recall the sweet smell of grasses beneath their feet, the time before they had strutted their pride before the Lord of the Living and been reduced to gloomy darkness. They hated the King's court and yearned for the Queen's light, but they wished to continue even at their forges rather than to cease their existences.

Aenor was caught between pleasure at her mischief and a faint sense of sadness she could find no reason for. The sorrow grew until it was a heaviness in her throat, a necklace of song which lay in her chest like a stone. White Folk would perish as surely as if she had cut them down with the sword at her side, and that was somehow not what she wanted. She wanted light, sun and rain, and the feel of clean air in her lungs, not death and destruction. She clenched her hand around the jeweled hilt of the sword until its facets cut into her palm.

She looked at her grimy hand, licked the wound and tasted ash and salty sweat and sweet blood. The song surged up the column of her throat like a sudden spring of water, flowed across her tongue and rang across the echoing chamber. The notes were sad and joyous at once, full of memories of green life and golden life.

Alphonze dropped his hammer as if it burnt him, and the half-made circlet in his hand rolled off the anvil and into the glowing coals of the forge, unnoticed. For a long moment his face was transformed with joy at the beauty of her voice. Then his eyes widened in something like horror as he realized who the singer was.

Alphonze gave a harsh shout and Aenor faltered. The forge masters and the King stared at her as the song paused within her, half completed. She looked down at her hand, at where a slight cut had existed and vanished, and remembered the taste of blood. Aenor shuddered slightly. She wanted light and life, not bloody death. She gazed down at the beryl, now reflecting redly in the forge light, and saw it as a thing both grand and dreadful. She would have flung it into the molten stream if she possessed the strength. Her shoulders bowed a little under the burden of the unfinished song. There was so much she did not understand, so much that mere memory did not provide.

"How did you . . . how dare you sing!" Alphonze was caught between puzzlement and outrage.

"I have been a long time with the Queen," she answered, musing.

"It is not possible. You are clay, a nothing. You have no beauty in you."

The sullen rage kindled in her breast once again. "Beauty! What do you know of beauty, you grubbing mole? This trash you pound out on your anvils is nothing . . . to a rose." For a moment she recalled a heady smelling bloom, the petals red and crystal-limned with silvery dew.

"You cannot make a rose, you ill-gotten monster."

"Are you certain?" She explored the possibility as she spoke, feeling a new song murmur in her heart. It was so filled with yearning that her eyes brimmed with forbidden tears. They cascaded down her cheeks and slid onto her throat.

"No," whispered the King. Then he turned to the masters. "Get back to work. I . . . I will inform the Queen."

Aenor watched him leave and returned to her chamber. She folded the scraps of her blanket into a pad and sat on it, crossing her ankles tailor-fashion and resting her elbows on her knees, her chin on her palms. She swallowed in a dry throat, aware that her sudden display of power would probably bring the Queen and her spell singers down into the King's court to send her once more into mindless oblivion. *I will not forget this time. Somehow I will remember all that I yearn for. My song . . . is so weak. They are too skilled—and I am alone. So alone. Would that I could sing another into being, a host of those I remember. But they are dust and moldering bones. I will not despair or surrender. I have power, and I must think how to use it. It is like the sword; it requires practice.*

Aenor found she was weeping again, so she brushed the tears away fiercely, straightened her shoulders, and struggled with her nearly overwhelming terror at the power of the spell singers over her mind. The chill of the cavern crept into her bones, and she felt small and helpless. Her hand brushed the hilt of the sword, and she stared at it. *I wonder if I could slay them?* She bit her lip thoughtfully, then stood up and untied her makeshift sword belt.

She lifted the sword above her head, pointing at the ceiling, her feet a shoulder width apart. Aenor felt a strange sensation, a surge of energy from her soles to the hand which held the weapon. It jolted her almost painfully and she heard a roar from the forge gallery. Screams and shouts followed, and she dashed out to see what had happened.

The molten stream seethed and bubbled, overflowing its confines on one bank and sending huge lumps of red-hot rock flying through the air. The forge masters and dwarves scurried around in confusion as anvils and forges vanished in a glowing tide. She watched a hapless dwarf get smashed by a huge piece of burning rock, then turned away, weak and heartsick. *I have all this power, and all I can do is destroy things with it,* Aenor thought as she stumbled back to her cavern, huddling under her inadequate blanket in misery.

VI

Dylan rubbed his eyes, yawned, and stretched. Then he curled his arm under his head and focused unseeing eyes on the deserted hall. He had a vague wish for the strange and bitter brew his mother sometimes conjured on wintery mornings or when the wine had flowed too freely. It tasted dreadful, but it sharpened the wits. "Coffee," she called it, and said it had civilized the Vikings. When he asked her what a Viking was, Eleanor just smiled, shook her head and said, "Men in funny hats."

The fire was out and the hall was chilly. Dylan sat up and set about rekindling it. His dreams had been odd, and he was not quite certain what had been real and what a product of sleep. Had he really danced with a woman who was part dragon? Or was it part of the dream of that other woman, the fair one, who lifted the sword she bore and made mock battle with her shadow upon the wall? He chewed bread and cheese and tried to sort out the images. She was quite able with the weapon, he decided, and discovered he did not much care for the picture. The only woman he had ever known who wielded a blade was his mother, and she had never done so in his sight. He had, however, seen her use her rowan rod as a quarterstaff once upon a drunken ruffian in the streets of London. She'd caught him first in the belly, then upon the jaw, and stepped across his groaning, fallen form with a brisk shake of her wide skirts and an audible sniff of disdain. Why couldn't women just stick to their knitting and leave swordwork to men, as was intended by nature? And why did his mother intrude at every turn?

Finally he gathered up his belongings and quit the hall. He stopped at the well in the courtyard and pulled up a bucket of water and splashed it on his face, then wiped himself dry with his sleeve.

The licorne stared at him across the wall. "Good morning, big fellow." It bobbed its head and pawed the flagstones in response. "Have you ever been to Paris? And will you bear a man's weight upon your back, I wonder?" The beast regarded him with silvery eyes and made no reply. "Probably not. Besides, what saddle in the world would be fine enough?"

Dylan left the ruined keep and the licorne came with him. They passed the yew alley and returned to the tangled forest while the man tried to find his sense of direction. This was difficult, since he was uncertain where he was, and the grey overcast hid the sun sufficiently to make him unsure. Finally he set off in a direction he believed to be east.

A snort and a nudge between his shoulders startled him. The licorne clamped strong white teeth into the leather of his jerkin and pulled.

"What?"

The animal half dragged him backwards and gave a high squeal. After a minute, Dylan decided that he was either heading wrong or the dark beast wanted him to ride.

He shifted his packs and the animal released its teeth. Dylan found a low stump and got on it. The licorne stood at right angles, just as a well-trained horse might, and with a little trepidation, the man swung his leg over the narrow back. It was considerably less comfortable than a horse, and he was not used to riding bareback, but it was possible. Dylan clung to the rough mane, longed for a bridle of some sort, and the licorne plunged into the forest.

After a very short time, Dylan leaned forward and lay his chest along the splendid neck and drew his arms around it lightly. It was a bone-rattling ride, for the licorne was gaited differently than a horse, and its sharp spine dug into his groin rather painfully. He longed for a pad, a saddle or just about anything between him and his strange steed. After a time his well-trained body stopped complaining, or rather the aches became so general that he ceased noticing them.

By dusk he was exhausted, and when the licorne halted in a birchwood copse, he slid to the ground in a kind of mute misery. Dylan forced himself to his feet and stretched cramped muscles and aching arms into motion. The licorne was damp with fine sweat, and smelled of exertion. Dylan was filthy with dust and sweat himself, but he wiped the beast down before he did anything else. The licorne bore these attentions with calm majesty and seemed none the worse for the wild ride, but Dylan was more tired than he had been after a day's tourneying.

Dylan unfolded his cloak—it was chill already—and put it around his shoulders, then began sorting out dried meat, cheese, and hard bread for an evening meal. His pack was a jumble and he set it in order, hanging his extra hose from a convenient limb to air out. They were still a bit damp and smelled of salt water from his brief walk to the shore. His fussing over his belongings made him think of his mother, who had the most unlikely notions about cleanliness, and he smiled to himself. Prince Geoffrey often teased him. "How many baths have you had this year, Dylan?" he would ask. At the moment, itchy with sweat and dried salt, he would have enjoyed one of his mother's fragrant tubs—or even a dip in Sal's sacred well, as his mother was supposed to have done. Icy water from a spring or stream might wash away his grime, but it would not ease aching muscles or comfort him. With a slight pang Dylan realized he was homesick and even a little frightened. These unmanly emotions piqued his pride, and he promptly banished them to a darkened corner of his mind. He munched meat and stale cheese and tried not to think of one of Eleanor's savory stews, accompanied by his sister's warm loaves and fresh butter. He was so successful in this endeavor that his food tasted like boot soles and he quite lost his appetite in mid mouthful.

A soft giggle startled him. Dylan looked around into the darkness. The licorne was a silvery glimmer on one side of the grove, and he was sure the sound had not issued from that noble throat. He turned around completely. Something soft and green shimmered at the base of a large birch tree.

"Humans are so amusing. I had almost forgot." It was a girl's voice, a very young voice; the shimmer solidified into a pretty maid with pale hair and snowy skin. Huge green eyes dominated a heart-shaped face. The laughing mouth was small and generous with a hint of cruelty about it. The girl's body was unclothed, and it was almost a child's body, with tiny immature breasts and a skimpy fuzz of pubic hair. Embarrassed, Dylan averted his eyes.

"Oh, do you not find me pleasing?" The voice was sulky.

"You are very fair, milady, but isn't it a bit chilly to be out in your birthing clothes?"

"But—I am never cold. Oh, very well. I never would have thought you such a prude. There. Now I am as proper as a lady at court."

Dylan looked again and found she wore a shift of green and silver leaves. It was almost transparent and enhanced rather than disguised her nakedness, but he decided to accept the thought for the deed. He knew enough of feminine fashions to realize that any of his sisters would have starved for a length of the stuff. In a gown of it, his sister Rowena would have been quite irresistible to Prince Geoffrey.

"Very pretty. Are you a . . . dryad?" He had to hunt for the word.

"Oh, no. If you had ever met one, you wouldn't make

such an error. They are quite droopy and have no conversation whatever. Well, most of them. Those of the holly are rather prickly." She mused for a moment. "And impatient," she added.

"Pray forgive my ignorance. We seem to have very few dryads in Albion."

"Nonsense. That island is fairly crawling with them. But they are somewhat shy, you see. The trouble with you, Dylan, is that you think the magic went out of the world when you were breeched. Even my sister Sal is but a dream of a dream to you."

Dylan reddened. Her words were true and precise and they stung him like a whiplash. It felt like the birch switch his mother used upon him on those rare occasions when his childish wickedness merited such attentions. That memory, plus the girl calling Sal her sister gave him a clue to her identity—the Lady of the Birches—but he hesitated to name her. This pretty girl frightened him as the ancient dragon Melusine had not. The great green eyes seemed like mirrors, and he could see his hidden fears and rages—those things he had kept locked away in his mind. He found he didn't like it one bit and tried to turn his gaze away.

"No, no, my cautious poppet. You cannot evade me so easily. Ah! That dame of yours! She has so much to answer for, but all parents do. That is why they come to me to exorcise the wickedness they themselves have made in their precious offspring."

"I bow to your greater wisdom, my lady Chastisement," he said quietly.

She chuckled. "Save your charming gallantries for someone who cares for such things. You do not bow to anyone, like your father before you. And you do not know yourself."

"No doubt you will enlighten me." Dylan kept an iron grip on the fear that fluttered within him.

"No. I will not."

"You won't?" He was surprised.

"That is something you will have to do for yourself." She giggled again, and now it sounded like the cackle of some mad beldame. He was cold with more than the chill of night. "You mortals all expect such miracles. I do not do revelations. The answers lie within you, if you will but seek them."

"Milady, I do not even know the questions."

"Yes, you do, you silly boy. You simply do not wish to ask them, since the answers might not please you. It is the way of your kind, to sweep dirt under the floor reeds and pretend it does not exist because you can no longer see it. Why are you afraid?"

Dylan plunged into the wells of her eyes, into swirling memories of his childhood. Everywhere he looked he saw his mother, strong and vital and tall, holding her rowan staff with the four faces of the moon upon it. He sheltered in the wild folds of her robe. For the first time he saw that Eleanor's bravery was a disguise for her terror that some terrible, unknown fate would take him from her; and he loved her for her love and hated her for the shackles of weakness it made within him. The revulsion and his dinner rose as one from his stomach and he spewed them out onto the patient earth.

Dylan wept.

Cool fingers brushed his cheeks. "There, there, *mon brave*. 'Tis but a fever. 'Twill pass, as all things pass." She stroked his tousled head against her shoulder. They were a mother's gentle words to chase away the nightmare, and Dylan knew that if he lived for a thousand years, he would always bear within him a tiny scar to mark that clutching, obsessive fear that had been Eleanor's first gift to him.

Abruptly, he pulled himself free of the lady's embrace and glared at her with tear-reddened eyes. "I do not require any comfort."

She laughed, a silver sound in the darkness. "Oh, no. Of course you do not. Foolish man. We all need comfort—

even I. When my ancient sister Demeter lost her beloved daughter, Persephone, all the gods wished to ease her grief, but she would have none of it. She masked her rage in a veil of sorrow and punished all the living for her loss. The earth was dry and barren in her mourning. She died a little, all because she was too proud to accept a little comfort. That is a cold and bitter place you have within you, Dylan—a child's sulky petulance when he is forced to eat his porridge before he gets his cakes.''

"I did not ask to be born into such terror."

"I did not ask to be the Mistress of Punishments, to have my supple limbs used to whip the wickedness out of the generations. The world is not fair. It is full of mindless cruelty and carelessness. But, too, it is full of unexpected joy and kindness. Your mother did the best she could."

"It was not enough."

"It never is." She smiled a little. "Wait until you have your own children."

"Perhaps I shall become a monk."

"Oh, Dylan," she trilled.

He found himself laughing at the idea in spite of himself. "I was not cut out to be a servant of God, was I?"

"Well, not that jumped-up little dunghill cock that the Pope fancies. You must discover the God within you—as all men must. I can tell you this much. He is no tidy, distant fellow in some celestial palace with sexless angels singing hallelujahs in his ears."

"No. He's a wild man, like my father. Why, when I think of him, do I only see my mother?"

"She stands between you, a doorway to his past, and your future. Do you have the courage to pass through her womb a second time, as he did?"

"I am not certain."

"A very sensible answer. Your mother would have said yes in a moment and regretted it later. She has, in a way, protected you from her own impetuousness. In that moment, years ago, when Bridget told her that her children would continue her task, she set her face against the Fates. She is stubborn, that one. An odd mixture—but all mortals are a motley, a bit of this and a dab of that.''

''Unlike yourself.''

''I am that I am.''

Dylan discovered he was shocked to hear her use the words out of the burning bush. ''And what is that?''

She looked into his eyes, and he knew a terror and a joy beyond any words. She was the bravest of the brave, the first tree to set leaf in the dead of the year, and the most fragile as well. Her gaze promised rebirth, but also death. Beside her, his mother's womanliness was but a memory of a shadow of the thing itself. He dropped his eyes and found he was trembling.

''Do not think less of your mother for her fear, nor of your father for not crashing through her fortress and rescuing you from her eternal womb. They did not ask to have their lives become a poet's lay, nor to bear a child of such dimensions. They did their tasks as best they could—and very well at that.''

''But what am I?''

''Not 'who'?''

''I am Dylan, the Son of the Wave.'' The grove vanished at his words, and he could hear the roar of the sea crashing against the shore. In Eleanor's womb he had ridden the cold ocean and seen the weedy tresses and solemn face of the Mother of Waters. He had longed for her embrace and chilly comfort. For an instant he saw the fair woman of his dreams, now made of pearls and coral, resting in the bosom of the sea, and he knew only her touch would ease his ache and release his loneliness. He had a moment's panic, for she seemed so still, so dead. Where was she? Asleep in the deep or perished in some dreadful cavern?

The vision faded, and he looked at himself seated before the Lady of the Birches, as if he rode the night breezes like an owl. He saw his skin flayed away and saw his anger and his fear, both black as pitch like molten rock oozing from the tortured earth, concealing the light within. His face changed. It became a snarling wolf, slavering fiery spittle, a boar with bloodstained tusks, a ravening bear with yawning maw, and finally an eagle screaming its challenge.

He was a beast, a fearsome, mindless creature, full of blind hungers and lusts. He defiled the earth with his rages. Once again his form altered. He was a stag, noble and brave, his seven-tined antlers pulsing with the green light of the birches. The eyes shone like the moon, and he knew himself for both the jailor and prisoner; that within the bear, the boar, the wolf, and eagle lived both the fiercest and gentlest of the beasts. He saw the licorne as himself, and he felt a mild chagrin at what a bone-wracking and uncomfortable ride he had had. We *were not intended to be ridden*, he thought.

The light of the stag's eyes and antlers mingled, and the grove brightened so that he could see each leaf upon the birch trees and each hair of the lady's tresses. He studied each leaf in turn, marvelling at their perfection, their promise of life and death. And for a moment he loved her as he had loved no other. His mother, his sisters, even the dream woman faded into insignificance beside her serene strength.

"My lady! Beth!" He cried her name and tumbled head first into her soft lap. He pillowed his head upon her thighs and breathed deeply the sweet green scent of her womanhood. She coiled supple fingers into his curling hair and he heard the murmur of earth in her song. Dylan slept.

Mornings, he decided, were for the birds. Indeed, every avian in Franconia seemed to have journeyed to this spot to herald the new day with every note they had within them. He groaned and sat up.

The birch grove was rainbowed by the colors of their feathers. He saw the red of robins, the brown of wrens, the gold of finches, the white and taupe of cooing doves, the bright azure of bluebirds, and the glossy black of ravens, plus a dozen sorts he knew no name for. They were all caroling, honking, cawing, and tweeting. The result was quite awful.

"Be quiet!" he bellowed, and his head throbbed.

They went still and silent, eyeing him with brilliant orbs. A plumb dove waddled over to him and climbed onto his knee, tilting her head to one side. She gave a soft coo.

Dylan found he was holding his breath. He released it slowly, and lifted a finger to stroke the soft plumage. Stuck to his palm was a birch leaf. It was green on one side, silver on the other, but it had never grown on any earthly tree. It must have dropped from the lady's gown, though it was no cloth he had ever seen before. What had happened was more than a dream.

For a moment he experienced a sense of disloyalty to that other goddess, Sal, Lady of the Willows, who had in some sense sent him upon this adventure. He almost heard her rare, rippling laughter in his mind. Sal was his mother's mentor, and perhaps his sisters'. Beth of the Birches was his own, and he would wear her single leaf upon his sleeve, his lady's favor, no matter what claims any mortal woman put upon him. He had dreamt upon her lap and found within the dream the courage to endure the winter of his fears.

For the moment, he tucked the wondrous leaf into his belt pouch and then noticed that the glade was occupied by more than birds. A solemn badger peered at him from under a tree, while a dozen squirrels raced up and down a trunk. Ferrets and field mice were plundering his dried bread and hard cheese, and a vixen and two kits sat calmly near a pair of rabbits. Within the dappled shadows of the trees he saw a fawn, and behind it a doe, still as statues. The birds began to chatter again as one of the ferrets climbed onto the leg not occupied by the dove. It swarmed up his chest and stood on his shoulder, nuzzling his ears with a wet nose.

It tickled and Dylan laughed, which made his head throb. He lifted a hand to his forehead, and above the brow he found two spots which were tender to the touch, as if the stag's antlers were about to grow out of his head. He looked at his hands and arms, but they were still quite human, and he was silently relieved. Dazed and dazzled in the pale sunlight, he watched the consumption of his food by ferrets, mice, squirrels, and rabbits with almost complete disinterest. He was not hungry, and he wondered dispassionately if he would ever eat flesh again. He was Lord of the Forest, and any of these beasts would die for him, but the sense of command made him uneasy. For the first time he understood his mother's reluctance to accept her own powers and magics and her unwillingness to do more than minor domestic conjurings.

Were it not for the leaf in his pouch and the animals gathered around him in unnatural harmony, he would have thought the whole thing a pleasant dream. *Not pleasant, entirely,* he amended, rubbing his forehead. Dylan could not understand why he felt as if he were about to sprout horns. For that matter, he wondered what he had done to attract the interest of the Lady of the Birches. Some rough ancient god like wild Pan seemed more likely than pretty Beth. Then he chuckled, for Pan was a master of music, and he had no gift for that. It was not a problem to be solved in the pale light of morning, or ever, perhaps. The powers of the world were simply not ruled by any logic he could perceive.

"Who said I would not regret my choices," he asked a raven that had flown down to investigate a bit of meat the rabbits were ignoring. The bird gave him a look and a shrug of wings and went back to his breakfast. "Well, I will never get to Paris, sitting here. Be off, little friends. The audience is ended." The birds rose in a flutter of color, darting off to the four winds, and the beasts hopped, ran, and scurried into the shadows. In a minute all that remained was a collection of discarded feathers and the droppings of mice and hares. The licorne appeared from the trees, and Dylan rose to greet it, stroking the soft nose and the strong neck. Then he gathered his belongings and prepared to set out once again.

VII

Aenor dreamed, smiling. She saw a forest glade dappled in golden sunlight. Little purple flowers poked out around the roots of slender trees. If only she could recall their names. But she could not. A woman sat at the base of a tree a little larger than the rest. Her hair was almost white, and her gown was palest green, like the first leaves of springtide. The face of the woman was sweet and gentle and she looked at Aenor with eyes the same pale green as her gown.

"Good day, daughter." The voice was low and honeyed.

"Greetings, mother." She saw herself sit down at the woman's feet, ashamed of her ragged gown and dirty face. She rubbed a sleeve across her cheek, careless of the scratchy remnants of metal embroidery, but it did no good. Still, she was content to be with the strange lady.

"You are troubled, child."

"Yes. I am weary of my captivity. Why cannot I just give these folk this accursed jewel and return to the sunlight?"

"You gave your word." The sunlight seemed a bit less golden with these words.

"I did, but to whom, and for what purpose? I cannot remember."

"Keep your word, and you will reap a great reward. Falter, and you will never see the sun or the sea again."

The sea. The word brought a rush of memory, of other dreams perhaps, and Aenor saw huge waves and white horses cresting upon them. There were other beasts as well, great sleek creatures who leapt from wave to wave and uttered sharp shouts in the sparkling air. One shot straight up in a huge spray and sped towards the shore. It touched the sands and became a man. He swept the strand with grey eyes and shook the sparkling droplets out of his curly black hair. He held a long object in his hands, brightly colored and covered in strange patterns.

The dream of a dream faded and she was back beside the pale lady. "Mother, I am weary. I am hungry and thirsty and dirty and cold all the time."

"I know. But you do not have to be. A song will cure thy ills."

"A . . . song?"

"Your song, Alianora." The lady gave a tiny chuckle. "You can make beauty, more beauty than even your captors can imagine. They will be sick with envy. Just remember the sea and the sun, the moon and the sound of licorne hooves upon the bosom of earth, the smell of apples and roses. Sing *that*."

Aenor woke abruptly, her mouth watering at the thought of a ripe, rosy apple. The tangy smell of its flesh filled her nostrils and she was almost sick with longing. She rubbed her temples to drive away the persistent headache, and swallowed her hunger. She rose and shook out her worn blanket and the ragged skirt of her gown. The clang of anvils made an ugly melody in the cavern beyond.

She grinned a little. It had taken them days to get the molten river back to its course, and the Queen had had to send one of her best singers down to the King's court before it was done. Alilian Garnet Singer had accomplished it, but it had tasked her badly, and the dwarves whispered she had returned to the Queen's court powerless, her song faded beyond recall. The dwarves had been driven cruelly to clean up the mess, and for that she was sorry. She had no dispute with the poor, twisted forge slaves. Now they were back at their work, and she hated the noise. She wished all their hammers would turn into rushes and reeds.

There was a river near the castle which had been her home once, a broad current of water, and she had often played amongst the shallows, when she could escape the watchful eye of her nursemaids. There was one place where the reeds and cat willows grew thickly, and she would hide amongst them, watching the tiny silver fish who swam between the stems, and the insects with multi-colored wings which darted along the surface of the stream. Sometimes an unwary one would be gobbled up by a trout, and she would grieve a little for the ruin of its iridescent beauty. In her mind she could almost hear the steady croak of frogs at evening.

Aenor pushed back one of the long braids of her hair and shifted the sword to a less awkward position. Her fingers brushed the slender rope of licorne hair that still ran through the beryl, and unconsciously she began to hum. It was a tuneless humming, more a series of rhythms, hoofbeats and frog croaks, than a song, but she could almost hear the gurgle of the river beneath it and smell the rich wet scent of mud and growing things.

Aenor remembered a day in the Queen's court, years before, very early in her captivity, when no memory of sunlight pierced her mind. There had been a solemn cele-bration of some sort, and the singers had lifted their voices into a wonderous melody, in words which had no meaning but which conveyed a picture of a huge hall of white stone. Great pictures in colored crystal pierced the walls, and beyond them she knew there was a nameless light. It was then she had begun to waken from the living dream the White Folk had woven around her.

Knowing that her voice was like a raven's compared to the least of the Queen's spell singers, she wove a portion of that antiphonal melody into her humming. The words were a blur in her mind, a montage of visions of grasses and flowers and the way sunlight touched the leaves at springtide. It swirled in her mind as she paced the narrow confines of her chamber. The cavern smelled odd.

Aenor paused in her pacing and tilted her head to one side. She sniffed. The scent was delicious, sweet and spicy. Where could it be coming from? She peered into the dark corners of the rocks.

A flash of white caught her eye. She went to it and bent down. There was a flower there, a star-shaped blossom nodding on a slender stalk. She touched a petal with one finger and caught a shining drop of moisture on the tip. Aenor brought it to her tongue and tasted a sharp tang, as if green had a flavor.

"What is that infernal stink?!" The King stood at the entrance to her chamber, his pale face almost rosy with fury.

Aenor gave a guilty start and turned, stepping in front of the fragile flower. "Stink?" she asked hesitantly.

"What are you hiding?" He was bellowing and his eyes were like coals.

The little stream of song bubbled within her. Behind it, she knew, was a mighty river, a veritable ocean, a thing which might destroy the very vessel which contained it. That was how spell singers perished, by making songs too great for their powers. The thought that she might possess such energy surprised her. Aenor realized she had been learning all those years in the Queen's court, without knowing it.

"What do I have to hide? I have a blanket I would not ask a dog to lie upon. Here." She thrust the thing at him.

The stream gurgled in her throat as she spoke, pushing, threatening to breach its banks and flood the hollow room with a roaring torrent of music. Aenor hissed a ripple of notes out of a dry throat.

The King ignored her and peered towards the back of

the small cavern. He sprang forward and pointed at the shimmering blossom. "What is that?"

Aenor pressed her back against the wall, her hands clutching the rough rock, trying to contain the song which seemed ready to burst from her straining lungs. Her breathing was deep but ragged. She fought for some control and found enough to speak. "It appears to be a flower. A jonquil, I believe."

"What is it doing here?"

"I have no idea." That was quite true. She had not been thinking of jonquils, and she did not think that the King would believe her in any case.

The King stared at her. His face had thinned in the past days and his eyes were circled with a darkness which did not come from the smuts of the forges. The rainbow circlet above his brow seemed dim and grimy, and his dark locks were lank against his skull.

With a quick move he smashed the flower with his boot. Aenor gave a little cry, as if she had been kicked. The small compassion she had begun to feel for the King died stillborn. The song thrummed along her veins, not like fire, but like chill water, clear and clean.

Aenor lifted her hands off the rock and moved towards the King. Her touch might not kill him, but it might make him wish she had. He gave a sort of squawk and pointed behind her.

She turned. The imprint of her body stood upon the rock, a mass of wild white roses, irises, and poppies. A single stalk of gladiolus, red as blood, lay along her hip, where the sword rested. The scent of roses filled the room, and where her foot had rested, lilies sprang. The King rushed away, leaving Aenor alone with a growing bower.

Alphonze, King of White Folk, was worried. He had failed twice to exercise command over one troublesome mortal female, and several of his lesser relations were eyeing his rainbowed circlet with open covetousness. When the Queen had exiled Aenor to his domains, he had been certain he could accomplish quickly the recovery of the jewel she possessed. A few weeks of cold and hunger would reduce the girl to such abject misery that she would be glad to hand over the thing. It would be quite a coup to do what the Queen and the court had failed to do.

But Aenor had surprised him. She showed little if any fear of his awesome might. She was rude and defiant, and she had eroded his authority by her critical presence amongst the forges. Something she had done had certainly caused the eruption of the metal river and the ruin of his workshops, though he had not spoken his suspicions to the Queen. It had been humiliating enough to beg for the offices of a spell singer to clean up the mess. The Queen suffered greatly under the curse that Aenor had laid upon her, but he considered that to be a sign of Elpha's own weakness and incompetence.

Now he could not get the memory out of his mind of a silhouette of hateful blossoms springing from the bare rock where Aenor's body had pressed. The terrible scent of these flowers disturbed him. Once, long ago, he had rejoiced in such things, in the sweet music of breeze on leaves, the soft fall of petal upon grass, for he had been very young when they had come to these caverns. Now the thought of such things was painful and loathsome. The Clay Folk were inferior, short-lived, and brutish. It hardly seemed possible that they were heir to the Blessed Lands, fouling it with their stone houses and loathsome habits. How could the Lord of the Living have chosen them over his earlier and greater creatures? Why, in his vanity, had he given them imperishable spirits, those souls which made them unique amongst his creatures? As he had been many times before, Alphonze was enraged at the injustice of it all. *We are beautiful, the fairest folk to ever walk under the sun and moon, and they are ugly and stupid.*

With an effort he set aside these futile musings and concentrated upon the problem at hand. Aenor had somehow learned the secrets of the spell singers. If he was not careful, she would be leaving patches of daisies all over the workshop floor. He ought to send her back to the Queen and wash his hands of the whole matter. It had not been his idea to steal her from her bed and bring her to these caverns. He had dwelt several millennia in the now-abandoned Crystal City beneath the green sun of the beryl, and in truth he preferred his sooty workshops. And Alfgar the Accursed had certainly shown the folly of treating with mortals. Alphonze sighed. Alfgar had been the finest flower of the Fair Folk. How could he have loved a silly wench? How could he have stolen the sun for lust?

He arose from his great stone chair, unable to penetrate these mysteries, and began his preparations. Fresh clothing, for the Queen hated the smell of the forges, and new boots, for the sole of the one still stank of jonquils. He would swallow his pride and ask for aid a second time, though it left a bitter taste in his mouth. They would take the girl back. He would demand it. It was Elpha's fault anyhow. They never should have let Aenor run tame at court, learning who knew what secrets. They should never have brought her into the realm, as they never permitted those others who bore White Folk blood in their veins, the Guardians of the Way who hid the avenues between the sunlit world above and that below. There were merely servants who could bear the light, and while they possessed great powers compared to the miserable Clay Folk, they were still tainted by their human heritage. Vile creatures, neither one thing nor the other, performing their meagre magics in pale imitation of their betters. The only good they did was to prevent the Clay Folk from entering the realm with their dreadful swords.

Alphonze raged silently as he prepared himself to go again to the Queen's court. He was unwelcome there, the more so since the Queen had begun to sicken from Aenor's curse. The efforts of the spell singers had thus far sustained her, but they had not managed to undo the damage.

How was it possible for one silly slip of a Clay Woman to
wreak such havoc? He thought of the roses in her chamber
and shuddered. The spell singers had sworn that Aenor
was harmless, bound by their powers forever. Accursed
females, all of them, with their endless chantings. They
were just waiting for Elpha to pass, so that one of them
might become Queen. They probably were not really trying
to cure the Queen. It was unthinkable that Aenor could
have been so effective.

Alphonze shifted his dark belled baldric into place over
his tunic and contemplated the candidates for Queen if
Elpha perished. They were all quite young, and none of
them his allies. They might wish to put another in his
place. If only Eldrida were a singer. He considered the
woman, an odd female, always making visits to his forges
and asking all kinds of questions of his masters. She was
too cunning and flattering by half. Still, she might be
useful, somehow.

His thoughts returned to Aenor and the imprint of her
body in living blossoms upon the bare wall of the cavern.
*I, the greatest lord of the White Folk, will not be undone
by any half-clay mortal.*

Aenor lay stretched out on a bed of sweet grass. Her
small cavern was warm and humid with the moisture of a
thousand blossoms. A small cascade of clear water tumbled from one wall and spilled into a pool upon the floor.
She had washed her face in it, then had removed her gown
and unbound her golden hair, and cleansed herself to a
glowing pink. The song within her had altered to a soft
murmur, a melody that mirrored the ripple of the water.
She felt a vast peace. The beryl-hilted sword rested beside
her on the grass, but she had forgotten it.

A whisper broke her reverie. She sat up, her long silky
hair falling across her small breasts and sheltering her
nakedness. She felt the presence of another song nearby. A

spell singer! Who? She racked her brains to identify the maker.

Ah, Angold. She was the youngest and most vigorous of the Queen's singers, and her song was fresh and innovative by their canons. Indeed, she was almost a renegade amongst her kind.

Another whisper. The King, of course. Aenor tensed. What were they up to? The room seemed cooler, suddenly, and her body felt heavy. Her eyes drooped.

The grass beneath her was no longer soft, but cold and glassy. Aenor forced her eyes open and looked around. The flowers were turning to stone and glass, the merry waterfall to crystal. Angold was stopping her song!

A flicker of fear touched her, replaced by a flood of rage a moment later. Her song was gone—almost. A faint echo of its power rang in her mind. Her head nodded as a terrible sleep began to envelope her. She dug her nails into her thighs and the pain roused her a little.

Aenor clawed the crystal grass and closed her hand around the hilt of the sword. She was heavy with Angold's song now and could barely move. Somehow she dragged the sword towards her, and clasped it to her chest. Then she sagged back, clutching the sword to her body, the great green stone upon her heart. A pearlescence covered her body, and she became a statue resting within a glassy bower.

"Is she . . .?"

"Dead? Hardly, Alphonze. She merely sleeps. My song was barely strong enough to do that much, and how long the spell will stay I cannot say. I am weary beyond all measure."

"You mean she might awaken? Get her out of my court, witch woman!"

"Mind your tongue, you miserable artificer." They glared at each other. "She is no more touchable in this state than waking, for she holds the sun against her heart. And let so much as a drop of moisture touch her lips and she will rouse . . . and my song shall cease.''

Angold leaned against the rocky wall at the entrance to the cavern. She was a tall, pale-haired woman with smooth features. Now she seemed shrunken in her blue pleated gown, and Alphonze looked at her bewilderedly.

''What do you mean?''

''I had to twist my song into hers. You cannot understand.'' She gave a terrible laugh. ''Now we are sisters. I wish we had never brought her here. I cannot bear the sight of her. She is our doom, Alphonze. You will be the last King of the White Folk, and no one will remain to tell our tale.''

''Have you added prophecy to your other gifts?'' he sneered, ignoring the chill the singer's words aroused in him. ''I shall have this place closed in with stones, so none may see this . . . horror.''

''Do what you will; it will not suffice.'' Angold turned away and he followed her. Neither of them heard the slight slither of leathery hide over rock.

VIII

The smell of Paris reached Dylan long before he reached the edges of the city. It stank like all the sheep in Christendom rotting in the August sun. A grey mist rose off the river, full of flies and midges and biting gnats.

When he could see the shield wall, Dylan slid wearily off the licorne and patted his flanks. "This cesspit is no place for the likes of you, nor me either, if the truth be told. But I must go there. Somewhere in there is a bit of my grandmother's hide pretending to be a scabbard. I do not know if we will meet again, dear friend, but if we do not, it has been a privilege to have known you. Thank you for bearing such a clumsy burden so many leagues." He stroked the mane and plucked a cockleburr from the tail. To his surprise, some dozen hairs came away with it. He wound them back and forth between his fingers into a luminescent coil and tucked them into his pouch.

The licorne gave a brazen bellow and turned away. It vanished into the woods, and Dylan stood for a long time after it had gone, feeling a little lonely. A tiny melancholy frisked in his mind like a playful puppy, and he realized that he had lost his taste for the haunts of men, for the bustle of commerce and the shrill voices of his kind. Too, he was disturbed by his dreams. Beth shimmered in his sleep, but the other woman did as well. She slept, it seemed, or perhaps she had died, for she seemed so still, unmoving in a glassy bower, her pale skin gleaming like pink pearl, the lovely hand clutching the sword against her breast. He was no Prince Charming to wake the Sleeping Beauty with a chaste salute upon the wide brow, like one of his mother's tales. He had the niggling fear that somehow the Fates would cheat him, unreliable as they were.

Banishing these thoughts as well as he could, Dylan walked up the left bank of the Seine until he came to a bridge. It was a clumsy affair of poorly cut stone, new by its rawness, but already missing blocks from its sides and center. It looked as if the masons had been drunk when they made it. He shook his head, comparing it unfavorably with the fair span across the Thames that Arthur had built after he became King to replace the one ruined by the dreadful sound of the King's pipes. Then he picked his way carefully across it. Huddles of beggars crouched here and there upon it, and they called to him for alms. They were miserable and diseased and he avoided them, for they had the same look of Shadow as had the peasants which had attacked the licorne.

An indifferent guard in rusting mail and filthy braies barely stirred as he passed. Inside the wall, the beggars were more numerous. He could barely comprehend their gabble, and he realized that many were missing lips and noses and had running sores upon their faces and arms. This was no Shadow sickness, he knew, but the dreadful white death called leprosy. Franconia's ruler must be a fool, to permit these folk to run free in the streets. Did Paris possess no lazarium where these people might dwell in decency, cared for by pious monks, without the risk of contaminating their fellows? Two scuttled towards him like crabs, claw hands out in whining supplication, and he waved them back in horror and pity.

A few steps further on an ugly fellow offered him a pretty girl of ten—or a boy about the same age, if he preferred. The children stared at him with empty eyes as they crouched in the litter-clogged doorway of a tumble-down shed. Dylan was disgusted and almost moved to pity. His better judgement told him that he could do nothing.

He passed a reeking alehouse and though his throat was parched, he was not tempted to enter its noisome confines. From the shouts, he suspected they were engaged in some sport he did not wish to know about. He was almost past it when there was a terrible roar, followed by screams and shouts.

He turned and saw a large bear, collared and muzzled, lumbering out, dragging a hapless youngster behind it. The beast was missing bits of fur, and a bloody froth rimmed the leather around his mouth. It reared up and batted the boy aside, raking sharp claws across his arm. The patrons exploded out of the alehouse and skittered to a halt as their victim turned to confront them, bellowing his ursine rage. A tongue of flame licked out between the planks of the structure, and there was an explosive *boom!* The customers, caught between an angry bear and a fiery building, screamed and darted this way and that.

One, braver or drunker than the rest, poked the bear with a cudgel while several others ran down the narrow street. The beast knocked the pole aside and the man fell down screaming. The bear lifted him up with great paws and dashed him down again to the paving stones. Then it turned and lumbered over to Dylan and groveled at his feet like a dog.

"Kill it! Kill it!" screamed the customers who remained.

Dylan felt his skull throb where the stag wore antlers, and he was almost blind with rage and pain. He looked at the bear's tormentors and they shrank back, mindless of the fire behind them. A pitiful bucket brigade swelled the crowd, but the alehouse was beyond saving. They splashed filthy river water on the flames in a halfhearted way and scurried away.

Dylan bent down and removed the muzzle and the collar. "Poor little brother," he murmured. The bear rolled brown eyes at him and growled in what passed for a friendly way in such a beast. Dylan stroked its rough head. For the first time he began to understand the power of the Stag Lord he had become, and it was not an easy thing. The bear had somehow sensed his presence and come to pay him homage. Otherwise it would have borne the teasings and abuse of its tormentors until it died in the mute agony of the beast.

Dylan looked disgustedly at the faces of the little crowd, sickened by the pointless cruelty of his own kind. They were avid for some excitement, some occasion to forget their own misery and pain. He remembered his mother's strange tales of Prince Siddhartha, who was quite happy until one day he saw hunger and death, disease and old age, and had then left his beautiful palace to seek an answer to these terrible curses. The Prince, Dylan remembered, had become a great holy man, and he almost regreted that he had no gift for contemplation. He could abandon his quest and return to the forest and live out his years among the beasts, but that would not change anything.

"Go back to the woods, little brother," he told the bear. The animal stood on its hind legs and gave a bellow, then turned on all fours and lumbered down the crooked street with amazing speed for such an ungainly beast. The crowd parted as he passed.

"That was my bear," said a fat man with a ruddy complexion. "Who gave you the right to turn him loose? He was very valuable. Give me—"

"Piss on yourself," Dylan said succinctly. He turned away from the fat man, and the crowd snickered and elbowed the ribs of their fellows. If they could not have a bearbaiting, a brawl would do as well.

The man grabbed at Dylan's shoulder, and Dylan felt the fury rise. He twisted around, picked the man up by his underarms, and tossed him back into the cackling gaggle. They parted like wheat before the wind, and the man hit the paving stones with a guttural grunt. A couple of other men sprang forward to defend their friend, and one landed a glancing blow with a short stick on Dylan's brow.

He was dazed for a second. Then something filled him; a wild, singing rage, a storm of mind that rushed into his blood. Dylan snarled. He caught the man's stick as it descended again and twisted it away. Then he grabbed a wrist and turned the arm up in the socket behind the man until there was an audible pop. The man screamed as he fell, and the crowd decided to find other amusement. They vanished, abandoning the fat man and his friends—one fallen, one standing—in front of the burning alehouse. The one standing eyed Dylan, then his cronies, shrugged and slipped away.

"So much for loyalty," Dylan muttered as he bent to pick up his fallen packs. He heartily wished he had never come to this miserable city. He wondered why the Seine did not overflow its banks and wash the place away.

"Monsieur," came a quiet voice.

He looked for the speaker and found the pretty little boy he had been offered further down the street. He was crouched in the shadow of a broken wagon, boney hands clutching the shattered wheel.

"Yes. What is it? Do not be afraid. I will not harm you."

"I do not want Jacques to see me."

"Is he your master?"

"Yes, sieur. Please, take me with you. He stole me. I want to go home."

"Do you know where your home is?"

"No, monsieur. It has been two years."

"Your name then."

"Philippe. Philippe Sangrael."

"Why have you not run away?" Dylan was not sure if he should believe the child.

"He beat me." The boy lifted his tattered shirt and displayed a collection of welts and sores. "I was afraid."

"And the girl. Is she your sister?"

"No, no, monsieur. She is very wicked. She beats me too."

Dylan found that difficult to believe. The girl had looked so weak and listless. He studied the boy for a long moment. There was something subtly wrong about the child, a glitter in the eyes, a tension in the fingers. He wondered at himself, that he would nearly kill a man over a bear yet hesitate over a small boy. Then he realized that within the shadow of the wagon Philippe's body showed no light, no aura. The Darkness did not always deform the body. Sometimes it merely twisted the soul into a pit of evil. And like his mother, Dylan had a gift for perceiving the difference. With a deep sense of regret he realized he could not save everyone.

He shifted his packs into a more comfortable position on his shoulder and started up the street. The boy followed him, clinging to the shadows. Dylan ignored him, trying to make some sense out of the tangle of alleys and streets that made up the district. After several turns he came into a wider street—one where he could not touch both sides with outstretched arms and a swords length—with sturdier houses. The steady clack of heddles from several open doors told him this was a weaver's enclave, and he paused for a moment just to savor the simple domesticity of the sound. It reminded him of home, of cleanliness and security.

Then he noticed the avid little face of the boy Philippe peering at him from the shadow of a doorway, and he wondered if the boy's master had sent him to spy on Dylan. Shabby as his garments were after several days in the wild, Dylan was still better dressed than the miserable beggars near the gate, and that alone was sufficient to attract the attention of thieves. The sale of his sword would feed a large family for a week or more.

"Please, monsieur, I will do anything you wish," the boy began to whine. He continued in graphic detail all of the services he would perform, reeling off unspeakable acts in a little singsong voice, until Dylan had gone beyond shock into outrage. He had an urge to clamp a hand around the child's throat and throttle the life out of him and to run back across the nearest bridge and away from the city.

"Go back to your master, brat!"

"But, monsieur, he will beat me." The boy crawled towards Dylan's feet and touched his boot. Dylan pulled his foot away, but the child grabbed his other leg and cried piteously. He swarmed up the leg and embraced the man's waist, so his fair head rested against Dylan's pouch.

A second later Philippe howled and jerked himself away, clutching his head and dancing on the paving stones like one possessed. Heads popped out of doors and windows to see what was causing the ruckus, and one sturdy woman advanced on Dylan with a stern expression on her plain face.

"He's got a demon in his belt," shrieked Philippe. "It made me feel . . . light! Oh, it hurts. Make it stop."

"He's a thief, and I cuffed him when he tried to steal my pouch," Dylan said, improvising something he hoped would be believed.

The woman grabbed the boy's hair and peered at his face. "Stop this racket! There is not a mark upon you!"

Philippe gave a strangled sound and opened his mouth. A tangle of dark, slimy worms hung out, then slithered down to the street. The boy vomited more things up while the woman moved hastily away. A stench that overcame the persistent odor of the Seine rose from the mess, and the boy tried desperately to push the dreadful things back into his mouth. Finally, he fell moaning into the pile of his own making and his blue eyes fluttered and he died.

There was a silence in the street, and then a small man came from one of the houses. He carried a handful of rages dripping oil and a burning brand. He dropped the cloth on the still-twitching body and set it alight. The fire blazed, first on the rags, then on the tattered fabric of Philippe's poor garments and finally spread to the flesh of child and worms alike.

A huddle of weavers stood around the body and watched in quiet.

The woman studied Dylan, who watched the whole proceeding in horror, and patted his hand in a friendly way. "The priest says to burn them, for they have no souls and cannot lie in sacred ground. I can see you are a stranger. You are very pale, monsignor. Perhaps you will come into my house for a cup of wine and a bit of bread and cheese."

Dylan nodded dumbly, and she led him into a doorway. It was dim inside, for the shutters on the window where the weavers set out their goods on market days were closed, but he could see it was tolerably clean. There was a tiny fire in the grate and a bench against the wall beside it. The trestles and tabletop used for meals were stacked opposite, and a few bolts of cloth stood in the corner, their edges oddly unfinished.

The woman cocked her head, then shouted. "Marie-Louise, get to work, you lazy girl." He heard footsteps on the floor above and a few moments later the thump of a loom. She shook her head and clacked her tongue, then bustled through a small doorway into the larder. Dylan could just make out jugs of wine and a large, pale cheese in the dimness. She returned after a minute with a small cup of wine and a plate with bread and cheese.

"I thank you for your kindness, madame," he said, remembering his manners.

She chuckled. "My neighbors will no doubt think I have invited you in to warm my bed—the gossips—for I am a widow now. But you looked so dazed, my heart went out to you. And the church tells us that it is right to be kind and generous, though the priest takes more than he gives. Sit, sit. You are from the south, perhaps?"

She was obviously puzzled by his accent and curious as well. "No, I am from Albion."

The woman goggled. "Albion! Why, no one has come from there for a long time. My cousin Denise was a servant in the ambassador's house. Perhaps you have come to . . . see him?'' She looked doubtfully at his travel-stained clothing.

Dylan scratched his jaw, for he had several day's growth of beard and realized he must look like a wild man. He had a letter in his pack for the ambassador, one Giles de Cambridge, signed by Arthur's own hand, but he had been so intent upon just reaching Paris he had forgotten it until this moment. He sipped the vinegary wine, then set the cup on the bench beside him and picked up the bread and cheese. He had eaten little besides nuts and apples for three days, and had almost forgotten how good reasonably fresh bread could taste.

''Or did you come about the King?'' the woman persisted.

''The King?'' he asked, his mouth half full.

''He's dying, you know. Been at it for three months,'' she added, disapproving of such a laggardly departure. ''The priests have been around him like a swarm of bees.''

Dylan swallowed and took more wine. ''I am sorry to hear that.'' He wasn't really, for the little he knew about Louis VIII was that he was both proud and ineffectual, but it seemed a good idea to be polite.

''Pah! Do not waste your sympathy. Paris will be well rid of him, for he taxes us to pieces.'' She gestured towards the cloth. ''See those. I cannot sell them until I have sent them to the selvedger, but I cannot pay the tax of one sou on each ten ells, and that I do not have—unless I rob it from my daughter's dowry. Paris goes in rags from Louis' taxes. And it will be no better when that pious son of his sits upon the throne, for even as his father wastes away, he prepares a holy army to take against the Shadow. He will tax us for God as his father taxed us for glory. Still, if he can do it, I shall be glad to be rid of creatures like that boy.'' She paused for a moment. ''I cannot understand what you did to make his evil leave him, monsignor. Are you a monk?''

Dylan had to laugh and found it felt wonderful. He had

finished the bread and cheese and his stomach was so shrunk that he had no desire for more. The wine and the company of the woman had warmed him, and the horrible feeling of alienation from his own kind had diminished.

"No, madame, I am no monk. Besides, if sanctity could cure the evils of the world, the Shadow would not be amongst us. We would drink holy water instead of wine and sing like angels."

She roared with merriment. "How true, how true. But most priests are like dogs whining under the table for the scraps and growling when you do not give them the whole roast. I pray to the Blessed Mother, but she does not answer. Perhaps she is too busy. But I pray she will deliver me from priests and tax collectors, and perhaps that is wrong. The priests say to pray for goodness, but I am already a good woman, you see."

"Indeed you are. And generous as well. I do not know what I did to that boy. He put his head against my pouch and started screaming."

"Ah! You have a relic there, no? You are a pilgrim, perhaps?"

He liked her lively mixture of practicality and curiosity, all leavened with superstition. "No, madame. Just some hairs from my steed's tail and a pretty leaf I found in the forest. And I came to Franconia to find the woman of my dreams." His admission surprised him, and he wondered why he had said it. Had he come for the sleeping woman, or for the sword which lay upon her breast, or simply to escape his mother's apron ties?

"Ah ha! I always heard the women of Albion were rather plain. It is a quest of love. You better wash your face first though."

"Madame, if the Seine weren't little better than a sewer, I would jump in clothes and all."

"This is nothing. Wait until the summer really comes. All who can, leave the city, for the fever comes and we die like flies. That is how I lost my husband. By the end of

September there was hardly a weaver in the street with the strength to lift a shuttle and there were three funerals every day. Come, I will heat a pot of water and you will wash the dirt off your face. You have eyes like my Jean when he courted me. The Blessed Mother knows I miss him. Do you have a clean tunic? I can wash the one you have on and we can dry it before the fire, though the taxes I pay on wood will beggar me.''

"You are too kind. I have a clean tunic, yes, but if you use more wood, you must let me . . . contribute to your daughter's dowry.''

"I knew there was a gentleman beneath all that dirt and hair.'' She bustled away and Dylan realized they did not even know each other's names. While the water heated he removed his leather jerkin, the mail and the sweat-stained tunic beneath it. His chest and shoulders were covered with curly black hair, and he looked down at himself in surprise. He smelled different too, not the acrid scent of a man but a muskier odor.

The widow regarded his half-naked body with awe, and, indeed, his muscles seemed stronger and more prominent to him. Dylan pulled out his clean tunic and shook it to remove the creases. The widow snatched it from him and peered at the cloth.

"Good wool.'' She rubbed it between her fingers. "Albionese wool is fine stuff. In my father's time, we still could get it. Now we have to make do with Flemish. Or Iberian!'' Her words left him no doubt of the inferiority of Spanish sheep. She turned it inside out and looked at the sewing on the seams. "Fine stitching,'' she commented.

"My mother wove the cloth and my sister Rowena sewed it and did the embroidery. But I think it will be a little warm. I did not know Paris would be so . . . hot and damp.''

"It is not so bad away from the river, but you had best go to a tailor and get some linen made up.'' She cast a knowledgeable eye across his wide shoulders. "Two ells if it's an inch. Do not let them charge you for three. Those linen people are all Flems—and they would cheat their own grandmothers.''

"Our prince just married a Flem," he began.

"Fat and stupid and pink and yellow, no doubt. They are all the same.''

He smiled. It was a very accurate description of Isabeau. "She is not fat precisely, but she eats a great deal and will probably become so.''

"Did you go to the wedding?''

"Yes, I did.''

"Tell me. We have not had a wedding here—well, young Louis did marry, after his father dragged him out of the monastery, but it was a shabby affair. My cousin—the one who worked for the ambassador—invited me there to sit in the window and watch the procession, but I could have stayed home. Prince Louis was dressed more like a monk than a future king, and his bride was a drab little thing. It was more like a funeral than a wedding. Why, even the horses drooped their heads, they were so ashamed. I was not surprised. The King never spends a sou on anyone but himself.''

As he told her all he could recall about the manner of dress of Prince Geoffrey and his bride, Dylan wondered if the burghers of London were as critical of their monarch as this woman. He had never considered the burden of taxes before. Still, he could remember no complaint and thought perhaps that Arthur was a better King than Louis. Certainly London had fewer beggars and they were not as miserable as the people near the gate.

"My mother wore a gown of blue with silver crescent moons woven into it, and my sisters wore green and white. They are all dark-haired, and looked very lovely." He smiled fondly. "But I think my sisters are lovely at any time.''

"I can see you are a good son and brother. Here. The water is warm.''

Dylan washed before the fire, enjoying the sensation and feeling the dirt leave his skin. The woman handed him a rough cloth to dry himself and he re-dressed. He would have liked to strip off his filthy hose, but he felt a bit modest.

He stuffed his mail and jerkin into one of his packs and put his belt back in place. Settling his sword on his hip, he reached into his pouch and removed a coin. He held it out to her.

"For your daughter's dowry."

"Mercy, monsignor. That is gold! I would be thought a thief if I had such a treasure. It is old too. From the time of Philippe Auguste. Have you not something less valuable." She was caught between greed and caution.

Before he had left London, Dylan had secured as much Franconian money as he could. There was not a great deal to be had, since trade with Franconia was almost nonexistent, and such as there was was mainly in the hands of Flemish merchants who charged a ruinous exchange rate. He groped around again.

As he pulled his hand out, the coil of licorne hair and the birch leaf came out too. The leaf floated to the floor like a butterfly, shimmering in the dim room. The woman bent and picked them up.

She looked at him with wide eyes. Then she turned the objects over curiously and handed them back to him. "That leaf never grew on a tree, monsieur, and that hair never came from a horse."

"True. Will this do?" He handed her two silver louis.

"You are too generous."

"Nonsense, madame. You have fed me and sheltered me and restored my belief in the goodness of mankind. Now you can send your goods to the selvedger and save something for your daughter."

"Never again shall I complain that the Virgin is deaf." She tucked the money under her apron into a concealed pocket. "Tell me your name, that I may mention you in my prayers."

"I am Dylan d'Avebury. And you, madame?"

"Marguerite." She made a face. "De-lon. What a strange name. But it is no worse than a fat old woman like me being a pearl."

Dylan laughed, and put an arm over her broad shoulders. "You are indeed a pearl of great price and a good woman." He kissed her lightly on the brow. "Now, tell me how to find the residence of the ambassador."

"Ah, Monsieur d'Avebury, I will do better. I will have someone lead you. Paris is a warren, what with the King tearing down the good old to make way for the bad new, and I get lost myself sometimes. I know just the fellow."

Madame Marguerite darted out into the street and came back with a rat-faced boy who looked about fourteen. His back was twisted and his arms were shriveled and weak, but he smiled broadly and his aura was a clear, pale gold in the dim room. He made a clumsy bobble of a bow and regarded Dylan with lively curiosity.

"This is Pierre-Louis, and he will show you to the ambassador's."

"Thank you for your many kindnesses, Madame Marguerite."

"It was nothing. Besides, I can now tell my friends about your royal wedding. Go with God, my son, and may the Blessed Mother watch over you."

Dylan thought of the Lady of the Birches, and of that of the Willows, and smiled slightly. "I think she already does." He and the boy walked out into the street.

Two filthy men were shoveling the burnt remains of young Philippe into a refuse-laden wagon. It was late afternoon, and the street was darkened by the shadow of the houses on one side. The steady beat of looms broke the quiet as they went up the street.

Pierre-Louis, for all his unprepossessing appearance, was a pleasant companion. As they walked he pointed out various things of interest, winding them into local tales or old legends. They first turned back towards the Seine and moved along its course to the east. A large motte with attendant buildings came into view. This, Pierre-Louis assured Dylan, was the Louvre, built by Philippe Auguste some forty years before to defend the city. The King was dying within its walls. Dylan studied it with a martially educated eye and decided that perhaps the French had no talent for fortress building. It was in desperate need of repair, for there were several breaches in the walls. A crew of masons seemed to be making a halfhearted attempt to fix one.

A bit further up the river he could see the Ile de Paris and the spires of a cathedral. The boy informed him this was Notre Dame which was very wonderful but damp. Dylan could believe that, for the street they were walking in was green with slimy mosses, and the Seine smelled, if anything, worse than further downstream.

It was a relief when they turned inland into a fairly wide road with great houses on either side. Pierre-Louis pointed out one where the duc d'Argent had lived with seven wives—one for each day—like an eastern potentate until his ladies had murdered him in his bed one night, and another said to have been the domicile of a great sorceress, Blanche Le Fay, who turned men into swine when the moon was full.

"Pierre-Louis, where have you learned all these wondrous tales?" Dylan wished his mother could meet the boy.

"By listening and asking, monsignor. Also, I can read, and though the monks will not permit me to enter orders, they sometimes have let me come in and see their books."

"How did you learn to read?"

"My mother taught me. She was educated at the Convent of the Genevieves and was a lady of the chamber to the duchesse de Loire. But she was indiscreet with one of the duc's valets, and she was cast out when I was born.

So, she went to be a seamstress in the tailors' quarters and married an old man who had buried three wives already. He was kind enough, but his older children were less so. God made me ugly, but he gave me a strong mind, and I learned numbers and letters and was a clerk to the old man until he died two years ago. My mother was already buried, and the fools cast me out before he was quite cold." Pierre-Louis gave a crack of laughter. "They spent his money within a year and lost the business. He left me twenty sous in his testament, but they cheated me out of it, and God rewarded them by taking away everything. The ones who did not die of the summer fever—it was very bad last year—are beggars, except Jean-Paul. He was a thief when Papa was alive, and so he is today. It is the way of the world, monsignor. If you pursue evil, it will catch you."

"You are very wise for one so young."

Pierre-Louis gave him a large grin. "I am near twenty, though I do not look it, and not so wise. I am practical and very, very careful. I keep the weavers from being cheated too much, and they feed me and clothe me and give me shelter. It is a good life."

"But why could you not take orders?"

"The priests think my body would offend the Lord. But they are just ignorant fools and I am glad not to keep them company. They exchange piety for money, unlike an honest merchant who gives you something for your coppers. Here is the *hôtel* where your ambassador lives. *Bon chance,* monsignor." He turned and was gone before Dylan could thank him.

The residence was made of ruddy stone, and the door was carved with the two lions of Albion. Dylan knocked and a surly-looking servant opened it.

"Go away."

"I have a letter for the ambassador."

"Give it to me and go away."

"I must deliver it into his own hands."

"Do I look like a fool to let a ruffian like you into—"

"What is it, Paul?" A soft, female voice asked the question from somewhere behind the servant.

"It is nothing, my lady. Just some scoundrel trying to get in and steal the silver."

The speaker appeared beside the servant, and Dylan found himself looking into eyes like blue flags. They were huge, set in a long face that was beautiful and sad at once. Her hair was as pale as wheat and it was coiled under a jeweled net beneath a fine veil. She wore a clinging gown the same blue as her eyes, so the flesh of her breasts was clearly visible beneath the cloth. She was quite the loveliest thing he had ever seen, fairer even than the woman of his dreams, and his breath was taken.

While he studied her, she studied him, taking in the clean tunic and the dirty braies and mud-soiled boots. "You do look like a robber," she said softly.

"Oh, do thieves come to the front door in Franconia? In Albion we always make them go around to the back."

She gave a delightful laugh and covered her mouth with a graceful hand. It was a tiny hand and remarkably white, as if the sun had never kissed it. She lowered her eyes and the lashes were dark against the radiance of her skin. "Why?" she almost whispered.

"It would not do to have them get above themselves, demoiselle."

"Send him away," snapped the servant.

"I bear a letter for Giles de Cambridge," Dylan repeated.

"Do you? Then you had better come in, hadn't you?" She gave a tiny smile and he caught a flash of glistening teeth. She stood aside and the servant grumbled.

"I am Genevieve de Lenoir and I am the ward of Giles de Cambridge," she said.

"I am Dylan d'Avebury," he responded, wondering what the devil the Albionese ambassador was doing with a Franconian ward.

"Come this way. Giles is in the library doing the accounts with his clerk. He will be glad of the interruption. Poor dear, he suffers so much over the ledgers. And he is cold all the time, so you will find the room quite warm." She led him towards the back of the house through a dimly illuminated central hall all hung with murky tapestries.

Opening a door, she said, "Giles, dear, I have brought you a visitor."

"What? A visitor? Who?"

The room was like a furnace. The large fireplace was roaring and the room was very bright. The ambassador sat in a thronelike chair with a large book across his knees. There were several other books resting on lecterns around the room, and there were shelves piled with codices along one short wall.

"He says he is Dylan d'Avebury."

"By gad, you are even taller than your father!" The ambassador squinted at him. He was the fattest man Dylan had ever seen, and his flesh was an unhealthy color like porridge. He wore a heavy brown robe and a shawl across his shoulders. "I would know you anywhere. Come in, come in. What a pleasant surprise. Go away."

It took Dylan a moment to realize this last remark was directed at the clerk who crouched on a stool, bent over a long sheet of paper. The fellow sniffed and rolled up his paper and left without a bow.

So much for Franconian manners, Dylan thought as he made a modest bend towards Giles de Cambridge.

"Greetings, milord. I bear a letter for you from the King."

"He isn't recalling me, is he?" There was a note of panic in the fat man's voice which puzzled Dylan.

"Not to my knowledge, sieur. I believe it to be no more than a letter of introduction for me." Dylan pulled the letter from one of his packs and offered it to the ambassador.

"You need none, of course. I have known your parents for many years. But the amenities must be observed. Genevieve, my child, bring us some wine, and a morsel or two. I am quite famished from all these wretched numbers.'' He slid the book onto the floor with a thump. ''Some Rhenish, I think, and a bit of ham, some cheese, a few grapes, and perhaps a comfit or two. I am nearly faint with hunger.'' His enormous jowls jiggled as he spoke.

Dylan stood patiently, although the room was stifling, and there was no other chair except the clerk's stool which was much too short for his long body. The ambassador broke the seal on the letter and read it.

''He commands me to give you all aids and comforts—which I would do without his direction—and he does not say a word about the funds I have asked him for. Ah, well. That is the way of Kings. I shall have to borrow from the Flems again. How was the wool last year? How fares Albion?''

Dylan was aware that there was some complex agreement whereby the Flemish merchants took a part of the wool crop in exchange for providing the support of the ambassador, and though he had no head for numbers he could not understand why Giles de Cambridge should have to borrow money. ''The wool was excellent, sire, and Albion is blessed with good fortune. The King's son has married now and no doubt there will be a young Prince or Princess in a year or so.''

''Married! My goodness. When I left he was a spotty boy. The wool crop was good, you say. These damned lying Flems! I knew I was being robbed. I am helpless. Was ever a man so plagued. I wish I had never come to this benighted land. My servants steal me blind, and if it were not for my sweet Genevieve, I would die of neglect.''

He continued to complain and Dylan only half listened. He was soaked with sweat from the heat and began to wish he had not come to Giles de Cambridge. The man was obviously incompetent and a fool into the bargain. He wandered towards one of the lecterns and began to puzzle out the words on the open page. He stopped, startled. It appeared to be some sort of formula for flying ointment, and it called for the fat of a new baby. What did his mother call such a book? A grimoire. She spoke of them with contempt, and he could see why. And what was the ambassador doing with such a wretched thing?

Genevieve de Lenoir returned with a large tray and he hastened to help her. She was such a tiny thing. She gave him a little smile and poured wine. There was an array of viands on the tray: white loaves and golden cheeses, apples, figs, and grapes, a slab of pâté and a hunk of ham, plus little pastries filled with dried fruits and creamy custards. Dylan held the tray while she served Giles de Cambridge a heaping platter, then set it down on the clerk's stool. The woman handed him a cup of wine with a flutter of dark lashes.

The ambassador stuffed food into his mouth and barely chewed before he swallowed. He gulped the wine and dribbled onto his robe front. Dylan was revolted by his greed and turned away to study another book. It seemed to be a history of one Simon Magus, an ancient sorcerer who appeared to have studied with Merlin. He toured the library as the girl fussed over the ambassador and found every book to be on some aspect of magic.

De Cambridge gave a gargantuan belch and sighed. "My boy, I do not see what I can do for you. I cannot even afford to offer you a good horse."

"A horse?"

"To go on your quest. The King spoke of a quest."

"I need information more than a horse, sire." Dylan decided not to mention that he possessed quite enough money to buy several horses. Despite his geniality, he did not quite trust the affable ambassador. "I seek an object, a jeweled scabbard, which I understand might be in Paris."

The girl exchanged an odd look with Giles de Cambridge. "There are quite a few jeweled scabbards in Paris, boy. Even the King has one."

"This one would not fit any modern sword, and the leather would have a complex and curious pattern of

Hibernian make.'' He had seen the sheath of the Fire Sword which was a treasure of Albion, and he had some idea what he was looking for. He also had a clear picture of the sword upon the breast of his dream woman and knew it was an unusually shaped weapon.

''I know of no such object.'' Giles de Cambridge's eyes seemed to shrink into the rolls of fat as he spoke, and Dylan knew he was lying.

''Then I thank you for the wine and will take my leave.''

''Oh, please,'' began Genevieve prettily. ''You have only just arrived, and Giles is so hungry for news of Albion. Will you not stay the night with us?'' She smiled a little too broadly, and Dylan saw her sharp, white teeth for a moment.

The hairs on the back of his neck bristled, and he was chill despite the heat of the room. There was something very wrong, very evil, in this house, but it was not of the Shadow.

The girl fluttered across the room and laid a white hand upon his. It was cold as winter. She turned her pansy eyes upon him beseechingly and brushed her breasts against his chest. ''Oh, do say you will stay. Giles will be heartbroken if you do not.''

For a moment Dylan was enchanted and beguiled by the promise behind the words. Then she smiled and he knew he had seen whores with more subtlety. He was not sure what she was, but he did not want to stay to find out. He put a finger alongside the slender throat and felt nothing there of human warmth. He must find out where the sheath was hidden, and he had no other informants, except the knowledgeable Pierre-Louis, now vanished into the warren of Paris.

''Where is the privy closet?'' he asked abruptly.

''Ah, you will stay then.'' She almost gloated. ''This way.''

Dylan stood in the foul little room and relieved himself.

Then he thought, searching his mind for some means to force the truth from the ambassador or the girl. He knew much, but it was disordered knowledge, for like his father he had few gifts for the magics that his mother used. The sort of nonsense that the ambassador's books were filled with was both useless and repellant to him.

"Beth," he whispered.

She shimmered above the stinking cesspot, all green and silver, and smiled. Lifting her fingers to her hair, she braided a tress and laid it across her own throat. Then she was gone, but another leaf from her glorious gown lay upon the soiled floor. He picked it up and turned it over in his hand, then tucked it away in his belt pouch. His fingers brushed the coil of licorne hair.

Dylan drew it out and stared at it. It was coarse and silky at the same time, and he uncoiled it. He took three hairs in his hand and put the rest back. Then he knotted the three together and held the knot in his teeth while he tried to plait the hairs into one. It was difficult, more difficult than he had imagined, and he admired the way his sisters' fingers flew upon their tresses. When he was done, he had a slender braid as long as his arm plus a bit and he tied up the bottom end as neatly as he could. He looped it over his hands and tugged. It was amazingly strong, and he cut his left palm where the thumb webbed to the index finger. He licked the blood away and wiped the droplet off the rope.

"Dee-lon. Are you well?" Genevieve's sweet voice cooed through the door.

"Yes."

"You are such a long time in there, I began to worry." Her voice was full of honeyed promise and Dylan felt his skin crawl again.

He opened the door and she turned to lead him back to the library. With a swift movement, he looped the garrote around the lovely throat, pulling it taut but applying only a little pressure.

Genevieve gave a tiny cry, like a strangling rabbit, and

clawed at her throat. She flailed and writhed and tried to twist away. Dylan turned the little woman towards him, holding the noose in one hand, and watched her features transform: the nose elongated and the mouth beneath it, deep teeth glittered and the blue eyes blackened. She snapped at him like a dog and he jerked the noose a little. The hands raked at his arm, but they were not quite human any longer.

"Where do I find what I seek?" He was not sure her mouth could form a human tongue, for she looked like a hideous fox.

"Let me go." It was blurred but understandable.

"Tell me." He twisted the rope a bit.

"Aargh! Beast! Foul monster." A fine rufus-colored fur began to grow from her cheeks and upon her throat.

"Tell me."

Huge black eyes stared at him, full of mute hatred. "Fool! He will destroy you."

"Who?"

"Stay here, with me." She wriggled her body in a parody of provocativeness. "I will make you forget. I am beautiful." She crooned the words and spittle drooled onto her gown.

"You grow less lovely each moment."

Genevieve lifted her hands to her face and touched her features. She gave a little scream. "No, no. You have broken it. How could you?" A tear rolled down a furry cheek. The reddish color began to fade into ashy grey.

"Where is the scabbard?"

"I must be beautiful. I must. Have pity, have pity."

Dylan might have wavered but for the look in her eyes. "You seem to be growing old before my eyes, demoiselle. I fear if you do not speak quickly you will turn into a crone."

"Old." A sound like laughter. "Old! I was old a thousand years ago. Go to Pers Morel at the House of the Bleeding Dragon. He knows where your precious scabbard is. I hope he turns you into the dog that you are. Now let me go, before I am ruined.''

Dylan believed she was telling the truth, but he did not release her. Instead he dragged her, still choking, into the stifling library. Giles de Cambridge goggled at the pair of them.

"What is the meaning of this?''

"I thought you should see what your precious ward really looked like,'' Dylan replied.

"Genevieve?''

"No, no. He has cast an evil spell upon me. Quick. Cast a fire upon him.'' She covered her face with one hand as she spoke, and her voice was rasping and rusty.

Giles waved his bonelessly plump hands about in meaningless gestures. He stared stupidly at them and repeated them. "I never was very good at this,'' he said weakly. "I say, Dylan, my boy, this is not very funny. It is not good manners to go about choking ladies half your size.''

Dylan could see that the fair hair beneath the coif and veil had faded to white and seemed to be falling out. The hands were raddled with age too, and he let her go, albeit reluctantly. She sprang away and leapt upon the ambassador's huge body. She buried her teeth in his throat and blood spilled down into her mouth.

"Gently, gently, my dear. Do not be greedy.'' It was the last thing he said before she tore his throat out.

The Genevieve-thing staggered away, ripping at her gown and screaming. The cloth tore and revealed shrunken breasts and a wrinkled belly. She moved towards Dylan, face smeared with blood and eyes gleaming. Her legs gave way and she crawled towards him while Dylan backed away and drew his sword. It was unnecessary. Her flesh began to rot away and in a minute she lay still, a thing neither human nor beast. The stench was incredible and he gagged.

Dylan grabbed his packs and went towards the door as quickly as he could. He paused for one last look. The body of Giles de Cambridge had shrunken to skeletal proportions, as if the flesh he had so much of minutes before had melted in the heat of the room. Of Genevieve de Lenoir there was nothing but a tumble of bones and the remains of her garments. *I wonder what she was,* he thought, and left.

IX

Dylan found the street outside in shadow as the day began to fade. His heart, he found, was pounding as if he had run for miles, and his mouth was dry with a foul taste in it. He moved down the street away from the ambassador's residence as nonchalantly as he could, but several hard-faced servants from nearby residences eyed him askance. A rook took flight from a nearby roof and landed on his shoulder with a thump and a rough caw. A mean-faced valet gave them a look that boded no good as he withdrew into a house, and Dylan wished he were not quite so large and noticeable.

He stroked the bird's glossy feathers and felt a fresh flutter of a black despair touch his mind. He had always been subject to odd moods, sudden fits of morosness, sometimes for no apparent reason. They were, his parents assured him, just something in his Hibernian blood. When it happened at Avebury he went for a long ride or lay by the river until it passed. In London he would have repaired to some alehouse to drown his sorrows.

Here, in Paris, he felt alienated from everything and oddly guilty. He had not been in this city a day and three people were dead, two were wounded by an angry bear, and an alehouse had been burnt to the ground. Dylan wanted to howl like a wolf.

He walked towards the river out of a need to keep

moving more than with any purpose. The rook nibbled at
his ear and croaked avian secrets into it. Dylan heard and
understood them almost without noticing.

He reached the river bank and turned west awhile.
Then, without full awareness, he crossed the bridge to the
Ile de Paris and found himself before the doors of the
cathedral. Although the huge square towers he had seen as
he walked with Pierre-Louis seemed complete from a distance, close up it was obvious the work would not be done
for many years to come. There were three sets of double
doors, but only one of them had the tympanum carvings
over them in place.

Dylan could hear the voices of workers nearby and the
sounds of their tools, but he could not see anyone. He
walked through the first doors into the narthex. It was
long, longer than Westminster's, perhaps, and a priest was
saying mass in one of the many small chapels along the
side walls. He spotted Dylan and the rook and glared at
them.

Dylan slipped behind a pillar and wondered what he was
doing here. Then he saw a little chapel on the other side
which had columns covered with stylized leaves. Inside it
was a small figure of the Virgin, her serene face radiating
beneficence. Unmindful of the large bird on his shoulder,
he went into the chapel and knelt before the statue.

Praying had never been an easy task for him, and he
found it was just as difficult as ever. He was too active and
impatient for such things. All he could think of was *Help
me. Forgive me*. He bent his black head forward in mute
supplication. After a time some of the peace of the place
seemed to steal into him.

A hard foot booted his behind. Dylan turned quickly and
the rook dug its claws in and flapped its wings to maintain
its balance. It was the priest, a tight-mouthed, half-starved
crow of a man in a well-worn and filthy habit.

"You cannot bring your dirty bird into God's house!"
Bits of spittle flew from his mouth.

Dylan wiped one off his face and stood up, angry. It certainly was not making his life simpler to have half the livestock in Paris leaping up to do him homage. The priest cowered a little when he saw how tall Dylan was.

"Dirty! Look at yourself before you throw mud. Why, you are filthier than the Seine." Dylan pushed past him, leaving the priest gabbling with fury, and went back outside. He crossed the river again and wished the Parisians would do as good work on their bridges as they were doing on their cathedral. A beggar whined at him.

Dylan stood undecided for a moment. "I do not suppose you know a place called the House of the Bleeding Dragon, do you?" he asked the bird. The rook cawed and the tender spots on Dylan's skull throbbed. He listened intently.

Surely, surely. I am the most knowledgeable rook in all of Paris. I am the king of all the rooks in Paris. All other birds bow to me. I know where the best carrion is. The King is dead, you know. Just this past hour.

He continued gossiping in this fashion for some time. Finally he said, *The House of the Bleeding Dragon is a very bad place. The carrion there is good though, if you like cat. He strangles cats, you know. Kittens too. Not much meat on a kitten. It is better to let them grow a bit.*

"Show me the way," Dylan commanded.

It is a bad place, O Lord. Surely, surely. We go up river a little. Here comes a messenger to tell the priests the King is dead. He was not a good King. He was not a bad King. Perhaps the carrion will be better with the new King. Into this street. They burn a lot of carrion in Paris. A sad waste. A terrible waste. Perhaps the new King will not burn so much. See the house with the acorns on the door. The stingiest man in the city. Never any garbage. Turn here. A mouse would starve in that house. Are you sure you want to go to the Bleeding Dragon? I can take you somewhere with good garbage. Quality stuff. You don't want to go to a bad place.

"I must go there."

If you must, you must. It is at the end of the street. You cannot miss it. Now I must go pay my respects to the King, even if he was not a good King. Farewell.

The rook departed in a flap of great wings as bells began to toll across the city. Dylan watched its flight for a moment, then continued up the street. A great metal door with a wounded dragon upon it caught his eye. It was a cunning piece of work unlike anything he had ever seen before. The blood dripped out in red droplets against the golden surface of the door. He peered at it in the fading light, but it was neither painted nor enamelled. The droplets were rubies as large as quail's eggs, and he was amazed that no one had prised them out. Such an ostentatious display of wealth was remarkable, and he noticed that the eye of the beast was an enormous sapphire. It seemed to stare at him in agony, as if the spear thrust into the scaled chest was painful. He almost lifted a hand to touch the creature, thinking of Melusine, then shook the feeling away.

Dylan lifted the wooden knocker and rapped. After several minutes the door opened, and a pale man stood before him. He was very tall, and his eyes were like bits of amber. Dylan saw that he was cloaked in an odd aura—a cool, pale light—and while this reassured him that he was not dealing with another creature of Shadow, he was also faintly uneasy.

"Yes." The man's voice was even, yet musical, in that single word.

"I seek Pers Morel."

"Then you have found him." Morel did not move, and though his voice had a seductive quality, Dylan thought it faintly chilly.

He paused a moment, unsure where to begin. "I have come from the house of the Albionese ambassador, Giles de Cambridge, and it was suggested that you might be the person to enlighten me in a certain matter." It was, he felt, a statement his mother would have been pleased with, being entirely true but avoiding all the dangerous issues. Dylan had an intense longing to see her again, and stand before her, proud and clean. She, he realized, would not have agonized over the Shadow-struck boy or the Genevieve creature, or at least not for long.

"If he has sent you to buy the—"

"No, this is a personal matter."

"I see." The amber eyes darkened almost to ruby and Dylan felt something like a feather brush his mind. It was gone almost before it arrived and Morel's eyebrows rose. They regarded one another in mutual puzzlement.

"Very well. Come in." It was a grudging and ungracious welcome.

"Thank you." He crossed the threshold and looked about. The walls of the room they stood in had been whitewashed and painted with a most remarkably lifelike forest. The very leaves seemed about to tremble with an unseen breeze. He did not recognize any of the trees, however, and that was a little puzzling. The trees of Franconia were not so different from those of Albion as these were from any tree he had ever seen. Perhaps they are Greek trees, he thought.

"I like your indoor forest," he commented.

Morel stopped in midmovement and turned a startled stare at him. "Why, thank you. So few people *notice* it." The words were stiff and the voice had lost its power. He gave Dylan a deep, piercing look, then shrugged.

"Too busy worrying about taxes, I suppose," Dylan replied.

"Ah, yes. The eternal occupation of the Parisian. Gold. A trumpery metal, at best." Morel's voice had recovered its quality of warm silk, but Dylan mistrusted it now. The man might not be evil, but that did not mean he was good either.

"If you have a surfeit of it."

"Come this way." Morel led Dylan towards the back of the house and into a small eating room with a big table and several chairs. "Pray, seat yourself. I will bring wine and we will talk."

Dylan didn't really want any more wine, but apparently no business was conducted in Paris without it. He removed his packs and settled down, his sword resting along his long thigh awkwardly. Morel returned with cups and a crystal flagon of exquisite beauty. It was rosy, though whether from the wine or the glass he was not sure, and shaped like some curious reptile neither dragon nor serpent. It seemed to be steaming slightly through the mouth of the beast which was also the spout.

Morel poured and seated himself. "Now, how may I aid you, sieur."

It was a polite demand that he make himself known to his host, and Dylan had a moment of reluctance. He could almost hear his mother: *You do not give your name to every Tom, Dick, or Harry, especially if they seem to have any Shadow about them. Or if they seem different. Never reveal more than you must.*

Morel had no Shadow on him, but he was certainly different. But to lie irked him. He was Dylan d'Avebury, and proud of it. Still, he had his share of nicknames: Dilly from his younger sisters and Sable as Eleanor called him when his black moods were upon him. Foolish names but suddenly dear to him.

"I am a knight of Albion and I am on a quest. My friends sometimes call me Sable, because I am so dark for an Albionese." That was true enough, as far as it went.

"I see." Morel sipped delicately and Dylan copied his gesture. The wine was warm as blood, and almost the same color. "And what is the nature of this quest?"

"There is a scabbard with a pattern of interlace and jewels which I seek." He traced the interlace upon the surface of the table with both forefingers, surprised at how clear his picture of it was. For a moment he saw a serpent's head covered with tiny braids all plaited together and knew where upon its body the scabbard had once lain.

Beady jeweled eyes stared at him, and he realized that in drawing the pattern he had drawn his grandmother into the room. The face was both human and reptile, and she gave him something like a smile before the vision vanished.

If Morel had seen the manifestation of Orphiana, the Earth Serpent, he gave no indication. "How . . . quaint. A quest." He made it sound stupid and childish. "I had no idea the chivalry of Albion still pursued such fancies. No doubt there is a maiden. Tell me, is she fair?"

Dylan was stung by his contempt, and the wildness stirred within him. His temples throbbed and his palms itched maddeningly. He took a deep breath. "I would not know. I have never *seen* her." He looked directly into Morel's eyes, and after a moment the man dropped his gaze. His hair was as black as Dylan's own, but smooth and straight, and it grew from a sharp peak in the center of his brow, so that when he lowered his chin he resembled a bird of prey.

"I have indeed heard of this scabbard. It lies in a keep beyond the city, to the north." Morel paused and lifted his head. "It is some distance, too far to reach before night, unless you are foolhardy. So, you will be my guest. We will dine together and talk. In the morning we will find you some sort of horse and send you on your way."

Dylan could not see anything immediately wrong with this plan, for although he did not doubt that Morel was certainly dangerous, he could not see any danger to himself. Unlike the fair Genevieve, Pers Morel did not set his nerves thrumming. His strangeness was of a different order than the woman's had been.

"How did you come to me, by the by?" Morel asked.

"The demoiselle de Lenoir thought you would be the one person who would be able to help me."

"I *see*." The words had a faintly sinister cast to them, though Dylan was not sure if it was directed at him or the woman. "She . . . ah . . . sent you here voluntarily?"

"Not precisely. I had to persuade her." *If a noose of licorne hair can be called persuasion,* he thought to himself.

"You must be a remarkable young man, then. At least I have never managed to persuade that young woman to do anything she did not already wish to do." He pondered possibilities. "I cannot see what mischief she might . . . ah, well. No matter. How is she? And sieur de Cambridge?"

"Dead." He couldn't think of a plausible half-truth, and the tale would serve to distract his host's attention for a while.

"Dead? Are you certain?"

"As much as one can be. We were in the library and I was looking at these strange books he has collected. I must say, I do not consider charms and spells to be the sort of thing a *gentleman* indulges in." He mimicked the faintly priggish tones of Arthur's chancellor. "The demoiselle began to look quite ill. Her hair began to fall out and she rushed upon the ambassador and bit his neck. I do not think, monsieur Morel, that she was quite human. In a minute he bled to death, and she fell to the floor and perished. I have never seen anything like it." He let some of his very real shock show in his voice.

"Incroyable!"

"Quite. She said something I did not understand— something about being broken, or that something was broken. Perhaps it was something in one of those books. I left hastily and went to the cathedral to pray for their souls—and my own."

Morel's eyes gleamed redly. "Something in one of those books, you say."

"I do not know, of course, not being conversant with such matters, except to know that only a fool plays with magics. Give me a good sword over a magic stick any day." He hoped his imitation of a yokel knight was not too obvious, but Morel seemed to accept it.

"Can you recall what book he was consulting?"

"It was very large and had a leather cover of grey."

"How large?" Dylan opened his arms to demonstrate the dimensions of the ambassador's innocent household account book, marveling at how simple it was to misdirect a suspicious mind. "I never sold him that!"

"No, monsieur?" Dylan affected polite uninterest.

"Ah, I weary you, do I not? Here, I will take you to the guesting room, that you may refresh yourself. We are of a size, though my shoulders are less wide. If it will not offend you, I will lend you a robe of my own for the night. And I will prepare a small repast." Morel gave a tiny gasp as a small brown cat materialized out of the wall and walked towards them purposefully. "If you would be so kind, monsieur, to remove that beast. They make me quite ill, you see."

Recalling what the rook had told him about strangled cats, Dylan rose hastily and grasped the little animal. It went boneless and purred passionately. He carried it to the front of the house and put it out. Morel followed him, dry-washing long hands anxiously. Dylan decided not to ask how the cat had come through the walls.

They went to a small room with a decent bed in it, and Morel brought a ewer of water and a basin, a soft towel, and a robe of woady blue. He left Dylan to his ablutions and thoughts.

Stripped to the skin, Dylan washed himself as thoroughly as he could, removing the stink of sweat from the ambassador's overheated chamber, and the offensive smell of fear as well. He had been frightened without realizing it, he decided. Then he dumped his filthy hose into the basin and poured the rest of the water over them. The simple domestic chore comforted him, and he hung the wrung-out hose on a hook on the wall to dry as best they could before he donned his other pair. He scraped the mud off his boots and sighed. They were almost ruined, and he would have to find another pair. He donned the loose robe which was a bit short in the arms but not uncomfortable, and put his belt and pouch back on. His sword he left with his packs.

As he was about to leave, a faint mew attracted his attention. Dylan turned toward the sound and a tumble of lean kittens appeared out of the corner of the room. There were five, all black and white, about three months old. They scrambled over to him and rolled at his feet, displaying their soft tummies in wanton abandon. He rubbed them as he wondered where the devil they had come from. The corner where they had appeared seemed solid enough. They fawned and purred and made small attacks on his fingers.

A bear he could understand, but cats? Something nagged at his memory.

Finally he dragged it up. One of the cats in the granary at Avebury had clawed him, and as his mother washed the wound she had said, "Cats only pretend to be domesticated. They never are, and the man with dominion over cats might well rule the world. Only he would be a woman, for men as a rule prefer a faithful dog."

"All the wild things of the world are yours to command, beloved Dylan." Beth had said that as he slept on her lap. So he told the kittens to stay put, and they climbed onto the bed all in a heap and fell into the profound sleep of their kind.

The table was set for two when he returned to the eating room, and Morel had changed his robe for another. There was a slab of beef in the center of the table, a sight which would have set Dylan's mouth a-water a week before. Now it made him faintly queasy, and he was glad to see there was plenty of bread and cheese, a platter of fruits and another of boiled carrots and onions, plus a fragrant mushroom pastry. Morel went into the kitchen and came out with a pot of stew—rabbit or chicken by the look of it.

"Pray, be seated, Monsieur le Sable. And excuse the poorness of my table. I was not expecting guests and—"

"It seems a feast to me. I have supped on nuts and

berries for three days.'' Dylan was suddenly ravenous and impatient with meaningless amenities. He served himself some steaming vegetables before they cooled and took his spoon. Nothing had ever tasted so delicious as carrots and onions and a slab of heavy bread.

"Some stew? A slice of beef?"

"No, thank you. I find flesh does not sit well in my belly. It is a flux, perhaps. From the water."

"Ah, *bon!* I do not care for it myself." He rose and whisked the stew and beef out of the room and returned with a custard in a crust, rich with plump currants and dried apricots. They ate in silence, Dylan wolfishly, Morel with more restraint. From time to time cats appeared out of the walls, and Dylan rose and removed them without request, putting greasy fingerprints on their soft fur from the fat in the crusts of the pies.

Replete, Dylan asked, "Will you not tell me, Monsieur Morel, what has brought this plague of cats into your abode?"

Pers Morel looked somewhat apprehensive and peered at the corners of the room. "It is a curse put on me by some foul witch," he answered without conviction.

"A witch? Surely you jest. Some old woman mumbling over her simples."

"Ah, the race of witches must have declined in Albion if that is what you think they are."

"But, surely that is all foolish superstition."

"Magic is very real."

"Yes, but it is for Kings, not women!"

"For Kings?"

"Well, Arthur of Albion has a magic harp and fearful pipes as well. I have seen them in the cathedral. They say the pipes can lay waste a city—throw down its very walls and set the roofs ablaze." Dylan hoped he was not overplaying his part. "That, at least is the claim of silly peasants. I have never seen it myself. But that is quite a different matter than cats in the woodwork."

"It does not disturb you?"

"Monsieur Morel, I saw a pretty woman age a thousand years and tear out a man's throat. I have no surprise left within me." He cut a piece of cheese with his eating knife and did his best to appear too stupid to be frightened. "Paris is a very odd city," he added, as if the locale might explain these strange events.

Morel chuckled. "Yes, it is. More than you will ever know. This particular witch is a cousin of mine, and we fell into dispute over a small matter. Thus, the cats."

"I see. Or rather, I do not, but it hardly matters. Now, tell me of this keep where I shall find this scabbard and shake the dust of Franconia from my feet."

Morel turned his head to one side and studied Dylan, looking like a puzzled hawk. "Very well." He cleared a place on the cloth and used the end of his spoon to indicate a rough map. Dylan suspected it was all too easy, and that some trap lay along the way, or that the keep housed brigands. Still, he could not think of any reason for his host to wish him ill, so he pretended content and more sleepiness than he felt and went off to bed as quickly as was polite.

His room was aswarm with cats large and small, all mewing and purring and staging mock battles. He sighed, undressed and told them to be quiet, then climbed into bed. In moments he was smothered by a living blanket of rapturous felines, pressing their warm bodies upon him in ecstasy. He tried to push them away, but they persisted and he finally fell into a sweaty sleep.

By morning there were more than a hundred cats in the small room, sleeping on his packs and the bed, climbing the bed curtains, wrestling, and preening their soft fur. Dylan re-dressed in his own clothes, and exited the room as quickly as possible, for it was quite rank with the territorial markings of various toms. They surged into the hall when he opened the door, and flowed along like a furry stream. He was surfeited with feline affection and felt quite sorry for Pers Morel. He led them to the front door and shooed them into the still quiet street.

When he turned, Morel was standing behind him. "You are very kind, monsieur."

Dylan shut the great dragon door and smiled. "It is nothing. You have been a kind host."

"I have sent for a horse. It will be here soon. Meanwhile, let us break fast with some gruel, and I will give you food to take with you."

Dylan agreed to this plan. He was eager to be gone, as eager as Morel probably was to see him leave. Within the hour he was mounted upon a decent steed and headed north out of the city. Dylan felt his spirits lift as the spires of the cathedral of St. Denis—where they would soon lay to rest the body of Louis VIII—faded from view amidst the trees. The road failed into a track, and the track into the faintest of trails between the great, silent oaks. The careful, polite Dylan of the night before slipped away and was replaced by another more earthy soul. The forest was alive with creatures eager to mark his progress, and he was certain no gold-crowned monarch had ever been so cheerfully honored. He found, too, that he felt less uneasy about his wildness.

Towards nightfall he found the keep that Pers Morel said held the scabbard. It was a square structure with towers at each corner and a squat and ugly one at its center. It was in good repair, the stones well mortared, and clear of growing vines along the walls. The gate was ajar, and he rode into the courtyard and dismounted.

Dylan led the horse into the stables and rubbed it down with some ancient, but clean, straw. He whistled a little as he worked until he realized how silent the place was. It was an oppressive silence, as if the stones of the walls were listening to him, and he decided he didn't much care for the place after all. The absence of creepers on the walls seemed somewhat sinister now.

He came out of the stable with his packs and headed for the donjon. The door was open, since it barred from the inside, and it moaned on its hinges as he pushed it aside. The central hall was quite empty except for some old bones. It was already too dark to explore much, so he looked for something to make a fire with. There was not so much as a scrap of wood within the building, and he dropped his packs and went back outside. The courtyard yielded nothing burnable, so he took some straw from the stable and decided to see what sort of fire one could make from bones.

The place loomed over him as he munched his dinner of dried fruit, cheese, and day-old bread. The fire light seemed to be consumed by the darkness of the keep, and his skin began to prickle. The noiselessness seemed to grow, until he could hear nothing but the thump of his own heart.

Dylan scraped his boot across the flagstones and there was no sound. A bone exploded on the grate, and he heard nothing. He strained his ears and lost for a moment the sense of his own heart and breath. In a panic he gripped the hilt of his sword and peered into the shadows. The darkness flowed into the fireplace and the light seemed extinguished. He reached a hand towards it and felt the warmth, so he knew it still existed.

He tried to reach into himself for some means to counteract the darkness, and heard, far away, the faint murmurs of earth beneath the stones. It was not a happy sound. Was this what his mother had heard so many years ago when she fought the Black Beast of Avebury? How awful, how dreadful a noise. He wanted it to stop. It hurt!

Dylan felt an agony seize his chest, a sense of something biting his heart. He put his hand to it and felt nothing, heard nothing. *I am dying.*

The thought grew, and he could feel his lungs deflate, his heart surrender to the now grotesque pain. He screamed and heard nothing—except a whisper of laughter.

Dylan crawled, each movement an agony, towards the

place where the door had been. He could not feel the stones beneath his hands and knees, and was not even sure he moved except for the cold pain. Twice he stopped and lay unmoving on the unfelt floor. Each time he heard the echo of a snicker, and with a kind of dumb rage clawed his way up again. He snarled into the darkness, or believed he did.

The third time he collapsed, he knew he had died and that it was fruitless to struggle onward. It was such a quiet death. He slipped into the darkness and the stillness. The anger leaked away and became despair, and that too abandoned him to utter emptiness. The void swallowed him.

X

Fejool the Fool unfolded himself from the rock where he had been contemplating this and that for several days. His fellow salamanders scolded him for behaving in a manner unbecoming his two millennia, but he had never found any reason to give up all the games of his youth and turn to permanent solitary meditation. Surely there was more to life than that.

The ring of hammers and the roar of bellows echoed from the forge cave nearby. He flicked his long tongue out to taste the air. It was acrid with fire smell and ash tang, and he pulled his tongue in again. He looked up and down the corridor cautiously, for if any of the White Folk caught sight of him they would try to capture him, to drain his blood for quenching and boil his flesh for soup. They probably would not succeed, but it would cause a ruckus, and right now he did not want to be seen. He would save his teasing for another day.

He was about to contravene the direct commands of Master Dimoolja, the current head of his tribe, and interfere in the concerns of the White Folk. It was not a decision he had made lightly, and he was still hesitant. It had been a very long time since the folk had gone on a real salamander hunt, but on the last occasion they had reduced the race to a mere remnant. Fejool was not such a fool that he wanted to start that sort of trouble. Dimoolja was an old bore, and his mind sometimes wandered, but Fejool did not consider him stupid.

He remembered the first time he had seen the young woman, Aenor. She had been wrapped in some ugly cloth, carried by four fainting half-breeds, three of whom expired shortly after relieving themselves of their burden. She had been in some sort of daze when she sat up from her wrappings and there was a dark bruise on her wide brow. He had been folded into a wall, unobserved by the miserable kidnapper who remained alive.

"Get up," he had told the girl. "You can walk the rest of the way yourself." He gagged and retched. "Cursed sheep coat," he muttered.

Aenor had staggered to her feet and leaned her hand against the wall of the corridor. "I cannot see."

"It is a just punishment for all the trouble you are, you miserable creature."

She had cringed away from the ugly words and put her hands right on Fejool's soft snout. It was a light touch, and she had curled her face in puzzlement. She put a tentative finger out and ran it along the ridge of his nose. Fejool was ecstatic. He had never felt anything so wonderful and he exhaled joyously.

"I smell . . . spice," Aenor said.

"By Elpha's milkless teats, there is a filthy salamander peering out of the rock! Come along, you wretched thing." He had prodded her side with a baton.

Aenor stumbled forward. "It didn't feel dirty. It was so soft. No cloth could be so fine. You are hurting me."

"Good! I would like to kill you for all the trouble you are. The Queen must be mad. Move, clay girl."

"Farewell, nice creature," she had whispered as she stumbled before her tormentor.

Fejool, entranced and unmindful of the danger, had flowed through the rock parallel to the girl and her captor, holding his breath so his presence would not be noticed. She had fallen several times and cut her hands and knees on sharp rocks. Aenor had moaned but given no other sign of her distress and had finally arrived in the blinding light of the Queen's presence, a dirty, tired, bruised female in a torn and filthy garment which barely hid her nakedness.

Fejool had withdrawn then, and backtracked the route, pausing to taste the blood which had smeared on the rocks and then to examine the dead abductors and the odd cloth upon the floor. His age was more than two thousand years, and for the first time he had some glimmer of the strange thing the White Folk sometimes sang of, the thing called love. It was such a new and wondrous experience that he had curled up in a stone and meditated for several months. Later he had tried to tell his fellows about it, but they just snickered at him and his new foolishness.

Often he had entered her chamber when no one was about. When she was absent he had rolled in her bedding to taste the sweetness she left, and when she was present he had rested his head in her lap while she stroked his nose. She had seemed mindless at first, speaking in single words, and he had discovered something of hatred. But always Aenor had been gentle and tender. Slowly her mind had returned, and with it hints of power. She had not known it herself, and he possessed no words to explain it to her. Rock he knew, and a thousand salamander lays, and these he shared as the only gift he had. Fejool rejoiced in her every small rebellion, and kept her company.

I am a fool, a very prince of fools, and I should not meddle in the affairs of the White Folk. With this thought he flowed into the rock and out into the crystal cave where she now slept. The entrance was blocked up by a spell-bound door from the King's forges—not song spelled, but made of blood and death—and he wrinkled his nose at the stink of it. The air was dry to his taste.

Fejool slithered across the floor and paused beside Aenor's body. Her soft, golden hair was gossamer glass and her flesh was like warm alabaster. One hand rested across the great green stone which the White Folk so coveted, and the other was upcurled as if she might stir at any moment. She was, he thought, fairer than all the songs of the White Folk.

He paused and looked around at the strange evidence of her power, the odd growths which had sprung from her first song. They were mineral now, blue and yellow jewels, but something of the life of them still remained, frozen in stone. The tiny waterfall was a tumble of crystal upon the wall.

Fejool gave a soft grunt. He breathed his spicy breath into her face, a favorite way he had of waking her when she still dwelt in the Queen's court, but she did not stir. He could taste the cold, bitter flavor of Angold's song upon Aenor's still and stony flesh. Then he pushed his snout against her cheek and touched his sensitive tongue to it. A minute drop of saliva rolled out.

Aenor opened her eyes slowly, as if she rose from a deep and profound slumber. For a second she stared at him blankly, and Fejool almost despaired. He could never forget her wretched mindlessness in their first times together. Then she smiled and lifted her hand from the jewel to caress his soft flesh as she had on their earliest meeting.

"Fejool, my dearest friend." It was a croon, a minor song, a benediction. "Once again you save me." Aenor sat up and embraced the salamander, brushing kisses against his nose. The tiny waterfall gushed down the wall with a cheerful tinkle and the strange green smell of her flowers filled the air.

Aenor made a face. "There is something rotten in here. And it seems to be me. Ugh. What a stench." She withdrew from the salamander and made a wiping gesture across her body. Her hand filled with crystal shards and she looked at them and grimaced. The crystals were twisted and coiled into hideous shapes and their color was a greyish red, like the feces of some diseased monster.

The woman flung them away from her against the wall, and they shattered with a metallic crash. "What an ugly song. Who made it, I wonder." She stood up slowly, deep in thought. "It is so hard to remember. I was singing. Yes. And flowers came. Do you like my bower, Fejool, dear?"

It is fair, but thou art fairer.

She gave a little laugh and bent to fondle his head. "You are not a fool. You are a poet. And a bit of a flatterer," she added, holding up the torn and filthy skirt of her gown, which she had slipped over her head.

Nay. Coverings are naught but rags. A bit of shabby artifice, like the King's men make. Thou art a song of light in the darkness.

"A very hungry song, my friend. And weary to death of this dreadful place." She turned and studied the door. "Now, *that* is an interesting bit of work. They must have slain half the dwarves in the forge hall to complete it."

More.

"Earth must suffer greatly to hold these White Folk in her belly." She paused as a shudder rolled beneath her feet. "Could I but see beyond the circle of the King's court, I would run away—again."

I will guide thee.

"No, Fejool. If we were caught they would kill you. And I could not bear that."

His heart sang. *Open the great door. I will lead thee, my song's own song.*

Aenor looked at him, at his long leathery body and his softly furred face, and felt his rocky threnody echo within the greater musical stream that flowed within her. It twined and coiled into her, full of his curiosity and fun, and within that the passion that led him to take so great a risk. It surprised her and strengthened her as well.

"Very well. Now, the door. By all that is holy, this is an abomination. To use blood like this." She stopped speaking and took a stance before the door. It was difficult and she wished she shared the salamander's ability to travel through solid rock. Aenor realized that if she took the time, she could learn that trick, and, distracted, she turned a thoughtful gaze upon Fejool. He regarded her with helpless adoration and, somewhat embarrassed, she turned back to the spellbound door.

After several minutes she closed her eyes and meditated upon the bloody patterns hammered into the metal. There was so much within her that was new, a thing between instinct and knowledge, and she saw that it was much greater than it had been when she sang her defiant little flowers into existence, as if her spellbound slumber had enlarged it from a single voice into several. Some of the voices seemed to be more like instruments: a viol, a flute, a tiny drum, and finally, a very large drum indeed. That last she considered for some time before she decided she did not know yet how to use it.

For decades she had watched the Queen's spell singers and web weavers in their work, acquiring their knowledge without realizing it. The craft of the spell singer was not grasped in a day or a year, for it was almost a living thing in itself: first a simple melody, then more and more complex variations laid upon it, until it becomes a corpus, a body of work. Aenor realized that her own song had come to her already partly grown, and that because she did not truly know the infant melody, her ability to use the variations was limited. She had great power and was somehow still powerless. The only way through the door was a sort of brute force that would have shamed a true spell singer. She was not as disturbed by the aesthetic problem, she decided, as she was worried about bringing the cave roof down on her head in her efforts to escape.

I want to live, to stand under the sun again. Or at least long enough to make them wish they had never been born! With this thought Aenor took her flute voice and prepared to shatter the barrier.

Angold, spell singer, Mistress of Opals, sat beside Queen Elpha's throne softly playing a curious crystal tambour of her own devising. All was as well as it could be. The Queen was fading, true, but Queens had passed before. That miserable child's curse was remarkably telling. Angold had a momentary flash of admiration for Aenor's clumsy but effective work. And, no doubt, she herself would be Queen afterwards. Her jewels were sung better than Elpha's to begin with. She was tranquil, past her minor panic in the face of Aenor's power. The threat was past. No drop of moisture would ever enter the sleeper's cavern, and if they had not regained their city jewel, at least there was no further danger. Content, she began a merry tune upon the tambour. Several courtiers smiled, and a round dance of five, the number of fortune, began.

She had an instant's warning, a dreadful sharp tearing in her long body, before the tambour shattered in her hands, cutting the white palms to ribbons. Angold raised her hands to her breasts as the pain increased. She knew her death was upon her, knew true despair.

"Aenor . . . wakes," she whispered, and felt her song rip out of her body, exploding organs. It hung in the air of the court for a second, the Opal Song, coruscating like a fiery serpent. Then it vanished, and she sprawled into dismembered pieces, spattering her blood upon the Queen's pleated hem.

Aenor felt the flute. It was a sweet-voiced instrument, properly used, but she found she must abuse it to effect her deadly purpose. The wrongness of this disturbed her and her stomach rebelled. She gagged and doubled over in racking dry heaves. Weak and shaking, she stood upright and pitched her inner voice, her flute, into an earsplitting shrillness.

The door stood for a moment, then cleaved into jagged shards, huge curls of crystallized metal that crumbled as they hit the floor. It was almost soundless, a sort of sigh of surrender, and Aenor was through the opening almost before the first piece shattered. Fejool folded himself through

the rock, not liking the spell stink of the dying metal, and
joined her in the corridor.

This way.

Aenor could see dimly at first, but about a hundred ells
beyond the influence of the King's court she was plunged
into blindness. She laid a hand on Fejool's neck and
stumbled beside him, the sword a clumsy burden against
her leg. Finally she untied it from her waist and carried it
in her hand, probing before her for sudden obstacles. They
crept along, hampered by her sightlessness, down narrow
corridors and through galleries where she could feel great
space even if she could not see it.

It seemed an endless journey, and her bare feet were cut
by sharp rocks, her knees scraped by repeated falls. Fejool
kept up a steady murmur of reassurance, but she barely
heard him. She wanted to scream at the darkness.

Be brave, my song. We come to the upper reaches.

A faint tinkle of crystal bells was all the warning Aenor
had before they ran almost headlong into a blaze of lanterns and a host of armed courtiers. They shouted their
own surprise.

"Hoy! A stinking salamander!"

"Kill it!"

Aenor, dazzled by the sudden light, blinked.

"Go, Fejool!" she cried.

It was too late. Six guards, frustrated by their inability
to seize Aenor, lifted their spears as one and thrust them
deep into the flesh of the defenseless beast. Blood spurted
onto the rocky floor and Fejool gave a piteous cry.

"No-o-o!" Aenor screamed. A rage surged into her
blood, a white hot blindness. She brought the sword down
upon the nearest foe and hacked his proud head from his
shoulders. Blood spurted up in a fountain from his neck,
and Aenor felt a deadly song overwhelm her. She raised
the sword again and again, mindless, and those closest by
fell one after the other. The rest dropped their lanterns and
their weapons and ran.

Aenor lifted the sword again, but she was alone. The rage drained away as quickly as it had appeared, and she was left empty and gore covered. In a sort of petty fury she cut the bell-laden baldrics off the fallen and smashed them against the walls of the corridor, screaming her frustration and something of her grief. Finally she turned to the salamander.

"Oh, Fejool." She cut the hafts off the spears when she discovered she lacked the strength to remove them, then knelt beside her fallen friend.

"I told you not to come," she cried, and burst into fresh tears. "Dearest and best of friends." She sat and took the dead head of Fejool onto her lap, stroking the soft nose as the warmth fled his flesh and he stiffened.

After a time her tears ceased and she crooned a discordant tune. It swelled from her breast, out of her heart, into a paean, a lay of his antics and his kindness that echoed along the walls.

The White Folk found her thus engaged and hesitated, pausing to ponder that one akin to them, however distant, could praise a lowly beast. The simplicity of her song moved them, so they looked at one another in uneasy astonishment and shifted from foot to foot with a continuous jangle of crystalline bells. The ruin of their comrades around the fallen salamander seemed as nothing to the grief of the woman.

Margold, the Amethyst Singer, sister to Angold, stood dumbly amongst the courtiers and felt the power of the singer. Slowly the body of Fejool began to change. It turned a dusky red, then green, and finally it crystallized to a bloody red, a gigantic ruby with a clearly visible heart of beryl. Margold shuddered as Aenor ceased her song, then gestured the dwarf servant Letis to take the girl back to her rooms in the Queen's court.

Aenor, dazed and exhausted, did as the little Letis told her, standing up and bending down to pick up her sword. She gazed at the blood-encrusted leaf-shaped blade, then looped the licorne rope over her head, so the green stone gleamed between her breasts. A little sigh went around the assemblage as it reflected the green heart of Fejool the Fool. They escorted her back to the court, but Aenor remained blind to their presence.

XI

The void was not silent. Although certain he was dead or dying, Dylan still found the capacity to be surprised at this. The stars sang, and not very well either, and the gods or the angels boomed at one another. It was, in fact, a beastly row and showed no respect for his tragic demise.

At this moment, Dylan discovered that wherever he was, he had left his body behind. He could hear and see again, but the other senses were still absent. He felt very free, but it was, he decided, not really any great improvement on the stifling oppression of that dark keep. He did not feel at all dead either.

So, this is Heaven.

No, no, you silly cub.

Dylan looked for the speaker and found a sort of gaseous emanation with a trumpet nose and donkey ears. *Hell, then?*

The thing made a very rude noise with its nose—it seemed to lack a mouth—and Dylan was annoyed. *This is the Place Between, the Overworld. And I do not have time to waste on foolish mortals.* It seemed to collapse into itself and receded away from him to a tiny pinprick of light, leaving him alone in the bawling, hooting, braying cacophony of the place.

Am I dead?

Of course, dear boy. The whole world is dead. But you

must not let that prevent you from getting on with your life.

The new speaker was a toad, a hideous warty beast with a gigantic jewel in its brow. *Everything that is not consummation is denial.* It flapped a long tongue out at him, and Dylan got angry.

Stop talking nonsense!

All sense is nonsense, replied the toad.

Dylan seethed impotently, and remembered a funny tale his mother told him often. *Move down! Clean cup,* he bellowed at the toad. The Overworld went silent for an instant.

Precisely. There is always another grail. The toad's jewel shone more brightly and the stars took up their disharmony.

The devil take the grail. Am I dead or not? He wished he had some hands with which to choke the answer out of the toad.

What do you prefer?

Prefer! Anything is better than this bedlam.

The toad looked almost sad, and the jewel dimmed. *I do my best. It is not easy to balance the humors, you know. I try to make it nice.*

Dylan felt a stab of sympathy for the ugly creature. *Are you . . . God?*

Yes, on midsummer. And it is always midsummer here.

I see. I do not think I belong in the Overworld.

None of us do. The toad seemed quite dejected. Its huge shoulders sagged and its belly splayed beneath it.

There, there. It is not so bad. If only those stars would sing together.

They are very proud, you see, and each assumes his song is finest. They do not like to obey an ugly fellow like me, either.

A moment before, Dylan had thought the beast quite the most hideous thing he had ever seen. Now, suddenly, he glimpsed a sort of tragic grandeur, a nobility greater than any earthly monarch's. The jewel coruscated the toad's body in an iridescence of indescribable beauty. *They are all fools.*

Yes. We are all fools.

O Toad, this fool wants to finish what he began.

Then you must not run away. Turn. Embrace the emptiness as a lover does. Eat the darkness.

Dylan plunged back into his body, into stricken consciousness again. He struggled futilely for some handhold on his own being. He willed his body to move but did not know if he succeeded.

Embrace! Embrace! The word banged like a tocsin within him, and he felt something darker than darkness flow into each opening of his body. It was a dreadful nothingness, something so loathsome that it revolted every part of his being. He wanted to escape its touch.

Dylan struggled not to struggle. He battled his own will and forgot about the other. The darkness invaded further until it reached that final spark, the last bastion of self that remained. For a moment or eternity it resisted, but finally it surrendered and was swept away on an endless black wave of nothingness. Beyond despair or fear or love, Dylan rode the wave until, at last, it faltered and crashed upon a bleached and light-strewn beach and was no more.

The faint smell of smoke stung his nostrils, then the stink of sweat. Dylan opened his eyes and found himself resting on his back in the dim and empty hall. The fire had died very little, which puzzled him. It was as if no time had passed.

It is always midsummer here. He remembered the words and decided that perhaps time was not quite what he had always thought it was. He was exhausted, more tired than if he had fought a dragon, and he rose from the floor and staggered back to the fireplace like an old man. Dylan opened one of his packs and pulled out the rest of the food Pers Morel had given him and wolfed it down almost without tasting it.

He stripped off his clothing and rubbed his furry chest and long legs with his tunic. Being cold and naked was preferable to sleeping in his filthy garments. Then he threw a few more bones on the fire and curled up in his cloak. For a few minutes he fought sleep, for it was too reminiscent of the terrible darkness, but in the end his body won the battle, and he slipped into profound slumber.

A tiny sound woke him. Dylan leaned up on one elbow and listened intently. The hall was bright, for the moon had risen and shone through one of the narrow, high windows, but he saw nothing. There it was again. A scrabbling noise, like a dog's toenails on the flagstones.

A mournful howl rent the silence of the night, and another replied. *A wolf?* There was nothing to fear. Bears bowed to him. So, why were the hairs on the back of his neck bristling? There was the rattle of many clawed feet in the courtyard.

They burst through the unbarred door, half a dozen lupine creatures with gleaming eyes and slavering jaws. Dylan leapt to his feet and grabbed his sword. The lead animal sprang at him and Dylan slashed the sword across the neck and deep into the chest. The sword emerged from under the left foreleg bloodless, and the wolf snapped, missing his arm by an inch. Its breath was cold, and he jumped backward.

The rest of the pack circled him almost lazily, and Dylan pivoted. His brows throbbed and the wildness rose within him. His leg muscles bunched and he sprang over the circle. White teeth snapped and just missed his exposed manhood.

Dylan growled a sound that never rose in any human throat, and felt his body *change*. It was fast and sickening, like fainting for an instant. The sword fell from a member no longer capable of holding it, and huge, crescent claws appeared. He felt his teeth turn into curving tusks, his nose lengthen into a bristly snout. His porcine eyes could see the tusks, and he knew they were not bone but metal.

The wolves rushed him and he slashed the nearest with his terrible claws and felt cold blood moisten his paw. The thing gave a terrible cry as it fell back and two more reached him. One clamped gleaming teeth around his paw and the other leapt for his throat. Dylan tore the throat out of the first and sunk the claws of his other paw into the glowing eyes of the second, snapping its head back. Then he buried his tusked mouth in the thick fur of wolf and felt a gush of foul-tasting fluid touch his tongue.

Another wolf leapt on his back as Dylan cast the two aside and bit deep into his great shoulder. Dylan roared with pain and tried to reach his attacker. The beast he was lacked the flexibility for such a maneuver, so he twisted sharply and tore loose the wolf's hold, then clawed its throat to a gaping hole.

He turned to confront the remaining two wolves, but they were howling over their fallen fellows and had lost their enthusiasm for the fray. Dylan paused, his beast mind and his man mind in conflict over what to do next. Finally, with some distaste and regret, he slew them in their terrible mourning, and cast their corpses into the fireplace. He barely noticed that he had returned to human form in the course of his labors, until his stomach rebelled at the stink of blood and burning bowels and the pain of the wound on his shoulder almost made him faint.

It was barely visible when he turned his head, a gash a handspan long of torn and bloody flesh. It burned intensely and Dylan did not want to think of what sort of putrefaction might arise from the strange saliva of the beasts. He took his remaining wine and squirted it ruthlessly into the wound, then bellowed with anguish. He sat naked upon his crumpled cloak and loathed the pain and the filth of his body. His hands were caked with dried blood, and bits of flesh were embedded under his blunt nails.

There must be a source of water in this benighted place, he thought, and struggled back into his braies and boots.

He lurched upright and stumbled out of the hall into the courtyard.

It was still and the pale moon silvered the cobblestones, but it was a natural stillness. All the sense of oppression he had felt about the place was gone. A tiny breeze brought the smell of oak leaves and moist earth to his nostrils, and he thought that no perfume could be so sweet. The almost silent passage of some nightbird—an owl, perhaps—reached his ears. The irregularity of the cobbles under his boots seemed quite marvelous, even in his pain, and Dylan rejoiced in the world of the senses. Even his growling stomach seemed good, assuring him that the night's adventures had not robbed him entirely of his humanness.

There was a well at one end of the courtyard and he looked down into its argent surface and saw his face. It was a stranger's face, with its black beard, and yet familiar. It was, he realized, his father's face, for Doyle had never surrendered to fashion and gone clean-shaven. He leaned forward to scoop some water up with his hands and stopped in midmovement.

Dylan saw the stag's antlers above his broad brow, and between them a crown of stars, like jewels in the water. He touched his forehead, but it was smooth, then he leaned his hands against the edge of the well and stared at the stag-man who looked back at him. His eyes were amber or gold, and there was a grandeur, a nobility in them he had never felt about himself. He was just the son of the heroes of Albion, a minor noble. At the time of his birth, his mother could have asked for half the kingdom, and Arthur would have gifted her with it. Instead, she had rejected titles and honors and retreated to the backwater of Avebury to be close to her Lady of the Willows and to keep her offspring safely away from the perils of the halls of power. She had somewhat grudgingly permitted his friendship with Prince Geoffrey and his entrance into the chivalry of Albion.

Dylan saw himself and his father in the silvered mirror

of water, and knew better his remoter parent. The stag-man was part of his nature, and he had always had the shape-changer within him. He remembered the dolphin's call and swore that one day he would indeed join them in their endless play. Then the pain of his wound blurred his vision, and his own face returned with blue eyes and a lip caught between strong teeth to hold back a groan.

He scooped chill water onto his shoulder, then scrubbed his hairy arms until they stung with friction. He washed his face and rinsed his mouth, until the foul taste of blood and vomit faded. His fingernails emerged from the gore, and he studied them a minute, for they were no longer quite pink and white. There was a slight silvery cast to them, as if a little of the strange metal claws had adhered to their surface. They seemed harder than before as well, but he could not be sure if that were just his imagination.

Satisfied he was as clean as he could be without soap and hot water, and now so chilled his teeth chattered, he hurried back into the hall and rubbed himself dry on his cloak. The hall reeked of charred flesh, and he was sorry he had been so hasty in disposing of the wolves.

Dylan glanced over at the fire. It had consumed the hides and meat of the beasts, and was now attacking the skeletons. One skull grinned at him, and it was not a wolf, but a human form. They had been shape-shifters too. It struck him that he might become like them if he was not very careful, and he shuddered.

Dylan rucked out his packs, looking for the bag of comforts his mother and sisters had sent with him. There was willow bark, which when boiled and drunk eased fever and headache, and dried parsley to brew into tea for bladder flux. There was poppy, bitter and acrid, to ease pain and bring sleep, and king's powder, basilicum, to sprinkle into wounds. This last he used awkwardly because of the position of his wound, and yelped at the sting of it upon the injured flesh.

He gathered his gear and quit the warmth of the hall for

the cold but sweet-smelling floor of the stable. A mouthful of poppy brought him painless sleep and dreadful dreams of utter darkness and talking toads.

Morning was dreadful. His shoulder screamed at the slightest movement and he had a pounding headache. Dylan gritted his teeth and turned his head to see the wound. The edges were pussy and it stank.

Dylan washed it again and put on more basilicum, then gave the empty keep a cursory exploration. As he had suspected, there was no sign of the scabbard. Pers Morel had simply sent him here to die, and he had stupidly played right into the trap. With a sort of grim stubbornness, he resaddled the horse and started back towards Paris. Pers Morel was going to wish he had died in his mother's womb.

XII

By nightfall Dylan was almost falling from the saddle. His left arm was swollen and puffy and the world was lost in a haze of endless pain. He was hungry and nauseated and so weak he could not unsaddle the horse. He made camp and somehow got a meagre fire ablaze. But the effort to fetch some water and boil it was too much. He simply collapsed on the ground and lay there, staring up at the interlacing branches of the trees overhead and the twilight beyond them. He was fevered and parched.

Thirst finally moved Dylan to the brook, and he thrust his great head under the water, then lifted it out and sucked and lapped like a beast. Runnels of icy water cascaded from his curly hair down his cheeks and into his beard. He thrust his burning arm into the water too. It felt cool and wonderful. Weakly he splashed water into the wound itself.

Dylan crawled back to the fire and got the little bronze pot he carried, then rested for a long while before he could fill it with water and set it to heat. He was sweating and cold at the same time, so he pulled his cloak up under the left arm and over the right shoulder, and huddled in misery. When the water began to steam, he put willow bark into it and removed the pot from the fire. He drank the bitter liquid and thought of Sal, Lady of the Willows, and his mother, who blended into one in his fevered mind. His stomach complained and belched in rebellion, but he kept the tea down somehow.

Sweat drenched his body, pouring out of him like rain, and he was wracked with cramps. With an enormous effort he got more water, draining the pot once before he refilled it again and set it on the fire once more. He shoved a few more pieces of wood into the coals, then curled up on his right side and lay with his knees bent against his chest. His body burned and froze simultaneously, and Dylan had a vain wish that he had not returned to the world of the senses.

Some while later the sweating stopped and the cramp in his limbs eased. Dylan sat up very slowly and made more willow tea, and drank it. He washed the gaping wound with some of the tea, startling the many forest creatures, who had crept to the edge of the firelight to see him, into flight with the violence of his howling. The wound superated messily, and with grim purpose Dylan fetched more water for another laving. He boiled willow bark this time, instead of infusing it as he had before, and let it cool no more than he had to. There were several fine linen cloths in his medicine collection, intended to be used for bandages, though his mother had often told him that to bind a wound was often more dangerous than to leave it open, so long as it was kept clean, and he dipped one into the hot willow water, then pressed it awkwardly into the sore. The injured tissue protested, and he cried out, but the pain eased after a minute.

Dylan set the bloody, puss-smeared cloth aside and took another. He wished the wolf had bitten him somewhere less difficult to see, for turning his head to look was both painful and frustrating. He used the second cloth and realized with some faint stirring of humor that his bare bottom had been hanging out all during the fight. He grunted with pain and continued cleansing the wound until he had used all the cloths.

The wound hurt less, and the puffiness was gone from

his arm. Dylan flexed his left hand, then bent his elbow cautiously. He sprinkled basilicum in the sore, rinsed the bandages out in the stream, then boiled them in the pot and hung them on a nearby bush to dry. It was exhausting, but he might need those cloths again, and if he did, they must be clean. He had seen enough friends sicken for weeks and months from tourney hurts, and he believed Eleanor was probably wise in her almost fanatical cleanliness.

The pain was still fairly bad, but Dylan decided against another dose of poppy. The aftereffects were too nasty. He banked the fire and put a pot of water close by him before he settled down to get some sleep. For a while he stared at the bush with the cloths on it, thinking it must look like fairy laundry, and finally slipped into a light doze. The fever returned, and with it, dreams.

The green and silver birch leaves crept out of his belt pouch like strange caterpillars. They humped across his back and settled on the wound like green leeches. They swelled and grew to twice, then thrice their original size, then fell to the ground.

Beth walked toward him through the moon-struck trees. Her face was sad, so very sad. Dylan wanted to comfort her, but he could not speak.

"I cannot help if I am not asked."

Dylan was ashamed, an ungrateful lout, an ill-mannered yokel unfit to bear the birch-leaf favor of such a great and gracious lady. He wanted to beg her forgiveness, but he was mute. He lifted a hand towards her.

Beth moved closer, a glorious shimmer of verte and argent. "You must follow your quest by yourself, but you do not have to do it alone." He wished she would not speak in riddles.

Dylan moved his lips to form her name. She bent towards him, lithe and supple, and her wonderful hair fell around them. Beth's lips touched his, her fair hand rested on the wounded shoulder. Her breath filled his nostrils. It was a green smell, cool, tender, and invigorating; and it flowed into his body, curling into his heart and lungs, into his limbs and finally into his manhood. She gave a little laugh and caressed his cheek with her other hand.

He felt marvelously alive, and lustful in a quiet way. His vitality needed no outward expression, and he drew it into himself so it seemed to ascend from his loins into his spine and fountain up into his skull, then cascade out into the stag antlers and across the glade, a golden green aurora which banished the darkness. Beth smiled and kissed him lightly as a leaf touch, and was gone. And he dreamt that he slept.

Dylan opened his eyes and peered at the morning. It peered back, a mist-fouled grey beginning of another day. He moved cautiously and found no pain, just a slight stiffness. He craned his head and looked at the wound. It was closed, healed into a ridgy white scar that might have been several months old. He touched it tentatively, but it was not sore at all.

Dylan sat up, ignoring the presence of various woodland creatures, and found the two birch leaves plus another on the ground, exactly where they had fallen in his dream. He picked them up and turned them over in his hand. The colors on the two leaves were darker than on the third, as if the silver were a little tarnished or stained. It had not been a dream. He put the leaves in his pouch and prepared to get underway once more.

Halfway through collecting his gear, Dylan was overwhelmed by an enormous feeling of listlessness. He had not, he realized, eaten anything solid for more than two days, and while he did not feel particularly hungry, he knew he should eat. He eyed a nearby rabbit speculatively, but found the idea made him faintly queasy. That left only the loathsome barley in his pouch to be boiled up for gruel.

Dylan made a fresh fire, unsaddled the patient horse while he boiled yet another pot of water, and finally cast a modest handful of grain into it. When he ate it, it was gluey and flavorless, but filling. The lethargy increased.

Dylan leaned back against a convenient tree and stared at nothing in particular. In just a moment, he was sure, he would leap up with his customary vigor and get going. Sometime later he discovered himself with a lap full of fox kits, a squirrel on one shoulder and a dove on the other, while a coney sat beside one knee and preened its whiskers. The pale sun was past the midpoint and sliding into the west. He tried to stir, but found himself fondling the soft bellies of the foxes instead.

This inertia disturbed him, for Dylan had never been much for sitting still like some old broody hen. In fact, he rather despised the occasional men he had met who wished to speculate on the nature of creation and other matters metaphysical. *I am just a down-to-earth fellow, a practical man, and I leave such nonsense to the priests and philosophers,* he thought.

Then he laughed and startled the squirrel, who leapt from his shoulder onto the tree trunk, tickling Dylan's ear with his fluffy tail. The kits pricked their ears and regarded him with sharp little eyes, apparently awaiting some explanation of the joke. The coney went right on with its grooming, too serene or too stupid to be alarmed, and the dove cooed. "A practical man who talks to toads," he told the foxes. Two of them promptly attacked a third in mock fury, endangering his manhood with their sharp little claws, and he dumped them unceremoniously onto the ground.

The effort exhausted him, and he sank back into his contemplations. Paris was a vague, misty dream, and the fair woman he had set out to find a phantasm. Even the treachery of Pers Morel aroused no spark within him. It was all too complicated, too twisted with unexpected events. The clear, simple world was lost in a mire of new experience that had been gifted unto him unasked for.

Dylan remembered all the times he had longed for some heroic deed that would give him distinction to rival his

mother in some fashion, and wished he had been content
to remain a simple country knight. No one had warned him
how he would change, so that he would barely know
himself. Storytellers, he decided, even his mother, related
only the events which were the least part of the tale. Those
were the bones, and pretty bare ones at that. The flesh and
blood was in the horror and joy, and that could not be told.

His mother had once fought a terrible beast just outside
the Avebury stones, and always, when she could be moved
to speak of it, he would ask, "But were you not afraid?"

Eleanor's face would go very still, her grey eyes narrow
to pinpricks for a moment. "Yes. I was afraid," she
would reply. And then she would relate the way she used
the Fire Sword, the cold breath of the beast, the charnel
stink of its body, the moan of the suffering earth beneath
its feet, the spattering of its blood where the sword cut it.
Dylan would shiver a little as she spoke, but with excitement, not fear. He could not feel her terror.

The rabbit claimed his lap and he stroked the long
tender ears and the soft coat. *Only I can know my own
fear, my own joy, and, in truth, I would rather not.* He
quietly envied all the many people who were not part
beast, who took no foolish quests, no great adventures. At
the same time, Dylan realized that they were a little beastly,
that they quested for gold or fame or just power over
others. The thought comforted him a little, that he had not
completely lost his humanity.

With something of a start, he realized that he almost
wished he could. That part of him that the animals adored
wished to be unfettered, to run free in the primordial realm
of the forest. It was newborn, but full grown, and it
warred with the Dylan of cities and clothing. The points of
his temples throbbed. *Just surrender and be free,* it
whispered.

Free? Of what, he wondered. *Free of evil people with
their terrible desires and twisted yearnings. Beasts were
neither good nor evil. They did not possess souls. But I*

have a soul, for good or ill, and I cannot wish it away, or run from it like a rabbit. I am a man—a beast of a man, but a man, nonetheless.

When Dylan set out the following morning, he discovered that he had not the faintest idea where he was. During his feverish ride, he had wandered off the trail and was quite lost. He tried to remember what he had done, and realized he had kept the sun to his back because it hurt his eyes. He must have gone west for half a day, then east, though probably not in a straight line, so that he might be either north or south of his starting point.

He struck south through the forest, seeking a path or trail, but found only more trees. By nightfall he had not reached any recognizable landmark, and he made camp rather dejectedly. He was lonely, and it was an emptiness no congregation of forest creatures could allay.

The forest was very quiet as the darkness increased. The moon was past the full and its light was pale and sickly. A faint breeze rustled the leaves, and made a sort of music with the ripple of the small stream nearby. It seemed to increase as the night advanced, and he knuckled his eyes to prevent sleep. His skin seemed to glow with life, and the beast struggled to join in the forest song.

One moment he was watching the flames of his tiny fire, and the next he was a stag. He shivered inside the smooth skin and tossed his antlers in silent challenge. With a leap, he was off between the trees, running as if the hounds of hell were after him. Faintly he heard their belling overhead, and he paused a moment to listen.

They poured out of the sky as if the air were a broad avenue, twelve huge white hounds with bloodred ears, and one bitch leading the pack. Their eyes were great and luminous, and their teeth shone with an unearthly light. They charged him with slavering jaws, giving their strange cries, then circled him fawning.

The bitch lolled her tongue out and flicked her flashing

eyes, then turned her rump towards him. The scent of her
heat crept into his nostrils, enflaming him, so his stag's
body began to alter. The hooves became great paws with
silver claws, the smooth coat roughened and thickened, the
antlers vanished, and he was wolf. She raised her tail in
open provocation.

Lust filled him, until it seemed to ooze from his skin,
but he did not move. The bitch whined. *The woman
tempted me.*

The words formed unbidden in his mind, and rage filled
him. He snarled, and the bitch yelped in terror. The stink
of her was revolting. It was alien, a false freedom. Mindless coupling was for beasts.

Dylan felt himself change again, and saw the world with
the piggy vision of the boar. The hellhounds tore around
him and darted to and fro in confusion. He grunted, then
bellowed, and they backed away. With a last look of
longing, the bitch belled a command, and the pack charged
into the empty air and loped away towards the north. His
boar self snorted, and Dylan stared into the dying embers
of the fire.

Another dream. Then he looked at his hands. The nails
shone silver in the firelight. *I am a man, but what sort of
man am I?* He curled into his cloak and let sleep take him.

By midday he had struck a river he believed was the
Seine, and he followed it west until he could see the faint
grey smoke of the city upon the horizon. Dylan was
relieved. He was not certain he could survive another night
in the forest.

The eastern entry to Paris was not better manned than
the western, and he was both disgusted at the laxity, and
strangely pleased to see the scowling countenance of the
guardsman. Dylan dismounted and began to lead the horse
up a narrow street, for he was stiff and tired. A clutter of
beggars whined at him, but he ignored them. What he
wanted most was a pot of beer.

Eight men-at-arms trotted towards him smartly, their mail tinkling cheerfully as their boots thumped on the paving stones. Their tunics bore a fleur-de-lys over the heart, and Dylan pulled the horse to one side to let them pass. He had no desire to get in the way of the King's men, whatever their business.

"Stand!" the foremost man bellowed.

Dylan dropped the horse's reins and stood calmly.

"Are you one Dee-lon d'Ave-a-buree?" The fellow made a face as he tried to twist his tongue around unfamiliar sounds.

"I am."

"Then I arrest you in the King's name for murder."

Dylan looked at them. The tallest of them did not reach his shoulder, and they seemed terribly nervous. A good shout would probably send them running. They clutched their sword hilts with white knuckles and rolled onto the balls of their feet.

"Murder?"

"It was sorcery, sergeant," said one of the men. He rolled his eyes and crossed himself.

"Yes. Let us just kill him here. I will get some wood," added another.

Dylan gestured to his filthy clothes. "Now, do I look like a sorcerer?" he said mildly.

"No, but you do look like a murderer," replied the sergeant. "Tie his hands."

No one seemed at all eager to accomplish this task, and Dylan could have laughed out loud. That seemed like a poor notion, however, for they were both serious and frightened, and frightened people do stupid things. So he bit his lip and waited while they looked at each other and fidgeted with helms and swords and twitched their tunics into more authoritative folds.

"Tell me, sergeant, whom am I supposed to have killed?"

"The Albionese ambassador."

"What? Old Giles de Cambridge? Why, I have known

him since I was a lad. He had grown sadly fat, but I suppose that is just your fine Parisian cooking." *I am going to turn into a fine liar if I am not careful. And what of the fair Genevieve?* Dylan leaned against the wall of the building and folded his arms across his chest. "I suppose that rat-faced servant of his told you this tale. I did not like the look of him. He was probably stealing the old man blind, and the ambassador discovered it."

The men-at-arms looked at one another. This obviously seemed a more plausible explanation to them. Dylan was too unworried to be a murderer. The sergeant was in an agony of indecision. Of course, if he got a good look at Dylan's silvery fingernails, he would fall back upon the charge of sorcery. Dylan sincerely wished he was a magician, for then he could vanish or turn them into frogs instead of standing here attempting to behave as if he had not a care in the world.

The sergeant studied Dylan and came to a decision, impressed either by his nonchalance or some other factor. "Would you be so kind as to accompany us, *monsignor*, until we can come to some conclusion?"

"But, of course, sergeant." He paused a moment. "As a chevalier it is my God-sworn duty to serve justice. And, by the Virgin, if Giles de Cambridge has been murdered, I shall not rest until his slayer is punished."

Dylan could almost feel them relax. He had established himself as a knight and a God-fearing man, and, for the moment, they lost their fear of him. Now if he could just stay clear of the superstitious priests, he might avoid any further problems.

Dungeons, Dylan decided, were for the dogs, and Parisian dungeons were probably worse than others. At least the one he now occupied had nothing to recommend it. The walls of his tiny cell dripped constantly, and the smell told him that the sewer of the Seine was probably the source of the moisture. The straw strewn upon the stone floor was moldy, and the corridor outside echoed with constant groans from other prisoners. The worst of it, however, was how confined the space was. He could not stand upright, for the ceiling was too low, and he was forced to sprawl on a louse-laden blanket.

For three days he had languished, apparently forgotten. They had been quite courteous about locking him up, courteous and inflexible. They had fed him maggoty bread and stale water, and changed his privy pot once a day, and ignored his protests and demands. It seemed unlikely that they had delivered his letters of introduction to anyone in authority, or if they had, that anyone believed he had not stolen them. And now the turnkey said his execution orders had been sent down. On the morrow, he would die.

Dylan coiled a bit of beard around one finger in unconscious imitation of his father, and flogged his brain for some way out. Shape-changer that he was, he could not walk through solid stone. They had left him his pouch, with Beth's leaves and the hank of licorne hair, but they were no help. Despair nibbled away at him.

I cannot help if I am not asked. The words rose in his mind, and Dylan tried frantically to remember where he had heard them. He saw his mother's face for a moment, then superimposed upon it Saille, Lady of the Willows. But neither of them had said those words. Sal's dark hair paled into silver, and she was Beth of the White Birches. Or was she? She seemed different somehow, but he could not put a finger to the change.

He did not want help, not a woman's help, not even a goddess's. It made him feel like a little boy, as if he had simply traded one mother for another. It was infuriating, the sense of powerlessness, as if the manhood he had conceived in the depths of the forest was nothing at all. Women were nothing but trouble. A woman he had never even met had gotten him into this mess in the first place!

Dylan indulged himself in this manner for some time, until it finally struck him that he was behaving like a sulky little boy. This enraged him at first, then left him miserable and ashamed. It was nothing but stubborn pride.

Dylan swallowed his pride—a bile-bitter gulp, he found—and tensed his shoulders. He gritted his teeth, then ground them together. "Beth, please help me," he whispered. There was no hint of her presence, no smell of green, no shimmer of silver, no faint tinkle of soft laughter. He was utterly alone, abandoned to his fate.

XIII

The stomp of booted feet in the corridor outside aroused him. Was it morning so soon? Dylan knuckled his eyes and combed his curling hair with his fingers. His mouth was dry and tasted like dirty hosen. There was some sort of argument going on outside his door, a low-voiced dispute, and he wondered if they were still undecided about whether to behead or burn him. Beheading seemed quicker and cleaner, so probably it was the stake for him. He hoped he wouldn't scream too much, and nearly laughed at this foolish vestige of dignity. He did not want to die well when he had barely begun living.

The door creaked open on unoiled hinges. A figure limned in an enormous aura stood in the opening. Dylan was dazzled. Even his mother did not shine so brightly. If ever there was a candidate for canonization, it was the man who stood before him.

His eyes finally adjusted, and he saw a slender man, clean shaven except for a pale moustache, simply dressed in the habit of a mendicant monk of St. Benedict. His hair was not tonsured, however, and he carried himself with great assurance. He had sharp, light-colored eyes above a prominent nose, a hawk's face. Dylan hoped the man had not come to confess him. Those eyes would have all his petty lies and venialities out of him in a moment.

Someone spoke from behind, and the man made an impatient gesture. "Enough."

"But, sire—"

"Enough, I say. This sty is an outrage! Come out of there, chevalier. Tell the warden I want clean straw in all of these cells before Vespers. How can we be men of God if we treat our fellows like dogs!"

"Clean straw?" It was a different voice. "But, Your Majesty, if we begin treating prisoners like . . ."

The King turned his head and the voice trailed off. Dylan stood up slowly and bent his shoulders down in a half-crouch until he was clear of the door. He then stood up straight and made a low bow to the man. Louis made a gesture like shooing away flies.

"I want this man fed and bathed and given decent clothing, and I want him in my audience chamber within the hour. Further, I want the documents on every prisoner in this hole brought to me before the midday meal."

"Documents, Your Majesty?" The speaker was a plump man with a clear sheen of sweat on his brow in the flickering torchlight. He wrung his hands across his ample belly. "We . . . ah . . . we have no . . . I mean . . . Your Majesty, common thieves and filch-purses do not have documents." He said the last with the air of one quoting scripture.

"Warden, any prisoner here without a written charge is to be released immediately. We are a Christian nation, and the least of us are still children of God!"

From the expressions on the faces of the men around Louis, Dylan thought the new King's piety was unappreciated and would probably come to be loathed after a very short time. Having a man so virtuous upon the throne of Franconia was going to be difficult, and he was glad that Arthur was in many ways an ordinary man.

His hair was still damp when a pickle-faced servant led him into a shabby room in the fortress palace of the Louvre. Dylan had not had time yet to marvel at what had happened, nor to puzzle out the circumstances. He had scrubbed away his filth in the large tub usually reserved for knights on their vigil, and was garbed in a clean tunic that almost fit. He was careful not to breathe too deeply for fear of splitting the seams, and the shoes they had given him were tight in the toes, but he was content with a belly full of lentil stew and fresh bread.

Louis came in a few minutes later, fingers flicking a rosary around his waist in a practiced manner and lips moving in silent prayer. In the greater light of the audience room Dylan realized that the King was only a few years older than he was, and that only the seriousness of his countenance made him appear more. He stood respectfully while the King completed his prayers.

The King smiled, and immediately looked years younger. "Sit down, please. I have had enough bowing and scraping to last me to eternity. Empty ceremony. I beg you forget my new estate and join me in some wine and conversation. I never thought I would long for gossip. I am pleased to fill the place that God has called me to, but I wish it could have been another. Still, I plan to leave Franconia a better place than I found it, if I have to work my advisors to death to do the task."

"Since you have saved my life, I am most happy to serve you in any way I can."

"We will come to *that* later." Louis paused, fiddled with his beads, and sat down. "Why have you come to Franconia?" He sat down at the table and Dylan joined him.

"Do you know, I am not quite certain anymore." He accepted a goblet of wine, looked into the pale, piercing eyes of the King, and told the whole tale, omitting nothing, though he glossed over his meeting with Beth and his encounter with the hellhounds rather hastily. Louis listened intently, and nodded.

The King sighed. "So, it was not the Virgin who appeared to me. *Quel dommage.* All these years of praying, and I am visited by a pagan tree spirit. Truly, God moves in mystery. I must see this Morel fellow is investigated. I cannot have such witch men practicing in Paris.''

Dylan, dry mouthed from his story, helped himself to more wine. He felt relieved. The King might be pious, but he did not appear shocked by anything he had heard. ''Witch men?'' The term puzzled him a little.

''There are sorcerers, there are magicians, and there are witches. These are the practitioners of the art of magic—as distinct from one like you.''

''Me?'' Dylan shifted uneasily.

''Yes. You are magical. It is not a learning. It is . . . a being. Your mother is a mage—a powerful one, by all accounts—but you will never be such.''

''Good.''

Louis laughed. ''Such a reluctant paladin.''

''All that I have seen of magic, except for my mother's, seems a pretty ugly business, and I wish no part of it.''

''Much of it is, for magic is about power, and that is dangerous stuff.'' He paused. ''They did not want me for a King, you know, for not only do I see all lies and all truths as clearly as you see your hand before you, but also I have the gift of magic in me. I have sworn it to God's service, but that is no comfort to those around me. There have been several attempts on my life, and there will no doubt be more. They would have preferred my brother, Robert, who is a weakling. Or the Devil himself, I think. I have sworn to drive the Shadow out of the land, as your King did in Albion, and that does not sit well. Too many profit in various ways from the Shadow.''

''I never knew a Shadow-held man until I came to this land, and I was surprised when I saw so many here in the city. My mother's tales of them made me expect living dead men, and those I have seen, but there are others who are less afflicted.'' He lifted his hands helplessly. ''I cannot explain it better.''

''But you have been most exact. It is like a fever. Some die but perish not, while others recover a little and become like that child you met at the gates. And many do not get the illness at all. Only the good Lord knows why.''

''And he has not told you,'' Dylan replied dryly.

''Well, perhaps he winnows the faithful. I shall do so, in any case. And you will help me.''

Dylan felt an icy finger of apprehension creep up his spine. ''I will, my lord?''

''I cannot drive the Darkness out of my land until I have driven it out of Paris. I cannot leave Paris full of vipers waiting the first opportunity to join forces against me. Therefore, I must cleanse the city, and I wish you to aid me.''

''I understood, sire, that you had been training an army for some purpose, and I assume it is to rid Franconia of the Shadow. But surely you have knights enough for that?''

''Knights I have, and priests as well, but only a handful who can see the presence of the Shadow as I know you can. A gift from your mother, if my 'sight' is true. You see, there are many here in Paris who would point a finger at their business rivals and say, 'He is Shadow man,' just for gain. My father's rule was slothful, and greed has become the faith of many. I need men like you.''

Dylan sipped his wine and thought. His mother had been charged with the task of restoring the heir of Albion and ridding the land of the Darkness, but he had no such appointment. No Bridget had spoken to him of saving Franconia, and he found he was enormously reluctant to become involved in the project. The office of knighthood seemed lusterless to him, and he did not wish to kill or to lead the slaughter of the hundreds he knew must die to accomplish Louis' end.

After several minutes of silent meditation, Dylan realized he was afraid of the killer within him. It was one thing to defend himself against attack and quite another to go looking for victims. The stag-man was wild, but gentle for all that. The other beasts were less so, but even the wolf did not slay for pleasure. It left a bitter taste in his mouth.

He looked up and saw Louis staring at him with awe. Dylan could feel the stag's antlers upon his brow and saw their shadow upon the table and the golden-green light they cast. He did not belong in this noisome city. The stone walls of the fortress oppressed him, and he forced the beast back into his mind. The antlers vanished, leaving him with a blinding headache.

Louis rose and leaned across the table. He touched a cool finger to Dylan's forehead and traced the cross upon the moist skin. The headache faded, and the King resumed his seat. It was a small healing, but Dylan sensed its difference from those of the Lady of the Birches. He was marked by both now, by the goddess and by the God of the priests and the cathedrals. He would bear the cross as long as he lived, an unwanted burden.

Dylan regarded the blazing man across the table from him. How could he have imagined this man a saint? Saints, he thought, did not ask you to help them slaughter hundreds of people. Then he remembered one of his mother's strange tales of the history of the strange world she had come from, of a holy war called a crusade and a man called Bernard of Clairvaux, who at the urging of the Pope, preached men to fight in the strange war. He too had become canonized. Dylan found the idea of a religious war utterly bizarre. Wars were to conquer land or to defend against invasion, and if the Shadow were more like a plague than an assault of arms, it still disrupted the peace of a kingdom. Louis, he decided, was a practical man, and a man who loved Franconia as much as Dylan loved Albion. He realized that if Franconia was healed of its sickness, they would be able to trade again with Albion, and that this would be an excellent result.

Dylan was about to give an answer when he saw another possibility. A Darkness-free Franconia would be very strong, and therefore a threat to the peace of Albion. Franconians had invaded them before, though except for Guillaume the Conqueror, not with any great success. Still, it was an unpleasant idea, and his mother had often admonished him to consider consequences, adding in a self-mocking tone that she rarely did herself.

"Very well, milord, I shall help you free your city of its pestilence, and then I will go on my way. But first I wish a treaty made that neither you nor your descendants will ever attempt to invade Albion, and Albion will not invade you. King Arthur is your vassal for Brittany, I believe, but perhaps you can persuade him to some agreement wherein he surrenders his claims to Normandy and Brittany and Anjou in exchange for peace between our realms. It seems to me, you see, that without the Shadow to keep you busy, you might begin to covet our little island, and I would not like that at all."

"I underestimated you, Dylan d'Avebury. You are wise beyond your years. Do you really believe your Arthur would sign such an agreement?"

"I do not know, but he is a thoughtful man, for all his rufus hair and headstrong disposition, and he has been a good King these twenty years. He would, I am sure, prefer to trade with you without the Flems."

Louis burst out laughing. It made his rather solemn face twist in unaccustomed ways and he looked years younger. "Ah, *oui,* the Flems. Grubby little merchants. I understand there has been a royal marriage between your two kingdoms."

Dylan nodded, and favored the King with a pungent description of the event. They gossiped for a few minutes about it, cheerfully assassinating the characters of the Flemings.

Then Louis became serious again. "I will set my councillors to drafting a treaty along the lines you have proposed. They will think me mad, but they do already. Perhaps history will remember me as Louis the Peacemaker. I would like that very much."

Dylan always remembered the next two weeks in a

nightmare haze of blood and screams and the constant smell of funeral pyres. He was given a troop of foot soldiers, doughty, serious men who wore a cross and fleur-de-lys upon their tunics, and a doleful priest who shrived them three times a day. It was a horrible, house-to-house business, an examination of every citizen—noble and peasant—and the swift execution of hundreds. Many fled, of course, but Louis' other troops caught most.

At evening they would return to their barracks, filthy and stinking, to drink vast quantities of wine, and weep for what they had done before they slept and dreamt it all again. Even the priest broke down after a few days.

The greatest difficulty was with the denizens of Paris itself, many of whom were not above a little expedient murder for personal gain, and Dylan found himself sending men and women to the same dungeons he had occupied so recently. Later, when the dungeons were full to bursting, he had the loathsome task of executing a few and tossing them on the pyres with their victims. There was barely a stick of wood left unburnt in the whole city, though the wagons creaked out of the gates each new, smutty dawn to gather more, and the Seine was almost black with falling ash. For two days there was no bread to be had, due to the shortage of wood, and the barracks were miserable and damp.

Somehow it stopped, and the city seemed to hold its breath. Indeed it was breathless, for the air was heavy and still except for the curling spires of the guttering pyres. The bells began, calling the faithful to worship, but Dylan was sick of God and everything else. He crawled off to his cot and slept like a dead man.

Later, he dreamt, first of twisted faces screaming as they died, then of a strange darkness filled with the sound of tinkling bells.

The darkness parted. She sat upon the edge of a huge bed formed like a golden swan, hands in her lap, weeping.

*Her golden hair was unbound and fell upon her sweet
breasts like summer straw.*

Dylan snapped awake. He had not thought of her for
days. Why was she crying? He sat up and tugged at his
beard.

"Chevalier?" It was the scrawny boy who ran errands
for the troop.

"Oui."

"The King wishes to see you."

"Very well."

Dylan did not hurry. He washed up, put on clean clothing, and dragged a comb through his hair and beard before
he let the boy take him to Louis. The King was in the
same small audience room they had met in before, and it
smelled of ash and incense and the rotting summer Seine.
It was hot though the sun was almost down, hot and
stifling.

Louis looked as if he had not slept in weeks. He was
thinner, and he had dark circles under his eyes. One cheek
twitched constantly, and his elegant hands trembled on his
beads.

"Your Majesty," Dylan said, bowing.

"Merde," Louis replied bluntly. "You look terrible."

"So do you, my lord."

"Sit! It is done, and well done, but what a cost. God's
work is never easy, but this! And I must carry this out
across the whole of Franconia. No victory was ever so
joyless. My heart wishes to break in sorrow."

"I think mine has." Dylan was almost in the grip of one
of his dark moods, and he thought that the cleansing of
Paris was no victory but somehow a wretched defeat. He
was no better than a murderer, no matter what Louis said
of doing God's work. The cross on his brow, the symbol
traced there a fortnight ago by this well-intentioned servant
of the Almighty, ached, and the stag in him bristled with
an impatience to be free of the smells and sounds of men.
When I have reclaimed this sword for my goddesses, I

shall find a quiet place, perhaps by the sea, and be alone.
I shall never return to this city. It is not that I hate men,
but I cannot pretend that I like them.

A boom like a giant clearing his throat rumbled through
the air. The tapestries rustled and the very stones of the
Louvre seemed to tremble. Dylan had a momentary thought
that his serpentine grandmother was shifting her body
before he realized that it was thunder. The heavens opened
up and he could hear rain pounding down into the nearby
courtyard. They listened in silence for a while, and Dylan
could distinguish the steady spouting of a gargoyle from
the rumble of thunder and the beat of raindrops. A wind
ripped through the narrow windows, bringing a clean smell
with it. Dylan wished he could go stand in it to wash away
the memory of the horror.

Louis placed an object on the table. It was not quite two
cubits long and wrapped in a piece of cloth of gold that
had seen better days. Louis flicked the fabric aside. "I
believe you were looking for this."

Dylan stared at the scabbard. The colors of the interlace
pattern were green and blue upon a silvery ground, and
there were gems at each intersection. It was an odd shape,
broader than any sword he had ever seen and tapering at
the point. He reached out and took it in his hands, turning
it over. The gems were amber and beryl, and how they
were attached he could not tell. The leather seemed almost
alive under his touch, as if it remembered its former
existence.

"Where?"

"It has been in the treasury forever. No one knows its
provenance—except you, I suppose—and it has taken my
clerks days to find it. Is it the one you sought?"

"I believe so. Thank you." Had Louis known he possessed it when they first met? Probably. It did not matter.
This was his thirty pieces of silver for being a slayer of
men, and he hated it and wanted to toss it into the Seine.
The river would carry it down to the sea, to the Ocean

Mother, and dolphins would play with it. He wished he could crawl into the grey-green bosom of the Mother of Waters, or change into some sleek sea beast and forget that he had ever had a hand to hold a sword in. He had no faith in the goodness of God, and his goddesses were jades and whores. There was everything in the world but hope.

"It is little enough reward for your valiant efforts, and, in truth, I am glad to be rid of it. It is magical, but it is not the sort of magic I care for. It is too old, too . . . primitive, and it makes me feel stupid." He paused and cleared his throat. His cheek twitched horribly and his eyes glittered with fatigue.

Louis mastered himself with an effort. "I have sought this Pers Morel, but he seems to have vanished into the earth. His house is empty." The King's shoulders sagged.

"Is it? I wonder . . . Louis, do you count me as your friend?"

"I do. 'Tis strange, for Kings do not have friends as a rule. Or rather, they ought not, for there is a danger that they will apply their influence upon a monarch. And, too, I have always had God." He sounded almost doubtful. "But your mother has been a true friend to Arthur, by all reports, and you seem very much her child. There is . . . a simplicity about you. You are no flatterer, and you wish no more than to do your job. I know how you have labored for me, and I even guess what it has cost you. And we are less alike than *bête* and *bette*." He chuckled over his clumsy pun, as if the making of a jest was a newfound game. "God knows my councillors seem to think I am no better than a beet, and you see more the inarticulate beast in yourself than the honest man. *That*, you know, is the great mystery—that the good do not see their goodness, and the wicked believe themselves virtuous. Still, it is no bad thing to be a humble beet of a King, to grow in sweet earth and feed my beloved Franconia with my flesh."

Dylan was acutely embarrassed by these reflections. "If I am your friend, let me ease your suffering a little."

Dylan reached into his pouch and removed one of Beth's leaves, and put it on the table.

Louis eyed it uneasily. "God will heal me."

"God is very far away, and I am here. You have put his mark upon me unbidden. I would return the favor."

"I do not like it."

"It is only a birch leaf, and the birch drives out evil spirits. Surely your faith is strong enough to—"

The wind gusted through the windows and caught the leaf up. It fluttered through the air and landed on the King's brow. For a moment his features twisted as if he was in pain. Then he relaxed and a beatific smile crossed his face. He stared at something—or nothing.

"Are you certain she is not the Virgin?" he asked, as the leaf fell back onto the tabletop.

"Well, she is *a* virgin, as far as I know."

Louis laughed. "I shall miss you more than I can say, and I regret our paths must part. I would wish you Godspeed, but . . ."

"I know." Dylan picked up the leaf and put it back in his pouch, and left the King of Franconia to his meditations. He paused awhile in the courtyard and let the rain soak him to the skin. Then he went to gather his belongings and to find out why the dream woman wept.

XIV

Dylan sat tailor-fashion on his cot in the barracks and listened to the roar of the storm. Several men-at-arms were dicing a few feet away, winning and losing imaginary fortunes and great estates. The rattle of the dice and the sounds of their voices was soothing and ordinary after the horrors they had endured. He looked at the scabbard which lay across his knees, seeking in its pattern some clue to his next move. No immediate inspiration arrived, and he wrapped it up and stowed it in his pack. He wished the storm would wear itself out, so he could depart the city.

Slipping into a reverie of silent forests, Dylan suddenly remembered the odd murals in the House of the Bleeding Dragon. Pers Morel had been puzzled that he noticed them. Why? he wondered. They were so lifelike that they must occasion comment from any visitor. Unless they were not visible to all and sundry.

Dylan stretched out on his cot and folded his hands behind his head and tried to visualize the murals. He had not studied them carefully, but he found that with concentration he could draw them up from the well of memory. The trees were smooth boled and almost shiny, and the branches were feathery, like great ferns. On one wall—the left, he thought—there was a low hill with a cave mouth almost hidden by curling vegetation. He sat up and the cot creaked ominously under the shift of his weight. One of the men looked at him curiously.

The wind outside dropped, and the rain began to slacken as the boom of thunder faded in the distance. The storm was breaking, and Dylan was impatient to be on his way. He wondered if the King of the Rooks was anywhere around, for Paris was still a maze of incomprehensibility to him.

Instead, he gestured to the man who was still watching him. "Do you know the House of the Bleeding Dragon?"

"Of course, sieur. My sister lives in that quarter and I have passed the place many times." He paused, reflectively. "It is a house with a bad name, chevalier, and an excess of cats."

"Will you show me there?"

"Why, monsieur?" He looked at Dylan's face, shrugged with Gallic fatalism, and nodded. "As you wish." He clearly thought Dylan was a little eccentric.

Dawn was breaking as they left the barracks, and the nearby Seine was quite audible, swollen with rain. The air smelled sweet, but an army of midges rose off the river and flung themselves at Dylan and his companion. It was warm and damp, and the center of many streets was clogged with sodden ash. Bits of unburnt bone and small trinkets from the bodies of the dead gleamed in the blackened sludge, and the two men kept to the sides of the streets to avoid the mess. It would need more than one storm to wash Paris clean.

Still, the city looked better to Dylan than it had when he had first seen it. A door opened and the smell of bread wafted out. A baby wailed and an urchin darted out and plucked some small ornament from the wet ashes, apparently unmoved by the recent horror. Some couple raised their voices in argument, the patois so thick that Dylan had trouble following it, though it seemed a woman named Alais was at the center of the controversy. He smiled, and so did his companion.

"Everything is love or money, is it not, monsieur?"

Dylan nodded. "I am sure you are right, Jean-Jacques. It is good to see that things are back to normal. The horror is over."

"*Oui et non.* We Parisians are strong and we respond well to adversity. Even so, we will be a long time forgetting the fires; a long time mourning. And our troop will go with *le bon roi* to other cities, to destroy the Shadow. Will you be with us?"

"No. Our ways part now. I have finished my part."

"But, are you not the King's good friend?"

"Perhaps. He saved my life. I do not know if that is a debt which can be repaid. Still, I came to Paris to find something, and, having found it, I must go on."

"The men like you, even though you are a foreigner. You have been a good captain."

"Thank you." Dylan had a moment's hesitation. Should he give up his foolish quest and help Louis drive the Shadow out of Franconia? All the killing had sickened him, but was it not his sworn duty as a knight? It was, but Louis had released him by giving him the scabbard. Probably with some feeling of relief, Dylan decided, for they would always be uneasy together. They saw too much of each other's souls, and saw each mirrored in the other. Louis was a man of God and cities, and Dylan faced towards the forests and the goddess, two sides of a coin. Dylan knew he would never really be content in the world of cities, that he was too wild, too like his father for keeps and castles.

"The King will do very nicely without my further help, I think."

"So you say, sieur. Of course, you are not Franconian." Jean-Jacques made it sound like that was a great mistake on Dylan's part.

They came into the street that led to Pers Morel's house, and found the great door closed. Dylan pushed it open and a musty smell of still air and many cats puffed into their faces. The entry hall was as he remembered it.

"Tell me, what do you see in this room, Jean-Jacques?"

"Sieur? I see a bench, a stone floor, reeds, a ceiling, wooden beams, and walls. It is a most ordinary room."

"Do you see anything on the walls?"

He peered at them. "Plaster and whitewash, *monsieur*. A good job. My cousin does such work. It is more difficult than one might think to get the surface smooth. I tried to help him on a job once, but I was hopeless. *Le bon Dieu* did not make me a craftsman."

Dylan coiled a curl of beard around a large finger thoughtfully. The strange trees were quite obvious to him. The leaves seemed to stir in a breeze that did not exist. There was a sort of path that wound through them towards the cave opening. He turned slowly, seeking the beginning of the path.

It took him several tries, for the light of the paintings dazzled his eyes slightly. Jean-Jacques watched him curiously. Finally Dylan saw that at one point the path seemed to touch the stones in the floor. It was on the wall opposite the cave opening, and he walked over to it and studied the point where wall met floor. He touched his toe to it tentatively, and felt a warm tingling.

Dylan shifted his pack and bit his lip thoughtfully. He had the scabbard, but he wasn't sure if the way before him was the right way. He wished he had a clearer idea of what he was about, that he had at least such cryptic instructions as his mother had received from Bridget. He thought of Beth and heard her soft laughter.

Go, she whispered softly.

Dylan turned and looked at the man-at-arms. Jean-Jacques returned his regard with open puzzlement. "*Au revoir, mon ami*," he said, and stepped into the wall. There was a slight sense of resistance, like moving in treacle, and he heard a startled "*Mon dieu!*" behind him. Then he was in a sweet-scented forest.

Dylan walked several steps forward, then stopped and looked around. The trees around him were ordinary trees, poplars and maples and pine trees. He saw nothing that even remotely resembled the ferny trees on the walls of Morel's house. A rabbit bounded across his path but did not pause.

He moved forward slowly, and as he set his left foot down he felt subtly twisted. Dylan moved to the right and the sensation vanished. There was a path here, but not one he could see, he decided. Dylan took a deep breath, closed his eyes, and groped his way forward, one arm held before him. It was exhausting, and he was sweating after a short time. He paused, wiped his brow on his sleeve, and kept on.

His outstretched hand met a smooth, warm flank. Dylan opened his eyes and found a licorne in front of him. A faint scar glistened on the left shoulder, and he was fairly certain it was the same beast he had ridden league upon league across Franconia a few weeks before. It seemed a lifetime ago, but he was glad to see his friend once again. Dylan stroked the soft nose and smooth neck. The licorne snorted and tossed its head.

"Hello, old fellow." The licorne stamped a hoof in reply and edged Dylan towards a low rock. Taking this as a command, Dylan mounted his steed. It was as awkward and uncomfortable a seat as he remembered, encumbered with sword and impedimenta, but it was easier than moving by feel with his eyes closed. The licorne trumpeted and bounded through the trees. Dylan clung to its neck and tried to ignore his discomfort.

The Queen's court was silent. The courtiers and spell singers moved soundlessly around the great chamber, their bells muffled, for the Queen was dying. Two web weavers, their long faces pale, stood on either side of the throne, trying to sustain her. They were haggard with the effort, aware of the sullen glances of their fellows. *Let her go*, the eyes said. The web weavers ignored them and continued in their sworn duties.

Elpha stirred, her light flickering like an aurora. She lifted her proud head and raised her arms with a great effort. The White Folk froze in their movements.

A ragged sound, a dreadful wheezing, came from her mouth. Elpha's lips were cracked and dry, and blood oozed from the cracks and spotted the pleatings on her bosom. The White Folk shuddered at the sound of her, hearing the faint parody of her song of power in the terrible noises. She had been a long time dying, and they hated her, both for being the cause of her own passing and for reminding them of their own mortality.

"Destroy," she hissed.

The courtiers looked at one another. Who? The accursed girl? If they could have accomplished that, the Queen would not be dying. But the elf stone, their own beryl, protected her, and now it was wedded to the dreadful sword it had come from and was even more potent. It could only be taken from her by love, and that was an emotion they were uneasy about. Love, after all, had taken the beryl away from them in the first place.

"Speak, Elpha!" Margold's voice seemed clamorous in the stillness, powerful and almost ugly. They glared at her.

"Destroy the Rock Folk!" It was a shrill command, and her last, for as soon as she spoke, her flesh withered and her silvery hair fell away from her skull. Her song ended and her body shriveled under the delicate pleatings of her gown. All her beauty faded, and a horrible mummy with puckered lips over great teeth, a dried husk, sat upon the throne.

The White Folk moaned and averted their eyes, though they kept glancing back at the monstrous vision until one of the web weavers cast a blue and silver pall across the corpse. A dreadful smell of putrefaction filled the chamber, and they gagged and retched.

Margold stepped forward, for she was the logical heir

after the passing of her sister Angold, and started to speak. To her surprise, another spell singer, Eldrida, came forward as well. Eldrida was young in the craft, and had only recently joined in the Great Song, replacing Angold. She was usually full of laughter and gaiety. Now she was solemn. The rubies of her singings clustered around her throat and encircled her wrists and her slender waist like great, glistening drops of blood against the grey of her gown. A circlet of ruby rested on her black hair and pale brow, and Margold wondered when she had sung *that*. None but the King or Queen might wear such an ornament.

It was a challenge, and an outrageous one, for Eldrida was no match for her. Margold decided to ignore it. The silly child was giving herself airs. "Remove the Queen's remains, web weavers, that I may take my rightful place. We shall celebrate Elpha's passing by fulfilling her last desire. We will rid ourselves of these wretched salamanders once and for all." Her voice trembled with strain.

Eldrida laughed faintly. "Your rightful place, Amethyst Singer? How . . . droll."

"What! My amethysts are the—"

"Are baubles compared to my rubies."

"You upstart wretch! How dare you challenge me!"

"I have heard cave toads with better voices." Eldrida's words were a minor spell, but an effective one. Margold felt her throat thicken with anger and the horrible smell of the dead Queen.

"Get Elpha off the throne, and purify it!" The words croaked out between her lips and she knew she sounded old. How horrible. She took a deep breath to regain her composure and nearly gagged on the scent of death.

"By all means, remove the accursed corpse of our unlamented Queen," Eldrida said, apparently unhampered by the stench. The web weavers moved like crones, already exhausted by their efforts to sustain Elpha, and one of them moaned, then swooned onto the smooth floor of the cavern. "Or does any of you have a kind remembrance of the Lady of Folly?"

Those present looked at each other in some confusion. The courtiers looked from Margold to Eldrida and back again, full of hesitation.

"Chamberlain!" Margold almost roared the word.

Tallis, the Queen's chamberlain, was ancient even amongst the White Folk, and his mind wandered. He stepped forward from where he stood near the shattered stone harp in the wall, and clutched at the embroidered front bands of his blue robe. His baldric chimed discordantly at his movement.

"Yes?" His pale eyes seemed witless as he looked at Margold.

"Proclaim me Queen."

Tallis seemed to ponder this demand while one of the courtiers appeared with a troop of dwarf servants to help remove the corpse. The dwarves crept nervously towards the throne, their grotesque heads twisting around to view the court. They bound the pall around Elpha's remains and lugged her awkwardly off the throne like a bundle of soiled garments. They curled their ugly noses and big mouths at the smell and muttered dwarfish complaints as they staggered away with their burden.

Tallis looked at Eldrida, then back at Margold. "Amethysts are not rubies," he began slowly, "and we have always—"

"I am the senior spell singer. I will be Queen," Margold interrupted him.

"There are precedents," quavered Tallis. "Precious gems are greater than age."

Eldrida smirked, and Margold fell into a rage. She jerked a little knife from her belt and flew at the younger singer. Eldrida lifted her left hand, and toned a single note. A shield of ruby, a roundel as large as a platter, covered her hand, and she brought it up in a graceful motion. Margold's knife shattered harmlessly upon its shining surface.

With a shriek she put her hands around the slender, ruby-hung throat of her adversary, and screamed in pain when her hands touched the stones. Margold tore herself away and backed as far as she could in the press of courtiers.

"What have you done?" Margold cried, holding her hands out. They were covered with bright sores.

Eldrida smiled serenely and stroked the jewels around her neck, like a cream-sated cat. She chuckled and the sound made the court shiver, their bells giving little shrill notes. "A little blood, a little song," she murmured.

"You abomination!" Margold shuddered, and the court shuddered with her.

"Blood!"

"She used blood!"

"But only the King's men can do that."

The whispers hissed around the chamber like a nest of vipers. The Queen's singers prided themselves on the purity of their craft, and held the King's artificers in some contempt for their use of substances like blood and bile in their work.

"What blood did you use?" asked Thela, web weaver, in a toneless voice.

"Why, Angold's, of course. It was such a lovely red."

The court paused and pondered this. Spell singing was "in the blood," so they said, and this meant that Eldrida possessed not only her own power, but that of the Opal Singer, Angold, as well. She must be mad to do such a thing.

Thela pressed her brow with white fingers. "And how did you achieve the knowledge to accomplish this deed?"

Eldrida gave her a look of hatred. It distorted the lovely face into something terrible. Then she smiled again. "The King's men do like their wine, and a bit of company," she replied.

"Which weakling did you seduce?" The web weaver seemed determined to know the worst.

"There were several. Now, ancient Tallis, proclaim me Queen so we can get on with our salamander hunt." She rubbed her hands together. "I have some interesting ideas I would like to try."

A dozen courtiers, men and women, turned as one and left the throne chamber. Thela continued her interrogation. "What ideas?"

"I shall make a new sun for the Crystal City—a ruby greater than any ever seen. Bring me Rock Folk blood by the tun, and I shall sing a spell of such magnificence." She paused, awed by her vision. "A bloody sun," she mused.

Margold was sickened. She turned blindly and stumbled into one of the courtiers. A firm hand clasped her elbow.

"Come, spell singer. Let us leave this monstrosity." It was Hamar, her friend, and she sagged against his chest and let him lead her away.

As he rode, Dylan was aware that the forest he was passing through was a little strange. While it did not resemble the fern tree place pictured on the walls of Pers Morel's house, being full of ordinary poplar, birch, oak, and maple, still it was different at the same time. Mistletoe grew in ball-like festoons along the tops of many trees, but that was not what bothered him. Finally he realized that the forest was utterly silent. No bird sang in the trees, and except for the single hare and the licorne, he had seen no animals. The stillness was oppressive.

Finally they left the trees and came to a swift, broad river. Reeds and mallow crowded the banks, and the water smelled clean, unlike the Seine. But no midges swarmed the banks, and no fish sported in the clear waters.

The licorne breasted the flow, careless of Dylan's new boots, and he cursed the lack of stirrups. He was wet to the knees before he could prevent it, though the water was pleasantly warm; he clung more tightly to his steed. It swam strongly against the current, snorting and grunting with effort.

The far bank was bare of vegetation. Limey tumbles of rock leperous with lichen were everywhere, leading to low cliffs of the same creamy yellow mineral. The licorne picked its way delicately across the rough terrain, its hooves sending rocks skittering away. The noise of its movements seemed very loud in the stillness, and Dylan craned his head around, seeking unseen adversaries.

The cliffs grew higher as he moved upstream until they shadowed the nameless river. Dylan was chilled by the shade and his wet feet, and he was starting to feel hungry, but the licorne showed no inclination to pause. The pale sun was westering, casting golden glints on the water and offering little warmth. Dylan shivered and felt out of his element. He could still see the forest on the other bank, and he looked at it with longing.

The licorne stopped before a narrow slit in the cliffs, a dark slot in the creamy limestone. Dylan slid off his steed gratefully and stretched his cramped legs. The beast snorted and stamped and nosed him in the middle of the back.

"What is the hurry, old fellow," Dylan complained. "The lady has waited for years. What is a few more minutes?"

The licorne gave a sort of squeal, and Dylan realized he was enormously reluctant to enter the cliffs. It reminded him too much of his recent sojourn in the dungeon. "What a paltry fellow I am, indeed," he told the animal, "to be afeared of the dark." He hung a long arm around the licorne's neck, savoring the warmth and the smell of it. The silence, except for the faint gurgle of the river and the sound of his own breathing and that of the beast, was disturbing. The sun slid below the horizon and the world turned to grey and creamy white.

Dylan got some bread and cheese out of his pack and munched them thoughtfully as the twilight faded into night.

He pulled off his boots and changed his wet hose for dry ones and chuckled, remembering his mother's complaint about how wet her own adventure had been. Of course, she would always add, if it had been in a desert, I would remember how thirsty and dry it was. *Will I tell my children about damp hose and the way a licorne's spine cut into my groin?* he wondered. He felt an odd comfort in contemplating his unborn offspring. A boy or two, he decided, and a girl, would be nice. He tried to picture them, and only managed to conjure up vague memories of his younger sisters.

Dylan put his boots back on, wrapped his cloak around him, so it stuck out oddly over the pack, patted the licorne once more, and went to the crack in the cliff. It was narrower than it looked, and he had to remove the pack from his back and thrust it through ahead of him. Even so, he barely scraped past the rocks sidewise.

His aura limned the tiny cavern with faint light. A damp, fungal smell rose to greet his nose, and he moved forward carefully, longing for a candle or a torch. A light seemed to flow out of his pouch, and Dylan paused. He reached in and removed one of Beth's leaves. It glowed with a greenish light, and he held it in his left hand.

A narrow passage opened at the back of the cavern, and Dylan bent his head to enter it. After about a hundred steps, the ceiling lifted and he could stand upright again, but his pack was an awkward encumbrance, as was his cloak. Finally he removed both, ignoring the chill of the caves, stuffed the cloak into the bag, and carried it in his right hand.

It was silent in the caverns, except for the occasional drip of water, and a rustling noise in the rocks. Dylan heard that several times, and turned to see what caused it. Blank rock stared back at him, though once he thought he saw a pair of reddish eyes. They were gone so quickly he decided it must have been a reflection.

Dylan could tell he was descending into the earth, and

the sense of mountains of rock above him disturbed him. His footfalls sounded like drumbeats in the stillness, and he was tempted to sing or whistle. He remembered one of his mother's tales about a deserted dwarf realm called Khazad-dûm and decided not to. There were, he recalled, several extremely nasty monsters in that place, and he had no desire to attract the attention of any such. Those red eyes looking at him from the rock might not have been a trick of light.

He thought he heard a shout, and stopped dead in his tracks. Yes, it was definitely a yell of some sort, and another answered. It seemed to echo from somewhere down the corridor. There was a rustling noise in the rock, and a reptilian head poked out a few feet in front of him. It looked up and down the passage, stared at him for a second, then vanished back into the stone. Dylan had the fleeting impression of ruby eyes and a soft snout, a sensitive tongue that flicked the air, and nothing more.

The shouts faded, as if the speakers had turned in another direction, and Dylan began to move on again. The passage widened, so he slung his pack up on his shoulder again, and relaxed a little. He turned a corner and halted.

A statue crouched on the rocky floor, a huge figure of red glass with a green heart. It resembled a dragon, except for the lack of wings and scales, and he could see spear heads and broken shafts embedded in the figure. Around the statue he could see evidence of a fight, for there were smashed bits of rainbow glass and smears of dried rusty stuff he suspected was blood all over the floor. Bits of torn cloth were scattered here and there, and he found a single crystal bell against the wall. He picked it up carefully, for it seemed a fragile thing, and it gave a faint tinkle.

A song seemed to fill the air, a dreadful lament, a terrible uneasy music that made his skin stand up in gooseflesh. The words were almost intelligible, but the sadness of them needed no translation. He put the bell down on a tiny ledge and edged around the statue. The song faded, and he hastened down the passage.

It was silent again for a short while, and then Dylan heard more calls. They were coming towards him, and he could see no obvious place to hide his huge body, so he waited, hand on sword haft. Faint footfalls whispered towards him, the rustle of cloth, and the ring of tiny bells.

Six men appeared out of the darkness. They had dark hair and pale eyes, and they all carried spears. Their long faces were sheened with exertion, and their eyes had a look Dylan had seen too often in recent weeks—the hunted look of the hunter. After a moment he realized they had a resemblance to Pers Morel, though they were obviously the originals and Morel but a copy.

They skittered to a halt and examined him with some intensity. They were dressed all alike in brief tunics of finely pleated cloth, heavy with embroidery upon the hems and sleeve edges, and each bore a baldric of bells across his narrow chest. Their feet were sandal shod, not booted, which struck him as quite impractical for running about in caves. One, he noticed, had run afoul of a rock and bashed his great toe rather badly. They grasped the shafts of their spears restlessly, but gave no indication that they were about to attack.

"How dare thee enter our domain!" one finally demanded. They spoke a strange tongue, neither Franconian nor Albionese nor Latin, and the demand was a trill of liquid noises for a moment. The leaf he still held fluttered against his palm, leechlike, and he understood, though it seemed a subtle language, unsuited to his unmusical throat.

"The door was open," Dylan replied.

That seemed to confuse them, and they conferred in hasty whispers.

"The door cannot be open!"

"Let us take him to the Queen."

"Which one?"

"Eldrida, of course."

"No, Margold . . ."

"Let us kill him here. It is simpler." That was the one with the bloody toe. Dylan grinned right at him, and he gave a shudder which set his bells jangling.

"True. He is an intruder. He cannot have gotten in. Only the half-elven . . . only they know the way."

"Are we betrayed then?" This idea seemed to exercise a powerful effect on them. They looked at one another anxiously and cast hard glances at Dylan, as if they might discern his nature if they studied him properly.

"What does he bear in his hand?"

"Who is he? He is no ordinary mortal. Gaze upon his lumen."

"I have. It nearly blinded me. He is a beast. All covered with horrid hair. Kill him, I say!" With this, Bloody Toe turned and flung his spear. Dylan drew his sword and deflected the shaft with a glassy clatter. It fell to shards beside him and gave a faint shriek as it disintegrated, as if it had been alive.

"You idiot!" snarled one fellow and slapped Bloody Toe across the face. "He bears iron!" He paused a second. "Go! Rouse the King's men. We are no match for this black-avised *animal*."

"You go, if you are so eager. Alphonze mourns the Queen, and he is in a foul temper. Besides, he fears a revolt. Already he has slain two of his rivals."

"What! When?"

"I heard it just before we started this accursed salamander hunt." Bloody Toe looked smug and uneasy at the same time. "The Queen is mad, and the King is mad, and now we find a beast-man wandering in our galleries as if he owned them. I tell you, we should never have let that girl be brought here. Angold named her well. Aenor Alfsdun. We will never get our stone back, and her song increases with each moment." He seemed quite pleased with his gloomy recital.

"Close your mouth, Nicor."

"I only speak what we all know is true."

"Yes, and if Eldrida hears of it, you will be bled for a ruby, you fool."

Nicor shivered at this idea and looked depressed, while Dylan tried to make some sense out of the information he was picking up. The girl they spoke of must be the dream woman he had been pursuing, and he felt a quiver of apprehension. What if she found him unpleasing? The goddess had made him no promise, he realized with a start.

Prompted by some unknown deviltry, he said, "I have come for Aenor." It was, he decided, nice to know her name after all this time.

The six elves looked at him with astonishment. Apparently they did not know he had overheard their conference. Finally, one said, "Come. We will take you to the Queen." *But, which one?* he wondered as he followed them down into the earth.

XV

The six guards trooped silently ahead of Dylan, still debating amongst themselves. They had made no attempt to surround him as he had half expected, and in fact seemed reluctant to get very close to him. When he moved near them, they wrinkled their noses, and he guessed he must not smell very good. Several times he heard the rustling noise in the stone walls of the corridors, and once another head popped out for a moment. He watched a slender tongue flick out before it vanished again.

"Those accursed Rock Folk are laughing at us," one complained.

"We will have the last laugh when we destroy them all," another replied.

"Of course. We have slain so many already," the first came back with unmistakable sarcasm.

"Why do you hunt these beasts?" Dylan asked. "They seem fairly harmless." He was not certain if the salamanders were part of his wild domain, but the two he had glimpsed had a rather pleasant feel to them.

"The Queen has ordered it."

"Which one?"

"Eldrida," was the sullen reply. "And it was Elpha's last wish. Curse her. She was ever a mischief maker. Women!" Reflecting for a moment on mothers and goddesses, Dylan almost agreed.

He moved up behind the troop as he spoke. "Are they difficult to—"

"Please, keep back, manling. The stench of cow and sheep upon you is quite dreadful."

"I do not understand you."

"It smells of . . . green—of grass and sun, of all that we have lost."

Dylan caught the pain and regret in the man's voice and dropped back a pace or two. The wool of his hosen and the leather of his pack had no particular smell to him, except those of his own body and long usage. He remembered what Melusine had told him of the terrible price the White Folk had paid for their pride, and almost felt sorry for them.

"Do you have some moon-tree stuff upon you, manling?"

"Moon tree?" He still had willow bark, and Beth's light-bearing leaves. He realized he was clutching one in his left hand yet. Dylan tucked it away, for the guards glowed with more than enough light to see by.

"It is the fairest of all that is green, first to leaf at snow-time-end, silver of skin and good against all that is dark. Perhaps you have hacked them all down with your hungry axes, for your kind is careless in such matters."

Dylan patted his pouch. "The woods still abound with such trees, and the lady who rules them is my guide."

"You lie, mortal," hissed Nicor. "She would never give her favors to a shaggy beast like you—unless time has changed her."

Dylan was outraged for a moment. He was tired of being apostrophized by these arrogant fellows. At the same time, he could not help wondering why Beth would care for him. Sal, he was certain, loved him because he was his mother's son. He felt a deep resentment that his mother seemed to stand behind each door he opened. How would he ever be a man?

When you stop being a fool! Saille's unmistakably acerbic

voice rang in his mind, a startling, refreshing mental slap on the rump.

Thank you, Lady of All Willows.

I should think so—a sound which might have been a laugh or a gurgle of water. It was gone before he could be certain which, and with it her presence. Dylan took a deep breath and stood a little straighter, assured of himself once again.

"Who are you to know the ways of a goddess, caveling?" Dylan asked.

Nicor stopped in his steps and turned to face Dylan. His face twisted horribly. "You raping, thieving animal!" He trembled all over, and his baldric jangled.

Dylan did not reply, and one of the others jerked Nicor and they went on. A faint musical sound began to echo up the passage, a harping that came almost from the stones themselves. A chorus of solemn voices seemed to drift in and out of the music, almost like a monkish plainchant.

They entered a spacious cavern. The music faltered, and Dylan found himself the object of several dozen eyes. He ignored them, and looked around the chamber.

On one side there were two large harps carved out of the rock of the walls. Their strings were crystalline, their beams covered with fair patterns. No player touched them, but they continued to tone, discordantly now, as if they required the guidance of voices to give them melody. Between the harps and somewhat forward, a woman sat on a seat of rock. Her gown was golden, pleated finely, and she bore a circlet of violet stone upon her pale brow. Huge purple gems bedecked her hands and wrists and girdled her narrow waist, while the bells across her almost breastless chest were the color of lilacs. Corn-colored hair flowed down her back.

She studied him with a quirk of pale eyebrow. Then she looked at his companions. "I was under the impression you were hunting Rock Folk for the usurper." Her voice was lovely, sweet and seductive.

The hunters shifted uneasily under her gaze. "We were, Your Majesty. We came upon this . . . person in the Windless Walk." The speaker paused.

"And?"

"He says he has come for the girl," another blurted.

"Indeed." The Queen regarded Dylan with fresh interest. "You were wise to bring him into my presence." She gave a smile he mistrusted immediately. "I am Margold, true Queen of the White Folk, and I bid you welcome, stranger."

He bowed awkwardly because of his pack, and heard twitters of laughter behind him. "Greetings, Your Majesty." Dylan stood up and gave the courtiers around him a look that silenced their merriment. They seemed to shrink into themselves, shivering with distaste.

"Come, come. We must have music for our guest," Margold commanded.

A sort of shrug went around the assemblage, and a few voices began to sing. It was a feeble effort compared to the music he had heard as he approached, and the harps seemed to be having some difficulty blending into it. A serious-looking fellow drew out a flute of alabaster and began playing. It was a clear, steady tune, and the singers seemed to take new life from it. Five courtiers, three males and two females, stepped out and began to dance. They moved in and out in an unbalanced pattern that he found confusing. Dylan looked away.

"Bring our guest some refreshment," the Queen ordered.

Those courtiers who were neither singing nor dancing looked at one another apprehensively. Finally, a pretty, boyish one poured something into a crystal goblet, placed it on a golden tray, and advanced towards Dylan in mincing steps. He stopped an arm's length away, curled his nose in distaste, and held the tray forward. Dylan remembered enough of his mother's tales of mortals who drank or ate of the food of the Fair Folk to be wary, so he shook his head and waved the elf away.

"But, surely, *guest,* you wish to quench your thirst— and fill your belly."

Dylan's mouth went dry as dust at her words, and his stomach growled noisily. He felt almost compelled to reach for the goblet still held towards him. It was filled with a liquid the color of summer apricots and its scent was terribly inviting. The Queen was trying to enchant him! He tried to find some anger to ward off the spell, but the singing seemed to wash it away. Everything was so beautiful—the music, the fair Queen, the stuff brimming in the cup!

With a great effort he opened his pouch and took a leaf between his thumb and forefinger. He reached forward and dropped the leaf into the goblet, then took the goblet stem in his hand. The server sprang away, snatching the tray against his narrow chest. Dylan watched Beth's leaf turn from silver to dreadful yellow. A terrible smell rose from the cup.

He poured the contents onto the floor and watched the leaf float down like a butterfly. "I do not care for rat piss," he said, and caught the leaf as it wafted towards the floor. It was still silver, still a shining piece of Spring, and Dylan wondered how something so small could be so potent. It was rather like his mother's kiss, banishing small boyish hurts.

Dylan looked up from his reverie. The singing had stopped again, the dancers frozen in mid pattern with looks of puzzlement on their faces, as if they could not remember what they had been doing. Margold, the Queen, was clearly furious. Her thin chest rose and fell in quick breaths and her pale cheeks actually had a faint rosy blush to them. Her eyes seemed brighter, too. A salamander stuck its head out of the rock between the two harps, an old one by the greyish color of its snout, and gave a gusty snort and a flick of tongue before it withdrew again.

"What sort of man are you?" demanded the Queen.

"Oh, rather ordinary, I think."

"Has the race of men become so powerful that they can resist the music of the True People?"

"Music? Was that what it was?" Impudence seemed a good way to keep the Queen off balance. Dylan scratched his head and looked more puzzled than he was. "I was not certain."

The pale blush upon the Queen's cheeks darkened. "Are you deaf—and a fool?"

"Neither, Your Majesty."

"I am the finest spell singer of an age, and the music of my court is—"

"Wearisome," he cut in. He waved a hand towards the wall. "Those harps could stand some tuning."

Margold glared at him. "They are new and not yet . . . harmonious," she said, eager to shift the failure of her spell off onto the instruments.

Dylan gave an enormous shrug. "I did not come here to listen to music or to watch such clumsy dancing. I have come for Aenor. I want her—now."

"And how will you force me to surrender her? Will you slay me? That is all your kind ever thinks of—lust and death."

Dylan thought of Paris, and almost agreed with her. "No, Your Majesty. I prefer to leave you to be Queen over this collection of asses. Even the Rock Folk laugh at you. But perhaps Eldrida will be more agreeable—or your King. I am impatient, but I can wait."

The courtiers around him rustled with murmurs, whispers of doubt hissing from lip to lip like the rush of the tide upon the shore. Margold raised her hand for silence, but it did not come. She rose from her seat and began to sing. Dylan marched up to the throne and slapped Beth's leaf against the hollow of the Queen's slender throat. Her song died in a terrible gobble of sound, a hideous parody of what she had made before.

Margold gasped and clawed at her throat, her face contorted in pain. "Take it away!"

"Bring me Aenor."

He heard a rustle of silks and watched one of the women leave the chamber hastily. Her hair, unlike the others, was braided, and he wondered what that signified, whether she was a servant, and what her errand might be. She might return with a horde of warriors, and then he would be in trouble. The spear-bearing courtiers he recognized as inept soldiers, but there were too many things he did not know about this strange world.

The woman with braids came back alone in a few minutes. She came up and stopped a few feet from him, made a dipping curtsey that rattled her bells, and addressed him.

"I am Elfrida web weaver, and I have sent for Aenor. Please release the Queen, for her song is our light."

"No!" gasped Margold, while Dylan noticed that the chamber was indeed somewhat dimmer. The crystal lamps which hung from the ceiling gave a pale silvery glow, when, before, their light had been golden.

"We will wait."

"You need not doubt my word, manling, for I cannot lie. The Web is always true."

"So you say."

Perhaps ten minutes passed, the lamps growing fainter and fainter, until a hideous little dwarf came into the cave, leading Aenor by the hand. She was, if anything, fairer than she had been in his dreams, but she had an air of grief about her that was almost palpable. Her blue eyes were rimmed with dark circles, as if they were bruised, and her rosy mouth trembled. She was dressed in White Folk fashion, a blue gown of finely pleated stuff girdled with a wide belt. The sword hung incongruously from it, along one rounded hip, the blade slashing the delicate fabric to tatters with each step, so he had a glimpse of long, elegant leg through the ruin of her gown.

"Release the Queen," demanded the web weaver, but Dylan did not hear her. He walked towards Aenor, a grin

splitting his heavy black beard. For a long moment they
looked into each other's eyes, and hers held a steady gaze,
full of sadness but no fear.

He knelt on one knee before her. "My lady. I have
come a long way to find you." To his shame, his voice
quavered and cracked like a boy's.

"Have you?" She sounded mildly curious, and reached
out a white hand to touch his curling hair. He felt her
fingers coil into it, caressing the scalp. "You are real.
How strange. At first I thought you were a dream."

Dylan stood up and found she was taller than he had
thought, a mere head shorter than he, so her head came
very naturally to rest against his shoulder. "A nightmare,
more like."

"Yes, that too. My, you smell . . ."

"I know, my lady, I know. These folk say I stink."

"No, no. You smell of sweat and dirt and sunlight. I
like it." She plucked at his beard. "This hides your
smile."

The web weaver danced around them, trying to penetrate their mutual absorption. "The Queen, the Queen,"
she squeaked futilely.

"Oh, yes." Dylan released his light grip on Aenor and
returned to the now livid Margold. He pulled the leaf off
her throat and moved back towards the woman.

"You monster!" Margold's first words were a raven's
caw. "And you, Elfrida, you traitor!"

The crystal lamps began to brighten, the stone harps to
thrum unharmoniously. Dylan realized that quite a few of
the court had disappeared quietly, and he assumed they
had abandoned their erstwhile Queen in her distress. Loyalty did not appear to be one of their virtues.

"I did what I had to," the web weaver answered primly.

The Queen seemed to recover her dignity a little. "I
suppose you did," she said quietly, eyeing Dylan and
Aenor in a thoughtful manner. "It may work out for the
best after all." Margold sat back in her throne, fingering

the necklace of amethysts that lay upon her breast, musing quietly. "He is nothing. A great, stupid beast of a man. And beasts rut." She laughed softly. "He is already eager to spread her limbs. And when he does, the sword will pass to him. It will be child's play to take it away from the brute." She touched the base of her throat, as if the outline of the leaf still hurt her.

The web weaver glanced at Margold. "And how shall we wrest the gem from the sword again? We paid dearly for it the first time."

"I am sure the brute can wrest it from its setting for us. Mortals have their uses, after all. I never noticed that before. And then I shall send him to serve in the King's court as a slave. And her, too. It will be a fine vengeance for my sister, Angold." She paused and smiled. "No one will doubt my domain when I have restored the sun to the Crystal City."

Elfrida web weaver pursed her lips thoughtfully. The gift of true foretelling was not hers, but she had moments of foresight, as did most of her people. The one she felt now was Margold's doom, but she said nothing. The dark beast of a man was much more than he appeared, for she had glimpsed a wondrous light within him, an illumination that was quite remarkable. If he was commonplace, if such fellows walked under sun and star beneath the green leaves of spring, then the White Folk were fated to pass. Surely the cosmos could not contain two races of such perfection. Who would make a song of their passing? Not the brute and the beauty who stood already half enchanted with each other in the center of the chamber. The Clay Men had no gift for music. For an instant she saw the possibility of another sort of song within the man and woman, a briefer, sharper sound than the endless paean of her kind, and the webs within her snapped and twanged disharmoniously. It was horrible and ugly. It was as unthinkable as rocks singing back to a spell singer.

She shuddered and tried to banish the idea from her

mind, but it was like a stone amongst her webs. It caromed from point to point, smashing the delicate magics of her spirit, destroying in a moment the aesthetic of a lifetime eons long.

Margold hummed, and the remnants of her court took up the languid, limpid melody. The stone harps thrummed very softly, and the flute player began to weave a counterpoint of caressing tenderness.

Dylan had been content to simply stand beside Aenor for several minutes, full of a sense of having reached his destiny. He would take Aenor into the sunlight and feed her strawberries and wine. It would never be night again, somehow, for she had been too long in the dark. And he would never see again the darkness of his own soul, because she would drive it out.

Almost swamped by a flood of tender emotions, Dylan's practical self struggled and shouted warnings. Strawberries do not grow on trees, and maybe she will not like you when she comes to know you. You are a prisoner in the bowels of the earth. You are a fool. The fair face may hide a shrewish disposition. Or is she a bitch?

He looked into Aenor's face and saw the slavering chops of the hellhound bitch who had so nearly enticed him into bestial carnality. Dylan's blood pounded and he felt a horrible lust. He reached a hand out and touched her soft, warm breast, and the silver fingernails flashed faintly in the lamplight. He was a beast without a soul.

Aenor trembled and laid a hand upon his cheek, then pressed the length of her body against him. She lifted her face and kissed him for an eternity. Her tongue was sweet and eager in his mouth. He could feel the rapid rise and fall of her breasts against his chest, the press of her thigh against his manhood. *Now, take her, take her! It is your right.*

Dylan wound his strong fingers into her hair and jerked it back. Aenor's eyes widened at the sudden pain, and she twisted her head free. He grabbed again, and she gave him a resounding slap in the face, then boxed his ears several times before he caught her wrists and twisted them behind her. The hilt of her sword pushed into his belly, and his ears rang with the ferocity of her blows. For a moment the blood-stirring lust abated.

The soft, cunning voice of the flute touched his hearing, and passion came with it. He was outraged and helpless in the same moment. His body wanted the woman, now, this instant, even as his mind knew it was an enchantment. His hand held her shoulder and he could feel the fingers bruising her tender flesh.

If only he could change himself, could slay the dark beast of his soul. *When what you are will not suffice, be other. Other, other.* The words echoed in him, and he focused on the glinting silver of his nails for a long time.

Change, change. Be other. Be lustless. The flute seemed to scream a promise of endless pleasure, and the beast trembled for it. *I am a beast. I am not a man. Only a monstrous beast.*

His sight seemed dimmer, and the music of temptation only a distant vibration. The woman knelt, horror-struck, and he put his head upon her lap. His body felt strange, cooler and longer somehow. Dylan wondered how he had gotten onto the floor. He did not remember lying down.

He lifted his head and looked. Something silvery and scaled coiled around her legs. It flowed like running water. He bent his head towards it, and realized it was himself, a great argentine serpent, chastely embracing his beloved. Had he possessed the capacity, he would have laughed. What would Grandmother think?

Aenor, wide-eyed, reached out a hand and touched his head. He flicked his tongue at her. Her eyes narrowed.

"You misbegotten monsters! What have you done to him? I will not have it!" Her face flushed with rage and the cords stood out in her throat. Aenor squared her chin, glared at Margold and said, "Cease."

To Dylan it was a simple sound, and yet more than that.

It seemed to resound through his body and the rocks of the cavern. There was a crashing noise, and he peered around. One wall of the chamber appeared to be disintegrating. A crystal lantern fell from the ceiling and smashed to shards as the wall behind it cracked. The harps jerked as if they were alive, then crumbled. There were screams, faint at first, then louder, as he returned to his man's body, mother-naked on the floor of the cavern.

He grabbed his cloak and covered himself, glancing quickly at the ruin of his hose, boots, and tunic. The White Folk were running for the exits in complete confusion. Where Margold had sat enthroned there was a huge stone. Blood leaked from under it, and one lavender-ringed hand lay beside it, the palm upturned in mute supplication.

Aenor was still trembling with rage, and she glared at him. She breathed rapidly for a moment, then calmed herself a little. "They will come back."

Dylan belted his sword and pouch around his naked waist, turning aside that she might not glimpse his bare thighs. "No doubt. Shall we go?"

"Where? They will look for us the way you came."

Dylan had the urge to smack her as he would one of his sisters for being provocative, a firm swat on the behind, and realized that it was more to release his still-aroused demon of desire than to hurt her. The enchantment the White Folk had put on him still lingered, and he knew it was not entirely of their making. It was a shame, really, that females were not as rutty as men. Then he thought of the way his mother sometimes looked at his father, even after twenty-some years, and decided that perhaps they were. Aenor's throat was flushed with more than simple anger. She was looking at him, not at his face, but at his form beneath the cloak, a sidewise glance of speculation.

"Do you often become a large, silver serpent?" she asked.

"Only to avoid rape," he replied. "At least, so far. I

am new to shape-changing. I am sorry if I frightened you.''

"It was not that," she replied cryptically. "I felt so strange, like Eve in the Garden. You are a most handsome serpent, for your eyes remained the same. I have been a long time in this place and forgotten much that I knew. Is it common for folk to become other creatures now?''

"No. You might say it is a family trait." He picked up his pack.

"How curious. And was your hand always argent?''

"What?" Dylan held his hands out and saw that while the nails of the right remained faintly silver, the entire left hand now shone with it. He flexed it tentatively and found it still felt like flesh and blood, but stronger too. "No. Do you know your way around these caverns?''

"No, I do not. For a long time I was unable to see at all outside the presence of the Queen's influence. I ran away, but they always found me. The last time I had a guide, but they killed him." She paused between sorrow and anger. "I killed his murderers," she continued in a terrible voice, "but it did not bring me back my friend. I have slain two Queens as well, the old one and this creature, with my song, but it did not bring me back my friend. What use am I, that I bring death?''

Dylan remembered the cleansing of Paris and understood her pain. "I regret, Lady Aenor, that I am not a bookish fellow with a quick answer to that question, which troubles me as well. Let us hope we can discuss it over wine and cakes in the clear light of day some time. For now, we must choose to try to retrace my steps, or to go in some other direction where these folk will not think to look.''

A rustling noise sounded in the broken wall behind the throne, and a salamander emerged from it. Dylan watched the sensuous body move across the floor and half reached for his sword. Aenor bent to fondle the soft snout, to caress it in a manner which gave him a sharp pang of envy. It was so tender.

"He says he can show us a path, though it is not an easy one."

Dylan looked at the broken remnants of his boots, opened his pack, and removed his soft shoes and his second pair of hoses and put them on. They were not suitable for caves, but they were all he had. Despite the chill, he left his other tunic off. It was unspeakably filthy. He made a mental note to undress before shape-shifting again, then laughed at such foolishness, and followed the woman and the beast out of the cavern.

XVI

They travelled downwards in silence for some time. Finally Aenor said, "I did not dream you were so . . . furry."

Dylan had thrown back his cloak on the left, to leave his sword hilt free, and his chest was half exposed. "I am sorry."

"Oh, no. It is rather nice, like a bear. Once a man came to our castle with a bear who danced. I thought it was cruel to keep a wild thing for amusement, but it was a friendly beast, so I do not suppose the man treated it badly. Still, if beasts have yearning, it must have longed for its forests. I have not thought of it for a long time." She spoke in a child's voice, half bemused.

"Where was your castle?"

"In a forest, near a river. I called the licornes, and they came to me." She reached down and touched the jewelled hilt of her sword, and Dylan saw there was a braided cord hanging from the great, green gem. With a start, he realized he still carried the sheath of the sword in his pack. He had forgotten all about it in the enchantment of her eyes.

Without pausing to consider, Dylan swung his pack down and pulled it out. The woman and the salamander stopped and looked back at him. Dylan held the interlaced scabbard and belt in his hands and reflected what a curious gift it was to give one's beloved. If that was what she was.

They were yet no more than companions in peril, and though he adored her fair face, he did not know her.

Dylan extended the scabbard. "This will save your gown from further ruin, milady."

There was no light except that cast by his aura, and Dylan realized that as far as he could perceive, Aenor did not have one. Like someone in Shadow. He peered, suddenly anxious that she might be some simulacrum devised by White Folk magic to betray him.

Aenor stepped towards him clumsily, as if she could hardly see, and bent her head towards the object. There, at the crown of her skull, was the merest spark, like a bright jewel nestling in the golden hair, and he released his breath as her fingers closed around the scabbard. He knew that somehow the White Folk had confined her light to that single point, and he felt a warm rush of fury. What sort of people were they to be so fair and act so foul? Melusine had said they were proud, but this was a strange sort of deliberate cruelty he found outrageous. A man's soul light was too precious to be hidden from view.

She turned the scabbard over in her hands, traced the designs curiously with an elegant fingertip for a moment. "'Tis a handsome thing," she remarked, and twisted around to slide it over the sword. The cave walls seemed to sigh around them.

Aenor gave a gasp and clutched her chest. Then she convulsed violently, her body jerking madly, as a gabbling scream came from her lips. Dylan leapt forward to support her just at the moment the spark of aura on her head burst into coruscating light around them both. He felt his flesh tingle as his muscles knotted and the hair on his chest and head literally stood on end with energy. It was a horrible, jolting sensation, like being lightning struck, and he fell to the floor with the woman clutched in his arms. She gave a little mewling whimper, like a sick cat, and shuddered all over for what seemed an eternity.

It passed, finally, and they lay together on the cold,

rocky floor, their arms embracing and the hilts of their two swords touching. Dylan could feel her heart pounding under his hand, and feel her ragged breath upon his bare chest. Her rainbow aura cast curious shadows on the wall of the corridor.

A soft snout nosed between them. Dylan felt a moist tongue flick his forehead. Aenor gave a slightly hysterical giggle.

"What?"

"He says this is not the time or place for coupling," she replied.

"Oh. A bed would be better, true."

Dylan released her hold, rose, and helped her to her feet. She was shaky and unsteady. "Are you ill?" He found he could not bring himself to ask her outright if she was subject to fits or had the falling sickness.

"No. But when I placed the scabbard upon the sword, it was as if something in me broke, like a crystal flagon shattering to bits. It must have been one of the spells they chanted on me, though I thought myself free of their bindings. I can see now clearly, not dimly, as before." She seemed thoughtful and distant suddenly.

They followed the salamander through great galleries of silent stone, the ceilings lost in darkness. Dylan ignored the constant stubbing of his poorly protected toes on rocks and pebbles, as he thought about what had occurred. It slowly dawned on him that his chivalry had been perhaps ill-judged. He had, in some way, departed from the plans which had been set in motion long before he had been born. He could almost hear some goddess, the cryptic Bridget who had dragged his mother into her adventure perhaps, gnashing firm white teeth.

Once, in a rare, candid moment, his father had said, "The deities are very able at grand scheming. The little details, however, such as the way mortals behave, elude them. Little pebbles that bring a great device to a grinding ruin. When I died—the immortal of me died, I mean—the sword returned to your mother, because she was its keeper. That was as it should be. But she bestowed it a second time, upon King Arthur, and *that*, I am certain, was not what Bridget had in her mind. The sword is surrendered by the keeper to a man she deems worthy of herself. We each paid our price, for it was a fair exchange of gifts, though I did not think so at the time. I wanted my freedom, my power, or so it seemed. Well, if I must bend a knee to anything, I would rather it be my Eleanor than otherwise.'' Doyle had sighed deeply over his wine cup. ''Women are the greatest mystery, son.''

Dylan recalled that Doyle had possessed the sheath of the Fire Sword, and that it had been a marriage gift to Eleanor. Now he suspected that some important detail of the story had been suppressed or eluded him, and he realized that the sword which Aenor bore held no particular fascination for him. He did not want it. Perhaps it was the faint air of regret his father expressed whenever he spoke of the Fire Sword. Or the sometimes shouted accusation of his mother, during heated arguments. ''You never really wanted me. It was that damned sword you were after,'' she would scream, her voice echoing through Avebury Hall to where Dylan was trying not to hear. The battles were infrequent, but enough to make him think that the magical sword had wounded their marriage in some fashion he could not quite discern.

So, let Aenor keep the sword. He would be content with a lesser blade and no midnight battles of rage and doubt. Let the plans of the goddesses go hang. Still, he wished he could speak to Sal or Beth for counsel.

''What is the number of the year?'' Aenor asked, scattering his thoughts.

''Twelve forty-one, milady.''

''Then, I am sixty-seven as the world counts years, though I think time has just begun again for me. Who are you?''

"I am Dylan d'Avebury, a knight of Albion and Franconia as well."

"Who rules Albion? My loathsome Uncle John or his vile get? And who rules Franconia?"

"No, John is many years dead. My mother had the dubious honor of slaying him."

"Good for her!"

Dylan was startled by the vehemence. "Albion's king is Arthur, son of Geoffrey Plantagenet and his wife Constance."

She turned towards him, her face glowing and her eyes begemmed with unshed tears even in the soft lights of their auras. "My brother lives! A miracle. How did he ever escape my uncle's ambition? Is he a good king? He was somewhat ill-tempered and headstrong as a boy. Tell me everything!"

Dylan chuckled at her eagerness, and told her how Arthur had been enchanted by John's magic for twenty years, released by the efforts of his mother and father; of the Fire Sword, and the death of John upon the broken bridge over the Thames. He said it simply, wishing he had the gift of tale making.

"You speak as if you had been there."

"I was, but safe in my mother's belly, yet. But I have heard the tale often, or bits of it, on winter evenings around the table. And, too, I have heard the King's own version, a fine lay of many stanzas."

"Now, that is an even greater miracle, for he used to squirm and fidget while the minstrels played, and pleat his tunic hem when the troubadours declaimed. But, is he a good King?"

"He is. Albion prospers under his rule. Is it so important to you?"

"Yes. And the Darkness? What of it?"

"Albion is free of it, but Franconia is still greatly shadowed. Still, the new king, Louis, has determined to cleanse the land, if he must make a river of blood to do it.

Which it will require, I think.'' Dylan gave only half his attention to his words, for he was busy realizing that his companion was not only several years his elder in time, but a royal Princess, the sister of a reigning monarch, and hardly marriage fodder for a minor knight. Even if his mother had accepted the duchy Arthur had offered her, it would not be sufficient. A black mood began to gnaw at him. She was Alianora of Brittany and he was a nobody.

He wondered if the Fates would play such a cruel trick on him to send him on the quest, to let him begin to care for this fair creature but deny him the reward of her love. They were, after all, three old women, and the rich heritage of his mother's many stories contained many with unhappy endings. If only Aenor had not looked right into his eyes, without the sidelong, demure flirting of most females! *That will teach me to fall in love with a dream*, he thought bitterly, as he envisioned a hermitlike existence as the Lord of the Forest broken only by chaste interludes with the Lady of the Birches. Worse, he saw himself as a grumpy old bachelor stumping around Avebury Hall kicking dogs and snarling at his sisters, who would probably marry and move away, leaving him alone. Eventually he would die, unmourned, and his nieces and nephews would breathe a sigh of relief and divide the holding between them.

Dylan focussed so intently on this lugubrious scenario that he did not respond to the woman's words until she demanded his attention.

''Dylan!'' His name sounded wonderful on her lips.

''Yes? What?''

''You are very far away.''

''Just some foolish woolgathering, milady.''

''But so sad! The White Folk have sad songs and happy ones, but their faces do not display it. When I looked at you the first time, your eyes were so happy, so glad, as if you were pleased to look at me. Your mouth curled in such a smile.''

"I was very glad to see you milady."

She gave a little snort, a delicate yet clearly impatient noise. "Do not 'milady' me, pray. That is not a word for friends."

Almost boiling with frustration and his own sense of despair, Dylan swore. "Damn all women! I do not want to be your *friend*."

Aenor shrank away a little. "Forgive me. I misunderstood the smile of your eyes." She drew herself a bit taller, a dignified withdrawal into regal reserve. "I need no one."

Her voice betrayed the hurt the words were intended to conceal, and Dylan wished there was a convenient abyss to fling himself into for his sad want of good manners. How could he have been so unkind?

"Forgive me. I . . . presumed to care for you before we met, and now I realize my error."

"What? I do not please you? I am ugly? I have an unruly temper?" She fairly sparkled with anger.

"No, no. But you are a . . . Princess, the sister of my King, and not for me."

"Why not?"

"Arthur would never permit such an alliance."

"Pah! My little brother can sit on the throne of heaven for all I care. How dare you set him between us!"

Dylan groaned. Once, when Doyle had been abed with a flux, Dylan had asked him how he felt. "As if I had an argument about something logical with your mother," was the reply. He had not understood at the time.

"I cannot do anything right it seems. You have been a long time down here, but surely you cannot have forgotten that a woman of your rank cannot wed as she chooses."

"I am a cow that the farmer leads to the right bull? I must marry a King or take the veil? I have been a captive in these halls for decades, and I shall not exchange it for another prison. My mother had such a cage, for she bore my father such loathing I wonder at my own existence. I refused a fat German princeling and a Flemish count who was dull. I will dispose myself as I choose.''

Dylan was shocked at the soles of his inadequate footwear. Women, except his mother, were fragile creatures, to be given at the whim or need of their fathers or uncles or brothers. He remembered that her father had died when she was fairly young, and he had a few memories of her termagant mother, Constance, from his days as a page in Arthur's court, enough to lay the blame for this aberration at that woman's door.

"You do not understand."

"I understand that all men are fools." She spoke bitterly and paused in her steps. "But I spoke of companionship, and you of alliances. *That* is not logical."

"Men and women cannot be friends."

"Why not?" She moved after the salamander, and he followed.

"It is impossible." He could not think quite why he felt this certainty, for he had often felt that his sisters were dear friends, especially Rowena. For all of that, it was not the sort of friendship he had with boys his own age. Even as children, his sisters possessed a remoteness he could not breach. They had a hidden kingdom behind their eyes, a fastness he could glimpse but never penetrate. A man might dally with a thousand maids and count their surrenders as his conquests, and yet never achieve complete dominion.

"Impossible? That is what Master Guillaume said when I wished to learn to use a sword. He said I would weep at the first blow. I changed his mind." Aenor spoke with grim satisfaction, and rested her hand confidently on the jewelled hilt of her weapon.

Dylan suspected she was probably quite competent at it, and he admired her bravery—and deplored such unwomanly activity—at the same time. His mother had wielded a sword, but only before she had met Doyle. He resented being who he was, the son of a heroic woman, and he realized that this woman was not unlike her. Dylan remembered that he had once wished for a wife as fine as Eleanor d'Avebury, and now he had found such a female, he did not know what to do with her. He had liked her better when she was still half enchanted by spells.

They started into a corridor and he noticed that they seemed to be ascending. The weight of earth above them seemed to diminish, and he felt a sort of tension in him begin to uncoil.

"Very well. It is not impossible. It is merely difficult."

Aenor turned to him and laughed until tears spilled down her pale cheeks. Then she coiled her arms around his chest and hugged him tightly. "Good. You will be my friend, then?"

Dylan kissed the top of her head lightly. It was all he would ever have of her, for once they came into the world again, she would belong to the realm of Kings and Princes, no matter what she believed. He hugged her back, feeling the warmth of her breath on his chest. "Yes. I will be your friend." His heart did not quite break, but he was sure it cracked a little. Poor thing. She must have been sorrowfully lonely down here to desire friendship with a great shaggy fellow like him. "If it is so important to you," he added hastily.

"Important! All those I counted as friends are long dead—or in their dotage, except my brother, who was not much my friend. We are too alike. And I had few companions—a waiting woman named Matilde who was older than my mother, and a younger one, Clarise; Master Guillaume who taught me swordplay. The rest were sour priests and toadies.

"And here, amongst the White Folk, I have been alone, except for my dwarf maid Letis . . . and Fejool."

He wondered if he could have survived without a human touch, or even the simple sound of real voices, without food or drink as men used them. His courage had nearly deserted him in three brief days in a dungeon, and he found he could not imagine living as she had, almost without hope, amidst the fleshless, pristine beauty he had glimpsed in Margold's court. "Who?" What a curious name.

"Fejool the Fool, one of the Rock Folk. He was my companion, my friend—and he perished of it. It tried to lead me out of the realm, but they found us and they killed him." Her voice faltered, and she took a ragged breath. "He broke one of their spells and woke me. I almost wish he had not—for what it cost him. Could you endure eternity without a touch, Dylan?"

Dylan considered this. He remembered the rough hugs of his father, the gentler ones of his mother and sisters, the bitter-scented caress of the Lady of the Willows years before, the ripe, fleshy embraces of tavern girls and the sweeter smelling ones of several ladies of the court who guarded their virtues well but were not above a clandestine snuggle in the shadowy halls of Westminster Palace. He recalled the soft lap of the Lady of the Birches, and how her hands stroked his brow, and the clutch of Melusine's webbed hand upon his arm, the brush of her breath on his cheek when he had kissed her. Dame Marguerite's earthy buss, and a hundred others floated in his mind, and he realized he took it for granted that men clasped arms and shoulders, that kisses were exchanged easily, a sort of human coin. He understood Melusine's endless loneliness with a fresh poignancy, and how the hunger for a simple caress might become a small madness. But he knew he would never feel it as the woman beside him. She had clung to him not from affection but from need. Once he got her above ground, she would doubtless find many to ease her loneliness.

"No, I could not. But I met someone who has endured a longer time than you without companionship, and I can guess how terrible it has been." *And why you'd clutch at a half beast fellow like me*, he added silently. "I saw a figure of a salamander after I entered the caverns—all made of ruby glass with a great green heart.''

''That was Fejool, for I made a song and . . . and then they bound me again. I have been caged in forgetfulness, prisoned in emptiness, but still the memories crept back. In the beginning I knew nothing, like a babe, and Fejool would creep into my sleeping place and lay his head upon my breast and whisper jests of his kind. And he would tell me tales of his tiny cousins in the world above, of great ancient wars the White Folk made, and long dead kings and queens. He told me of Alfgar the Accursed, my infamous ancestor.'' She chuckled. ''All my ancestors are notorious, are they not? My great-grandmother, Dangeruse, you know, ran away with my greatgrandsire, and lived with him without priestly blessing until the end of her troublesome life, and when she could not secure a marriage bond for herself, made content with wedding her child by her legal spouse to the son of her lover by his good wife, who first retreated to the Abbey at Fontevrault, and finally decently died. An infamous marriage, and not a happy one, I suspect. There is something wicked in wedding for power. My grandmother, Eleanor of Aquitaine, wedded twice to kings and was never happy in it.'' Aenor smiled at some memory. ''When she visited us, she always looked the young men up and down like good horseflesh, and I think she patted their bottoms in the shadows too. My mother did not care for her, but I liked her.''

''You sang the salamander into a statue?'' Dylan asked, brushing aside her reflections on her questionable heritage. ''How? A song is . . . only a song.''

''No. For the White Folk, a song is power. You heard a bit of it from Margold—a poor fragment, for she was not, I think, a great singer. The learning of it is the work of centuries, and it is a gift of the blood for all that. I do not know *how* I do spell singing, except that this jewel the White Folk want has something to do with it.'' She patted the hilt of her sword. ''It has hung upon my throat since my grandmother gave it to me, and perhaps something in it seeped into me. When I touch it, I feel phrases and fragments of something very old and both beautiful and terrible. The song comes to me unbidden, like a sudden fever, a thing more my master than my servant, though I had begun to seek it before the last binding. The jewel holds, I think, a song much older than any I have heard with my ears here, and much greater than the White Folk can make now. Some ancient Queen bound her song within it, and I can touch it, but I am clumsy.''

"Only Queens sing?''

"Only females sing in power, except for this same Alfgar who was my ancestor. It hardly seems possible that there is much of his blood in me though, after many generations. I would trade it all to have Fejool back with his endless jests and foolish tales.''

And you would snatch at a half man like me to comfort yourself. Oddly comforted by these morose reflections, Dylan began to be more observant of the caverns they passed through. Yes, they were definitely continuing to ascend, and the quality of the caves seemed different from the previous ones. He tried to put a name to the difference and finally decided that there was something less than natural about them. The down-hanging icicles of rock seemed too regular, as if some artist had come along and carved them into uniformity.

"Some great spell singers labored here,'' Aenor said quietly. "I can almost hear their melody in the rocks.''

They entered a short passage and emerged into yet another cavern. Here the effort of artifice was obvious, for the uprising icicles were subtly shaped so their surfaces resembled the bark of various trees, and the down-hanging ones had been removed. Where they had grown from the ceiling of the cave, the white rock was shaped like fluffy clouds. It was a burnt-out forest beneath a cheerless sky. Dylan could feel a great sadness almost seeping from the walls of the place.

Each cavern they entered was more realistic than the one before, each a greater travesty of a wood than the preceeding. Finally they came to a vast cave, the roof a glassy blue vault picked out in stars. Below it, the ''trees'' were branched in crystal and leaved in jewels. Birds sat on limbs, caught in songless perfection, and butterflies hovered in midair by some ancient magic. The floor was a carpet of crystal glass, with frozen flowers, scentless and exquisite, here and there. It did not look like any earthly forest, however, but resembled more the murals in Pers Morel's house.

Dylan moved carefully, trying not to smash the delicate things with his feet, as much out of respect for their beauty as to avoid cutting his feet to ribbons. As he had suspected, his soft shoes were not faring well on stony cave floors.

''They must have missed the land above to create such a work,'' he commented.

''To be sure. They have many songs of a world of trees when they were rulers of it. All of them are very sad. And they are only sung on great occasions. Once, even, they hoped to return to the surface, and a spell singer named Melys, who was Queen, led a great force of the White Folk up and out. The sun slew them, so the tale goes. She claimed her song would sustain them, and many believed it. Those who had not gone with her say that the loss was grievous, for they lost much knowledge and now can only sing little baubles of jewels instead of great ones.''

When they passed through the forest, they came upon an unseen barrier. The salamander went on, but they could not. ''What is it?'' Dylan asked, groping his hand across what seemed to be an invisible wall.

Aenor cocked her head, listening to something he could not hear. ''It is a shield song—Queen Elpha's, by the sound of it. Let me see.'' She walked a little way from him, her fingers extended in the air.

She paused, went a bit further, then returned to some

point he could not see was different from any other. He watched Aenor stand with her feet about a shoulder's width apart. She had an intent expression and she breathed slowly and deeply. Then she began to intone long solemn notes. The jewel on her sword hilt began to glow. Streams of green light began to pour out of it, then turned to red. Dylan lifted a hand to shield his eyes and felt stupid and useless. The cave moaned around them.

Aenor stopped her singing. "I cannot break this spell. It has web weaver threads in it, and I do not know how to undo them. The shield bends a little to my will, but no more."

"Does your jewel always light when you sing?"

She looked down at the sword. "No, not always."

"Can web weaver threads be cut with a sword?"

"What a cunning notion. I do not know." She drew the sword and extended it towards the invisible wall. Its point stopped. "It does not seem to."

"Perhaps if you sing at the same time," Dylan offered. He heard, he thought, a distant ring of little crystal bells. "I believe the White Folk have found our trail."

Aenor turned her head and nodded after a moment. "You have keen ears. Very well. A song and a sword it shall be." She took her stance, lifted the blade above her head, and began.

The nearby rocks started to hum after a minute, and the beryl glowed like a great red eye above her brow. Dylan could feel a pulse of energy, a power he could not define, throb across his body. The music of her song seemed terrible, and he covered his ears in a futile gesture. The sound seemed to vibrate along his very bones. He forced a scream back down his throat.

With a smooth gesture, Aenor brought the edge of the sword down in an arc. There was a flash that dazzled him for a second, and he felt Aenor's hand close around his wrist. She yanked him forward and he stumbled blindly after her. A dozen steps later he tripped, and they both tumbled to the ground, Aenor under him.

Dylan found his face buried happily in her unbound hair, and he could feel her breasts against his chest. The beryl poked into his stomach, but he barely noticed until he realized that he was sprawling atop a royal Princess, as if she were some tavern wench to be made free of by any man with a pence in his pouch. She wound her fingers into his beard, and he required no enchantments to know what his manhood was meant for.

He rolled off and stood up.

"Forgive my clumsiness," he half growled.

Aenor had a strange half smile on her lips. She extended her hand to be helped up, and simple courtesy forced him to comply. She rose in a single graceful movement and contrived to rest her weight against his body for a moment. She looked up into his face, a merry, curious examination, and seemed satisfied with what she found there. Then she stepped away calmly, except her breathing seemed a little short.

The salamander was regarding them with interest, and Dylan could not help wondering what the beast was thinking. It rose from its haunches and led them up a passage as wide and smooth as an ancient road. Dylan guessed a dozen men could march abreast on it without crowding. Pillars of white, translucent stone stood on each side of it—beautiful things, he thought, until he caught a glimpse of a pain-wracked face within one. The cavern over them arched away higher and higher, until he could no longer see the roof.

The avenue ended before a crystal trellis of stylized tree trunks and interlaced branches. It was enormous, six times his height, and a lovely work, the crystal a pale golden color. Beyond it Dylan could see shapes that might be buildings, almost impossible curves of glassy stuff, so fragile looking that he could barely believe in their reality.

They walked beneath the archway and their bodies' lights cast faint rainbow-hued gleams upon the strange structures. Aenor had a curious expression, as if she listened to ghostly voices, her head moving from side to side.

"The song of the White Folk has sorely faded since they made this place," she commented.

"It is hard to believe that the jewel you bear once lit the whole of this vast city. What is that?"

"What?"

"A sound, like mail dragged over glass. And where is our guide? He seems to have vanished."

Aenor looked around, but the salamander was nowhere to be seen. They moved forward towards the center of the Crystal City, and found the curving towers broken and smashed. Dylan moved carefully to avoid cutting his feet, and Aenor tiptoed. The further they went into the city, the more ruin they discovered. The rattle of glass became louder.

Finally they found a gaping pit in their way, a great, deep hole surrounded by smashed towers and crystal shards.

"Which way?" Dylan asked.

"You choose, for I do not know."

Dylan peered into the gloom. "It seems a bit less glassy to the right." He went before her, because the crashing sound disturbed him. His beast-sense informed him that something living caused it, but *what*, he could not imagine. The pit yawned on their left for several minutes.

There was a small stand of intact towers just ahead of them, a cluster of perfection in the ruins. Dylan eased a breath out of a tightened chest. Something roared. The towers shivered and one shattered into a storm of flying shards. Dylan pulled Aenor into the meagre shelter of his cloak and they crouched together, her head against his chest.

A huge head rose above the towers, eyeless and white as a leper's face. It swayed back and forth, smashing another tower in its movements. A maw opened and bellowed a brazen challenge. It blundered towards them, snuffling obscenely and moving fast.

"Come on," he urged. They stood up and moved as quickly as the glass-strewn footing permitted. It was slippery as well as sharp, and the thing slithered after them, braying horribly. Abruptly, they came to the cavern wall and turned to the right.

The beast swung its head down and yawned its mouth open. A smell like hot glass reeked from the maw as it closed around Dylan's body. It was soft and warm and Dylan could feel the tongue flex under his feet. He pulled his sword and hacked at the organ as the hard palate of the upper jaw threatened to squash him. Something thick and sticky spattered his arms and he felt himself being swallowed. His grip slipped and he lost the sword in the utter blackness.

Something thick and fleshy flicked his chest. Dylan grasped it in his huge arms and pulled with every ounce of strength in him. The beast screamed and opened its mouth and Dylan was flung almost senseless against the cave wall. His ears rang as he dragged himself away from the organ he had torn from the throat of the monster. He stood up and wiped away some ichor from his forehead and eyes as the agonizing bellows of the beast assaulted his aching ears.

His vision cleared as the noise ceased. Aenor, her face set in fury, hacked the dying thing into segments, spattering a thick white fluid on the ruin of her garments. Her aura flamed like a geyser, and she appeared like some warrior goddess out of an ancient tale. He watched her work in awe for several seconds before he roused himself.

"Aenor!"

She turned, a look like death upon her face, then smiled and rushed towards him. They embraced in gore-smeared camaraderie. "I was afraid you were dead," she said simply.

"No, not quite." A tinkle of many crystal bells caught his attention. "I think we are about to be intruded on."

"Yes, I hear them." She did not move from her stance against him. "Promise me you will not die," she said fiercely.

Dylan smiled a little. "I shall do my utmost to live to a ripe old age, but more than that I cannot swear."

"Then recover your sword, my friend, for I think you will need it in a very short time."

XVII

Dylan and Aenor stood almost shoulder to shoulder, despite the awkwardness of one being a right-handed and the other a left-handed swordsman, as a great host of White Folk picked their way across the ruins of the Crystal City. Dylan guessed their number at near a thousand, and he suspected they were the last remnant of an entire people. How many more of them there must have been to create the city! They were silent except for their baldric bells, and they were uneasy at the remains of the creature which bulked behind Dylan, a monument of rapidly decaying flesh. He could barely smell it over the filth of his own body, but he noticed the wrinkled noses and tight-held mouths of those closest to the front of the crowd.

The ranks split, and a couple walked forward—a dark-clad man and ruby-garbed woman. By their circleted brows he guessed them to be the King and the second Queen. He had thought that he would never see any White Folk who were not beautiful and fair, but this pair had a quality which made a lie of their fleshy selves. Perhaps it was the glitter of the woman's eyes or the little nerve that twitched under the man's cheek.

The woman smiled and Dylan felt cold all over. "I am Eldrida, true Queen of the White Folk, and this is my consort." She did not bother to give him a name and he glared at her. He bunched his hands into fists. "I suppose

I must thank you for removing that upstart Margold from her silly little throne.'' Her voice was deep and sensuous, full of enchantment and rich promise, and Dylan felt it begin to coil around him like a misty serpent. Aenor shifted her weight slightly beside him, and Dylan wondered if she felt the soft spell. With a sense of sudden impishness, he waggled his ears at the Queen, a rude, boyish trick, and several titters echoed in the silence. The Queen whipped around and looked for the laughers, but every face was priestly solemn. Dylan thumbed his nose at her back, and many suddenly found the rubble on the floor to be intensely interesting.

The Queen turned back towards him and began again. "We have not met, really, and I do not have your name." It was the same low voice, but it seemed as false as a moneylender's good humor now.

"Why would you want it? Do you not like your own?"

She looked pained and unhappy. "Why do you mock me? I wish only to be your friend, your good friend."

"I would sooner be companion with a leper," Dylan replied.

"But why? Am I not fair to your eyes? You will never leave this place, you know, but I am kind. Your captivity need not be onerous." She seemed aware of the wave of unease that moved through the ranks behind her.

"Fair? In a whorish sort of way I suppose you are." As he spoke he wondered why her magic did not seem to be affecting him as the other Queen's had. Perhaps she was less skilled in the art. He noticed that no droning chorus supported her, as if her people reserved their support until she had proven some power or other.

She frowned quite prettily and the man beside her smiled broadly for a moment. "Such hard words. Has dear Aenor been telling tales?"

"I would not foul my tongue!" Aenor snapped.

"How dare you speak!" The Queen seemed genuinely

startled that Aenor could talk, and Dylan wondered if her words had carried more meaning than he understood.

"Why should I not?"

"I command you silent!"

"Go back to your bloody rubies, you old bag of bones," Aenor said quite calmly. "A fine Queen you have yourselves. Elpha must be laughing on her bier!" Her voice carried well in the great cavern, full of contempt and derision. The White Folk glanced at one another and at the Queen's back.

The Queen shifted her weight and lifted her arms over her head, beginning a low intonation. Dylan boomed out a nonsense song he had learned from his mother, something about some people who lived in a yellow boat under the sea, clapping his hands to keep time, damned if he was going to risk another enchantment for himself or the woman. He was still a little deaf from the braying of the worm, and his ability to sing was never very good at the best of times, so what he produced was a fearful row of shifting keys and staggering rhythms.

Aenor looked at him round-eyed and many of the White Folk put their hands over their ears and shuddered, adding the jangle of glassy bells to the cacophony. After a second Aenor added her own clapping, and began to pick up the simple words.

The Queen screamed. The shrill sound echoed across the cavern, and several of the elves closest to her crumpled to the floor and appeared senseless. "Kill them both!" Spears whizzed through the air, but they were flung halfheartedly, and neither Dylan nor Aenor had much trouble ducking the missiles. One fell at Dylan's feet and he hurled it back into the crowd with better effect than it had been thrown at him.

The dark King suddenly smote the Queen upon her face with a balled fist, knocking the circlet from her brow. She fell backwards into the arms of several courtiers, and a cry of dismay rippled through the ranks. Some groups began to break away from the mass of courtiers, guards, and strangely sooty males, returning the way they had come, and Dylan decided that loyalty must not be much esteemed by the White Folk. At the same time, it seemed quite sinful to waste an opportunity to escape in the confusion.

"Let us steal away before they gather their wits," he told Aenor.

"Where?"

"Can you call one of the Rock Folk?"

"No. They do not obey me—or any man."

"Up, beyond the city . . . "

"Dylan, we could wander in these galleries for years."

"Perhaps." His pack had vanished in the fight with the worm, and all he had was the clothes he stood in, ichorous and bloody, and a sword and a pouch with a length of licorne tail and three shining leaves. No food of any sort. She was right. They required a guide. And the White Folk were hardly likely to offer them one.

The dark King stepped forward, his eyes glinting red, and he pulled a strange weapon, a swordlike thing yet different, from his side. It wriggled like a living thing. "You wretched girl! I should have killed you years ago." The sword dripped something from its point.

Dylan stepped between the King and Aenor. The King paused. "Get out of my way, manling!" When Dylan didn't move, he struck his weapon towards the man's bare belly. Dylan swirled and caught the point in the folds of his cloak for a moment. At the same time he cut across the King's chest with his own weapon. The edge cut the baldric in two and sliced into the flesh beneath the tunic a little.

The King stepped back a pace and crushed crystal bells beneath his feet, then struck again with his curious weapon. Dylan danced aside, whirled around and hacked at the King's thigh as a number of spears flew at him. The King howled, lifted his weapon again, then fell forward in front of Dylan. A spear shaft vibrated between his shoulder blades. The King's weapon twitched at Dylan's feet, and he felt a sharp pinprick through one soft and nearly ruined shoe.

He barely noticed it as he waded towards the milling crowd and grabbed the closest guard, now spearless and dazed. "Show me the way to the surface," he growled.

The Queen seemed to have recovered from her various trials, and she stepped towards Dylan and Aenor. "Give us back our jewel, and we will let you go," she offered, again in some command of her voice. The man he held wrenched away.

Aenor and Dylan exchanged a glance, and he watched her face stiffen with stubbornness. "The jewel belongs to the sword—and the sword belongs to the world," he answered. His foot seemed suddenly quite cold, but he barely noticed.

The Queen smiled as he stamped his foot to restore circulation. "Ah! So, he did not fail to kill you. Good. I can wait. I have forever." She was smug and sure.

Dylan felt the cold advance up his calf as the Queen began to laugh. It was too much. He reached out his left hand and closed the silvery flesh around the Queen's throat. She looked startled as he crushed the delicate structure within it into ruin, puzzled that forever was over so quickly. She sagged, dead, into his hand, and he let her fall to the floor beside her King.

He started to move and found his whole leg was chill and stiff. But the nearby folk were still too stunned by events to move, and he caught one despite his clumsiness. Dylan pulled the licorne hair from his pouch and hoped it worked on White Folk as well as it had on Demoiselle de Lenoir. He wound it around the throat of his captive and tied it into a slender noose and leash as the fellow squawked like a pullet on the block. One of Beth's leaves fell out and wafted gracefully to the floor as the chill invaded his groin and began to creep into his belly.

Dylan paused a moment to confront death yet again. It

was almost a friend, and if his last act was to free Aenor from this miserable half world, he would not be less than content. She bent and picked up the leaf, and Dylan remembered how the leaves had healed the wound in his shoulder. The cold began to grip his lungs. Clumsily he pulled another leaf from the pouch and pressed it against his belly, still holding the gabbling man with his left hand.

It burnt like a hot coal and he roared with anguish, but the cold in his chest diminished. Aenor stared at him for a second. "Put it on my foot," he gasped.

"Which?"

"The right. Aargh!" She rested the leaf where a toe had worn through the soft cloth, and it felt as if she had laid a burning brand against the flesh. It lasted no more than a few seconds, but it seemed like an eternity, the pain overwhelming all his other senses until it passed. He was drenched in sweat, and his only pleasure in it was the wretching and gagging of the man he held and those few others who had remained. Even Aenor curled her elegant nose a little.

"Now, show us the way out of here," he told the hapless captive. He glanced at the remnant of the host, a mere four dozen dazed courtiers and a few dark-avisaged men dressed like the King in sturdy tunics. One courtier, silver-haired and somehow old despite his unlined countenance, looked at the bodies of the King and Queen, and then at Dylan and Aenor. The corpses, Dylan realized, were already reeking with decay.

"Yes, Kalgor, lead them to the upper galleries," said the pale-haired man.

"But, Tallis—" some courtier began.

"No! It is done. We are doomed. Eldrida was the last spell singer of our kind—unless you wish to have Aenor's song in our halls." A sort of shudder ran through the assembly. "Go, child. Take the song you have into the sunlight we can never see and try to forgive our folly. Remember what our pride brought us." Tallis drooped his shoulders and clutched the bands of his robe with elegant hands. "Come. We have no Queen, no King, only me. And I bid you return to our caverns to await the end with as much grace as you can manage."

"Who will be our light, without a Queen?" asked one, as he grasped the enormity of the situation. A silence answered him as his companions turned away. Tallis led them back towards the entrance to the Crystal City and in a minute Aenor and Dylan were alone with several corpses and a sobbing guide.

"Come on," urged Dylan, feeling monstrous. Would he have stayed his hand from the Queen's throat if he had known her importance to the White Folk? He did not know. *I am not a man. I am a machine for killing.*

Aenor was silent for a long time, as they left the Crystal City and journeyed upwards through narrow corridors and echoing galleries. Finally she said, "It is all my fault. They wanted my jewel, which my grandmother gave into my keeping. She made me promise to give it to no man except my beloved, and if I found no man to love, then I must leave it to God. I did not remember that, for my mind was clouded, but I could not give it up. I have slain the White Folk as surely as if I had poisoned their waters."

"No," said Dylan. "I killed the Queen. I did not know . . ."

Their guide spat. "She was mad with blood. Her light would have destroyed us in the end. All you did was shorten the time of our fading, manling. If blame must be put, then Elpha must bear it for bringing Aenor into our midst. The foreseers warned her it would be calamitous— and she silenced them all. My dame was of their number." He gave a horrible laugh. "She always said 'We cannot unsing the song of our making and our doom.' I was born in these sunless caves and I remember when the Crystal City rang with endless song, the paean of Geldas the Great, before Alfgar stole the jewel for his mortal love and the beast we had trapped under the city arose, for the jewel had powers Alfgar, for all he was a singer, knew not. But Geldas' song was—is—in that gem you bear, woman, and she perished with its thieving. All those years you wore it round your throat, Aenor, you must have felt the splendor of it in your bones, half-breed that you are. For Alfgar was Geldas' son, and you are of his line, and hers. We wished that Elpha would tell you of your heritage, but she was ever envious of Geldas' power and commanded silence. If you knew, we thought, you would restore it to us. We knew not of your pledge, for we are not a people who make much of such things. But trouble not your minds. We made our own destruction when the world was young and your brief, foolish lives not yet thought of.''

"You are very forgiving," Aenor said a bit sharply.

"Nay. You are the last spell singer of our folk, and you have within you the greatest song we ever made. I forgive nothing. But I charge you to remember us more gently than you might wish to. When you look upon the light in the leaves remember that we loved them once.''

"Why could our two peoples not have been friends?" asked Aenor.

"Would you befriend a worm who resembled a man, but who would perish in but a day of your life?" Kalgor asked.

"I do not know. Did you even try?"

Kalgor shook his head a little. "I believe we did not, in our pride. You may release me now. At the end of this passage is a door into the world. Since I am doomed, I am almost tempted to accompany you, just to see the sun I have heard of, just once. But I will not, for the door opens into a place of your kind, and to see the good light smiling upon you would not please me. I would even wish you joy, but your miserable lives will be too brief to know what that is.''

Dylan and Aenor stopped and Dylan untied the noose. Kalgor looked at both of them, shook his head once, and loped away with a ringing of bells.

"I hope it is a city and has a bathhouse," Dylan said.

Aenor laughed and danced against him, brushing his cheeks with a brief kiss. "Oh, Dylan. How can you worry about such things when I have not seen the sun or moon for decades. You reek, and so do I, but I do not care. Come. I can hardly wait."

XVIII

Dylan and Aenor entered a great hall through a doorway that hid behind a large, dusty tapestry. Aenor sneezed and he coughed until his chest ached, but the noise brought no rush of anxious servants. Dylan wiped his watering eyes and looked around. The place appeared empty. What city were they in, he wondered, and whose house? A cool draft rippled the tapestry from the hidden door, and Dylan heaved the heavy fabric aside to pull it closed. A vista of fernlike trees was painted on the wall beneath the hanging, and he shut the door and lowered the cloth thoughtfully. A fresh pull of dust tickled his nose and he sneezed several times.

Aenor was standing near the center of the hall, her head cocked to one side, studying the tapestries and the empty fireplace. She seemed puzzled by something.

"What is it?" he asked.

"These hangings were made for my mother and hung in my home. You can see her device there, in that one," she said, pointing to a tourney scene. "But this is not my home, unless our hall has shrunk by half."

"Your mother is dead, and perhaps they were sold afterwards. She spent her last years in Albion, with King Arthur, and I suppose she discarded them."

Aenor shook her head. "My mother never sold or discarded anything."

This was consistent with Dylan's memories of the greedy and troublesome Constance of Brittany, so he shrugged. "Let's leave. I do not like this place." He moved to join her, feeling weary and ravenous.

A wraithlike woman walked towards them from the shadows at the back of the hall, all sable garbed, so her face floated like a disembodied mask in the still air. She had long black hair, unkempt and wild across her shoulders, and a narrow countenance. Dylan saw the resemblance to Pers Morel immediately. They might be brother and sister. She looked from one to the other of them and smiled.

"I see you have escaped from our kin, Alianora," she began sweetly. "I never did approve of the plan to take you below." Closer up, her eyes had a vague look, the musing vacancy of a drooling ancient.

Aenor moved towards Dylan a little, then took a combative stance, her hand resting lightly on the hilt of the sword. "Who are you and what are you doing with my mother's tapestries?"

The woman laughed and fluttered her long, slender hands. The draperies of her gown continued to move around the hem even though she was still, and after a moment a feline head poked out from under them and regarded Dylan with wide-eyed interest. The kitten, a bright orange-striped beast, emerged from under the fabric, mewing cheerfully, and promptly began to climb up his leg, to the further ruination of Dylan's hose and the flesh beneath. He plucked the animal up and it purred lustily.

"I am the chatelaine Brenna du Chanterelle. Welcome to my home." Another cat popped out from under her gown. It bounded towards Dylan and rubbed against his ankles.

Tired and dirty as he was, Dylan could not help chuckling at his effect on the cats. "You, I believe, set an affliction of these cats on Pers Morel, did you not?"

"Perhaps. I do many things. Tell me news of the kingdom below." She coiled a dank lock of hair around her
finger.

"The King is dead. The Queen is dead. The White Folk
are dying," Aenor answered brutally.

Brenna nodded, grave and amused at the same time. "I
thought as much. My crystal is so dark." Half a dozen
cats scampered out from her skirts. "Are you hungry?"
she asked, as if it was the most natural question in the
world.

Dylan's stomach growled audibly as the cats coiled
around his legs and gave little chirps of greeting. The
chatelaine was clearly a little mad. He was uneasy, but not
acutely so, and Aenor was bristling with energetic outrage.
"No. We have to go now."

"Must you? I have so little company. My relatives do
not like me," she added in a conspiratorial voice. "I have
a lovely chicken roasting in the kitchen. Surely you will
bear me company awhile. I will not harm you."

"Where is this place?" Aenor asked abruptly.

"Here. Near Saumur. Please, do not go. Let me give
you a new gown, cousin Alianora." Brenna reached out
and plucked at the gore-spattered pleatings on Aenor's
breast, and the girl shrank back.

"We would prefer some horses," Dylan said.

"Horses? Hmm. I have not conjured those in some
time. But if you will dine with me, I will do my best. I
warn you, though, I may only be able to manage donkeys."

Aenor giggled in spite of herself. The floor was crawling with cats, about two dozen, all fawning on Dylan and
batting each other to get closer to him, mewing and purring. "Can you sit on a donkey, Dylan?" Apparently she
found the idea amusing.

Disgruntled, he shrugged. "I have never tried. I take it
you wish to stay for dinner?"

"I am hungry too, years hungry," she answered simply.
"And I wish to remove some of this mess from me."

The unkempt lady smiled at them. "Come. I shall show you to the laundries. I have nothing that might clothe you, good sir," she added apologetically.

"It would astound me if you did."

"This way. I used to know a spell—I used to know many—for making a robe to turn away harm. Let me see. Rosemary and flax, the voice of an owl. Basil and birch." She was leading them towards the back of the hall, cats trailing behind her. She stopped abruptly, turned back and struck Dylan's belt pouch with her hand. One of Beth's leaves leapt out and floated into her outstretched palm. "This will do very nicely," she said, and tucked it into her bosom before Dylan could stop her.

The hairs on his neck bristled and Dylan wondered if he should take the leaf back by force. Aenor touched the back of his wrist with cool fingers and shook her head. At the same time he felt the presence of the Lady of the Birches within him, and was somewhat reassured.

"Why do you wish to do me this kindness, my lady?" he asked.

"Because it will infuriate my cousin, Pers Morel. He really is a terrible man, you know, refusing me. The cats were only a nuisance, but this—ah. You have a score to settle with him, manling, and I will help. I will have satisfaction." She almost purred as she spoke.

Dylan shivered a little and remembered that his mother had commented more than once that Hell had no fury like a woman scorned. It struck him as well that it might be unwise to treat Aenor lightly, for if she retained the powers of her voice she was quite capable of singing the house down around her ears. Even on brief acquaintance, he suspected she had a temper as monumental as any he had ever known, and had some of the same headstrong quality he had glimpsed in her brother. Why could it not have been simple and tidy? he wondered. Why were women so damnably complicated? And why had he ever wished for a woman like his mother? The thought of the two of them meeting made his knees weak. He would rather watch the Pope debate with the Devil.

The laundry was a small stone room with wooden tubs. It smelled of damp and mold and the lingering odor of soap. One tub was filled with cold but fairly fresh water, and their hostess left them to find a fresh gown for Aenor. Dylan doubted it would be clean, considering the untidy person of the chatelaine du Chanterelle, but at least it would be free of worm gore and sweat. Politely, he turned his back and studied the doorway while she undressed and washed.

Aenor came up beside him wrapped in a rough sheet, her golden hair now amber with moisture. The cloth clung to her small, round breasts and he could see the nipples beneath hardened with the chill of the room. Her skin was rosy with scrubbing and she looked more desirable than he had ever believed a woman could. She seemed quite oblivious to the impropriety of standing almost undressed with a man not kin or spouse, so he swallowed and turned away, removing his filthy cloak with a feeling of relief, and knelt beside the tub.

Dylan cupped chill and faintly soapy water onto his face, then plunged his head into the stuff to get the muck out of his long curly hair. Shaking his head to clear the water from his ears, he washed his bare chest and shivered in earnest. He longed for the great deep wooden tub at Avebury, with the firepit beneath it, where he could have cooked away the tired muscles and soothed the numerous small scratches that now stung his body. It might as well be on the moon.

Aenor came up and raised a corner of her drape and rubbed his chest with it. He caught a glimpse of leg and smooth belly, and cast his eye towards the low ceiling with a fervent wish to the goddess that she would stop being quite so lovely. He was certain he heard a faint laugh in his mind. The water had run down into the waist of his hose, plastering the wool against his skin and revealing his

desire as if he were quite naked. Dylan stifled a deep
groan, and Aenor moved behind him to continue drying
his body. He let out his breath and watched several cats
pick their way daintily across the damp floor towards him.
No wonder Adam had eaten the apple. Dylan would have
eaten the whole tree, roots and all, if Aenor had offered it
to him at that moment.

The return of their hostess, carrying a long gown draped
across her extended arms and tripping over playful felines,
banished these unworthy thoughts. During her absence her
hair had somehow become even more dishevelled and she
had a small smudge of soot on one fair cheek. Except for
the continuous occurrence of cats from beneath her robes,
she appeared terribly human, and Dylan realized that whatever other reasons she might have for her hospitality, she
was genuinely lonely as well.

"Alianora, here is a gown. I wore it at a ball in Paris,
for King Philippe, so it is rather out of fashion. But all the
others have been eaten by the moths. Silk, it seems, does
not appeal to them as much as wool. Such a dance," she
continued reminiscently, shaking out the folds and holding
it against her shoulders. "The torches, the music. 'Twas
splendid. I was a real maiden then, not just an old woman
no one loves."

The gown was a heavy white silk, cut very plainly in the
manner Dylan thought of as servant's dress, with deep
sleeves edged in bands of gold embroidery. It smelled of
lavender flowers and he suspected it had been carefully
tucked in a closet for at least two decades, since Philippe
Augustus had died when he was a mere babe. Probably
longer, he decided. How old was Brenna du Chanterelle?

"It is lovely," Aenor said, draping the gown over her
arm while trying to keep the sheet around her from slipping to the damp ground. "I am honored to wear it."

"Pooh. Dresses are like pearls. They die in boxes. Now
you, young man, get out and take the cats with you. Do
not frown at me, you great oaf. Alianora will suffer no

harm by my ministrations. Off with you.'' Brenna shooed
him out of the laundry before he could really protest.

Dylan found his way to the kitchen and sat on a rough
bench, pondering the wonder of women as half a dozen
cats attempted to occupy his lap. The room smelled of
cooking chicken, wood smoke, and dried herbs which
dangled from the rafters; they were homey and comforting
odors. The warmth and his weariness combined, and he
found his eyes heavy as he stroked the cats abstractedly,
pausing once to stare at his strange silvery hand. His head
nodded and he dozed.

Dylan!

Yes, Beth. She sparkled green and argent in his mind.

Do you love this Aenor?

I do not know. He felt himself pulled towards the shimmering goddess and the woman as well.

Do you love me?

Very much, dear Lady of Birches.

*Then love her that well, and I shall be content. And do
not draw back or hesitate, or you shall feel the sting of my
branches upon your very soul.*

Dylan snapped awake as a cat dug its claws into his
thigh to prevent itself from slipping off his lap. ''Stop that,
you little devil,'' he said, curling his hand around the soft
body to keep it in place. Another stood on its hind legs,
digging its feet into his groin, and butted his chin with a
bony head, buzzing noisily. ''I wonder Pers Morel did not
go mad.''

The faint rustling of skirts behind him made Dylan
dump his feline friends hastily onto the floor. He stood up
and turned around. Brenna de Chanterelle swept in with
Aenor, glorious in white samite with the sword once more
girded around her slender waist. Her hair, unbound and
almost dry, had millions of curls in it, and it caught the
color of the fire, so she was gold and white from head to
unshod toe. The scabbard made a gaudy streak against the
silk, and he gaped at her magnificence.

"Close your mouth or you will catch a fly," ordered Brenna. "If only any man had ever looked at me that way. Ah, well, regrets pay no debts. Let us eat." She scuttled over to the fireplace while Dylan pictured her dark hair contrasted with the gown Aenor wore. The Franconians must be paltry fellows, he decided, if they had overlooked the beauty of his hostess.

Aenor came close to him, so he could smell the lavender and the slight scent of soap on her body. She touched his wrist lightly, without wile but for reassurance. "Do not leave me again, friend," she whispered.

Dylan wanted to press her against him, to hold her until it hurt, but instead he stroked her face lightly with silver fingers. "No, I will not, friend. I like your hair unbound," he added lamely.

Aenor smiled at him and then seated herself on the bench beside the well-worn kitchen board. She looked out of place in her fancy dress, and he watched as she carefully folded the large sleeves, showing the pale blue of her undergown along the lower arms. Dylan wondered if he could beg a moth-eaten gown to wear on the road, then chuckled at himself as Brenna put a bubbling cauldron on the table. A thick vegetable stew, redolent of onions and herbs, steamed in it.

Brenna put out battered wooden bowls and large spoons, then rescued the chicken from the spit and put it on a trencher. Several bold felines leapt up onto the table with effortless ease, and she swept them aside with an imperious gesture. They retreated to the end of the board and sat on their haunches like statues, radiating aloof outrage. Dylan sat down beside Aenor, and several more cats leapt into his lap. One stuck a triangular head up and peered at the chicken raptly.

Dylan felt a prickle of his wild self, a tingle of staghorns on his brow. "Enough! Go sit by the fire and you may have the leavings!" He ordered the cats without any great confidence in their obedience. To his surprise, they vacated lap and board with boneless grace and retired to the hearth, glaring at him.

"So, *that* is what you are," Brenna said with some satisfaction. "Wine. We need wine." She gazed abstractedly around the room, as if a jug of wine might suddenly materialize from thin air. Muttering, she gestured, and an ornate bottle thumped into the middle of the table. It was silver and jeweled, covered with crosses and adorned with thorns around the lip, and Dylan was certain it belonged on an altar in some church. "Sacramental. Ah, well, the priests get the best wine." Brenna fetched some small wooden cups and seated herself across from them. "I steal everything," she said, calmly filling the cups.

Aenor's lips quivered with suppressed laughter. "Why do you do that, my lady?"

"Ennui, I suppose. Here, have some stew. Bread. I forgot the bread." She snapped her fingers and a still warm loaf fell about a foot to the table. "I once had servants, but they all fell into Shadow or ran away. That was long ago. I stole your mother's tapestries, Alianora. She did not need them, and I could not bear the sight of the True Trees another day longer. Do you want them back?"

"No, thank you. I only wondered how they came here." Aenor accepted a bowlful of steaming stew and spooned some daintily into her mouth. "Umm. Good. Did you steal this too?"

"No, no, just the makings. An onion here, a carrot there. The townfolk hardly notice." She handed Dylan a bowl.

"I hardly imagine the priest won't notice the missing wine flagon."

"Yes, but he's a scrofulous fellow—and I will return the container. Now, tell me everything."

Aenor exchanged a glance with Dylan. "You know I was snatched from my bed and taken to the White Folk years ago, and there I remained until Dylan rescued me

and brought me here. So, my everything is very brief."
She ate more stew.

Dylan, who did not feel much like a rescuer, was surprised and pleased at this description. "You are too modest, my lady. You rescued me as much as the other."

"Friends take care of one another," she answered. "But I would like to know how you came to find me."

Dylan chewed a large lump of carrot, swallowed, and tasted some of the wine. Then he launched into a somewhat edited narrative of his adventures, beginning with his dreams and skating over the horror of cleansing Paris rather quickly. Still, the chicken was reduced to a skeleton and the bread a mere heel before he was done. The cats got their promised treat before the fire, and he felt drowsily content.

"The mage comes to Saumur," Brenna said quietly.

"The mage? You mean King Louis?"

"Yes. He leads a great force of men to meet an army of Shadowlings which gather there—the Pers Morel and the other Guardians of the Way go there as well. It should be vastly amusing. You will settle my score with Pers Morel, won't you?" Brenna asked, her dark eyes boring into him. "And Alianora's. He took her to the caverns, you know."

Dylan felt the spell she tried to put upon him, and was annoyed. "I shall settle my own with Morel," he replied grimly. "Who is Morel—really?"

"He, we, are the Guardians of the Way, those born of the matings of mortals and White Folk, neither one kind nor the other. We are mortal but long-lived, and we possess something of the arts of the Fair Ones, though mine is little better than conjuring, for the most part. I did great magics once, ones far better than this mage-king, though he is rather good for a mortal. Nothing at all like you, shape-changer. *That* is a sort of magic quite beyond my powers, but I was good. And, having, I suppose, something of the pride of my ancestry, I thought that a wedding of my talents with Morel's, who is the ablest of the

Guardians, would be fortuitous.'' Brenna paused and drew a ragged breath. ''He felt we would not suit.'' She hesitated and her lovely face transformed into a nightmare of fury for an instant. ''He said the very sight of me sickened him!'' She closed her eyes and regained some semblance of control, though she trembled slightly, and Dylan could feel Aenor's hand clutching his where it rested on the bench. He glanced at her, and found her blue eyes sparkling with tears.

''Kill him for your own reasons, and I shall be content. Now, you are weary, and I still have much labor to devise you a tunic. Come. I will show you to the bed.''

Brenna du Chanterelle led them to a small chamber just off the main hall, a modest room which was spotlessly clean and, unlike the rest of the place, obviously well kept. There was a large bed with curtains around it, a small fireplace blazing merrily, a carved wooden chest and two high-backed chairs. Two of the walls were covered with tapestries, their colors bright and fresh, a courting scene and a wedding.

The chatelaine looked around. ''This was to be my bridal bed, but no one has ever used it.'' She gave them a strange look. ''I trust you will honor it,'' she added cryptically, and whipped out the door in a flutter of draperies before Dylan could protest. He heard a jangle of keys and the door was locked.

Aenor smiled and reached up and caressed his face. Dylan almost backed away, feeling trapped by an inexorable tide of feminine wiles. Aenor's smile faded and she looked puzzled. ''What is it?''

''Nothing,'' he muttered. ''Our hostess is just a bit high-handed for my taste. I can sleep in one of the chairs.''

She looked hurt for a moment, then angry. ''I will sleep in the other, then!''

''Do not be foolish.''

''The king of folly commands *me* not to be foolish! A fine jest, that.''

"Aenor, you have been out of the world for years and years. You cannot crawl into bed with . . . the first man you meet. You must . . . be practical."

"Practical! Phaugh! A fig for that." She snapped her fingers expressively and was every inch an imperious Plantagenent, a womanly mirror of her brother. "Why can't you pretend I am . . . a nobody?"

"Oh, fine. Just like a woman—no logic or sense! Tonight I should treat you like some maidservant or inn girl, but tomorrow, then what? What shall I say to your brother? 'I beg your pardon, my lord, but she insisted.' Shall I say I was drunk or ensorcelled? A fine figure I would make, with such a tale."

She slapped his face with a resounding smack, and Dylan, furious, grasped her wrist and jerked her arm. Aenor did not resist but leaned against his chest and put her ear over his heart. He had a clear sense that there was no way to win this particular battle, that Aenor would somehow go on submitting until he lost. He gazed down at the top of her head and glared at the golden hair.

"Don't you like me just a little?" she asked.

"No. You are as treacherous as any woman ever born." She was pressed against him tightly, and his body began to betray him again.

"When you dreamt of me, how did you feel?"

Dylan wished he could speak an easy lie and pretend he felt nothing, but that denial was impossible, for it would have denied Beth as well. The Lady of the Birches had given him too much, he thought, to merit such shabby treatment. "Great joy," he said simply.

Aenor slipped her free arm around his waist and lifted her head. He kissed her tenderly and was surprised at the fierceness of her response. Dylan released his grip on her wrist so he could put both arms around her. He held her tightly while he had a final wrestling bout with his scruples. The press of her mouth on his made rags of them. He drew away for one last effort.

"There are many men in the world, Aenor, better men than I."

"Shh," she said, putting a finger on his lips. "If ancient Zeus himself, or fair Apollo pursued me, I would count them as nothing to you."

"I am no god," he said.

"And I am no goddess, am I?"

"Well, you are more like one I am acquainted with than I care to admit."

She giggled. "Fine. You be dark Mars, and I shall be Venus, and we will make a mock of earthly Kings. I love you, Dylan, for my dreams of you were joyous, too."

"Life is not a dream."

"Are you quite certain?"

Dylan considered his adventures for a moment. "No," he answered.

"Then bed me and wed me, that we may know our joy together."

"It is usually done in the other order, and we do not have a priest." He could not help chuckling.

"Hush, or she will conjure one out of his bed, vestments and all."

"I do believe she would." He took her hand and kissed the palm. Her fingers caressed his cheek and the smell of her skin was sweet with lavender. Dylan took a long, deep breath and picked her up in his arms and carried her to the bed.

XIX

Dylan opened his eyes and gazed down at the tangle of golden hair that rested on his chest. Aenor was coiled around him, a leg across his so he could feel the silky nest of her pleasure against his hip, one hand curled around the scar on his shoulder, as if she feared he would vanish while she slept. He had been eager and a little clumsy, he thought, and he had been startled by her responses. She was like some fine horse, long trained for a contest and now finally allowed to run the course. She had run it several times, until he was quite exhausted. The doubts still gnawed at him, especially since King Louis was close by, but he found he had no regrets.

I should hope not. I thought you would never cease dallying about, young Dylan. You were made for her, and she for you, just as your parents joined by intention, so do stop your infernal fretting. It is noisy.

There was no mistaking the acerbic mental voice of the Lady of the Willows. *Am I just some pawn in your games, Sal? A healthy stallion?*

Do you love her?

Yes!

It was intended that you should wed her, but no god could make you love her. That is entirely your own doing. Now, do stop complaining because you like the task we gave you. Mortals! Sal almost snorted with contempt and left Dylan to some solemn ruminations on fate and will. *What if I had not loved her?* he thought in the peculiar agony of mind he shared with his father. He tightened his grip around Aenor's shoulders, and she stirred, yawned, and stretched like a kitten.

"Good morning, husband."

"Am I that?"

"I consider you so, and I will scratch out the eyes of any woman who casts a glance at you, and kill any man who attempts to stand between us."

"So fierce for so early in the day," he teased.

"I almost died when that beast swallowed you in the caverns." She clutched his upper arm and her nails dug into the bare flesh a little and she trembled. She took several breaths, and spoke in a voice strained with emotion. "We shall name our first son Geoffrey, after my father."

"That settles it, of course," Dylan answered, holding back both laughter and a strange desire to weep. He was almost afraid of her intensity and did not doubt she would carry out her threats against possible interference. He was not certain he wanted to be loved so deeply, and he was sure he was not worthy of it, no matter how many goddesses said otherwise. "You already have a nephew of that name, by the way."

"It does not matter. All the . . . the real *virtu* in my family is in the women."

Dylan roared with laughter, as much because he believed her as to relieve his tension. If even half the tales told of her famous grandmother, Eleanor of Aquitaine, were true, she had been a perfectly terrifying female. Like his own mother, he realized quietly.

"Get up, woman. We cannot lie abed all day. Stop that, you wretch." She did not, and Dylan lost his thoughts in the wonder of her hair cascading around his face like a golden waterfall. He rose to the occasion and surrendered to the inevitable with as much chivalric grace as he could muster on an empty stomach. It was some time later when he said, ''Shall we go see what milady has stolen for breakfast?'' They both laughed and hugged, reluctant to return to the world.

They emerged from the bed curtains and Dylan looked with disfavor on his dirty and travel-torn hose. The soft shoes were simply beyond aid, and he was beginning to wonder if he would end the adventure mother-naked. The gown Aenor had worn was carefully laid across one of the high-backed chairs, the sword's green hilt gleaming under its folds, and he was surprised that he had managed to take such care in the midst of his passion.

''Perhaps, *macushla,* I should just become a horse and bear you in triumph to Angers. These are hardly fit for a swine,'' he added, holding up the offending garments. ''And it would solve the problem of footwear.''

''What?''

''I just said—''

''What did you call me?''

''*Macushla?* 'Tis what my father calls my mother. It is Irish for 'my heart,' I think.''

''Am I? Your heart?'' Aenor was urgent.

''What is it, love?'' He reached out and folded his arms around her.

''I . . . just felt a coldness, as if someone stood between us.'' She pressed against him, frightened, her skin goose-flesh under his hand.

Dylan could sense nothing, but he knew that sort of magicking was not his gift. He pondered and finally felt a slight aching on his forehead, where Louis had marked him with the cross. Brenna had said he was coming, and if the King was indulging in some wizardry, Dylan supposed he might have noticed himself and the woman. Of course, Louis would know Aenor for who she was, now that she was outside the spells of the White Folk, and of course he would think in terms of alliances, not love. ''You are my heart, my life, my breath. Now, where is the fierce warrior-maid who was going to slay dragons and even Kings if they got in her path?"

"There." Aenor pointed at the small patch of dried blood that lay revealed on the bedclothes. "I am maid no more, and who ever heard of a fierce matron?" She sounded a little sad, and Dylan knew it for the *tristesse* that sometimes follows passion.

He kissed her once, then gave her bare bottom a playful slap. "My mother, dear Aenor, beloved Alianora, fought her way the length and breadth of Albion with me tucked up in her belly. You feel unlike yourself, as I did when the beast first came within me. It will pass."

"I do, yes. But it is more than that. There was *something!*"

"I do not doubt it. I shall make you a bargain. When we meet a man—or a woman—who would come between us, you may have the first stroke." As he spoke Dylan knew that in their joining a portion of her power had become his. He glanced at the sword hilt which gleamed greenly in the faint light, and for a moment he hated the thing and the deities who used him for their own purposes. It was his for the taking now and he wished no part of it.

Aenor followed his glance and her eyes widened. She slipped from his arms and disentangled the sword from the folds of the white gown. She held it towards him. "This is my bride-gift, for the man I love."

Dylan stared at her, nude and glorious, holding the sword just below the great jewel. "*You* are all the bride-gift I shall ever want, my Aenor. Let us give that troublesome jewel to God instead. It is a trumpery thing compared to you, my pearly lady." They had called her that, once, the Pearl of Brittany.

"That is a pretty refusal. Do you not want the sword?" She looked both pleased and irritated.

"No. I have all that I will ever desire—except some clean hose and a decent pair of boots."

Aenor laughed. "Are you never serious?" She reached for the shift and set the sword down.

"Good boots are a very serious matter, my lady, let me tell you." Her giggle was muffled in the folds of cloth as she slipped the undergown over her head. "Perhaps I can persuade our kindly hostess to steal me some."

Aenor's head emerged, golden ringlets in mad disarray. "You are quite mad—and I love you for it." She danced forward, twined her arms around his neck, and kissed him passionately. Then she slipped away to complete her toilet, and Dylan slipped into the loathsome hose, belted his sword around his waist, and prepared to face the day.

The door of the room was not locked, and the smell of cooking meat floated across the great hall. For the first time since he had begun shape-shifting, Dylan did not find the odor nauseating, and he was ravenously hungry. They found their way back to the kitchen.

Brenna was seated at the table, consuming eggs, thick chops, and bread at an amazing pace. Her eyes were ringed with shadows, and her hair was even more dishevelled. She looked utterly exhausted, and gestured them to be seated without ceasing to eat.

Dylan shooed a nest of cats off the bench and he and Aenor sat down. There was a platter of chops, a pot of porridge, boiled eggs, beer, and bread upon the board, and they fell to without amenities. The beer he found thin, watery stuff, compared to good Albionese ale, but he had no complaint for the rest, except for the lack of salt.

Brenna finished her repast, pushed her trencher away, and gave a resounding belch. "I had forgotten how hungry making magics gets one. Ah, I am not as young as I once was. Did you . . . sleep?" Her curiosity was almost lewd.

Aenor grinned widely. "A little. But do you not do magic every day?"

"Yes, but not *making* magic. A bit of crystal gazing and thievery is child's play, but to create something out of almost nothing, that is wearying indeed." Brenna gave a slow smile. "I have not enjoyed myself so much in decades."

Dylan slurped a little beer and regarded the last egg on his trencher. "My lady, is there a bit of salt for this one last hen fruit?"

Brenna shuddered. "No. We . . . cannot abide the stuff."

"Your pardon. I did not know."

"Of course you did not. Now, finish your food and we will see if my makings suit your fancy. I am afraid I got rather carried away."

Brenna led them into a curving stairwell and up into a little tower. Her crystal sat upon a table, and there were benches littered with flagons and bottles of every description, plus bits of cloth and bundles of herbs, little jars with unknown powders, and the reek of tomcat that almost drowned the senses. The floor was a-crawl with the beasts—sleeping, sitting, wrestling, and washing. They regarded Dylan with adoring eyes and dozens trooped over to rub against his legs and beg for caresses.

The chatelaine pulled an awkward bundle up off the floor and balanced it on the table while she untied a knot of cloth. She tugged out several garments and spread them over the table, covering the crystal.

"This, dear Alianora, is for you. I used the rags of your old gown in it, for it seemed a shame to waste the spider silk. I can say that no gown like this has ever existed in the world before or will again, and it was a real challenge to combine the world below and this above into a harmonious whole." She spoke with quiet pride as she held out a remarkable blue garment. It was utterly plain, without a hint of decoration, and it fell in the heavy drape of good Flemish wool. The surface, however, shone as no wool ever had, like satin, a vivid blue that almost pained the eye.

Aenor took it, rubbing the fabric between her fingers curiously. "Thank you, Brenna. You are very kind, and I cannot think how I can ever return the favor." She leaned forward, embraced the woman, and kissed her warmly on the cheek.

Brenna sighed and leaned against Aenor, her eyes closing, and an expression something like ecstasy lighting the exhausted face. Tears welled under the eyelids and rolled down her long face. Her lips trembled, and Aenor cast a puzzled look at Dylan as she continued to hold the woman. He shrugged.

"Your touch is thanks enough. I cannot remember when I last felt the warmth of affection." Her voice was very low, quavering the unspoken emotions, and Dylan thought of Melusine, haunted by the past and utterly alone. It seemed a horrible fate to be unwanted, unloved, and forgotten, and he had a sudden fear that he might somehow lose Aenor. The gods could be cruel in a fashion he could barely fathom, or kind for no reason at all. He made fervent prayer that they would continue to smile upon his ventures, and that he would never suffer the unutterable loneliness of this sad lady.

Brenna recovered herself, patted Aenor's face. "And why should I not be kind to my kin? I puzzled over it last night, and I think you are niece to me—or the daughter I wish I might have borne. Now, we must get on. My vile cousin Pers Morel draws nigh. Vengeance is a dreadful burden." She withdrew gracefully from Aenor's embrace and turned back to the table.

The chatelaine then picked up another garment, shook it out, and held it against her shoulders. Dylan stared at a large tunic which appeared to be made entirely of silver birch leaves. It looked both smooth and unsmooth, as if the edges of the leaves were curling out of the cloth, and it almost dazzled his eyes.

"This," Brenna began, "is my masterpiece. It will hide you in the woods and it will keep you from the harms of magic, though it will not turn aside the blade of a sword. But, if you change while wearing it, it will not rend or tear, but will change to a garland round your throat. I cannot have you running around half naked—pretty as your chest is—because it would not reflect well on the family.'' He heard the faint amusement in her words.

Dylan lifted the lady up by the armpits, as if she was a child's doll, and kissed her full on the mouth, like some tavern lightskirt. Brenna stiffened, startled, then she wrapped her arms around his neck and returned his buss enthusiastically, tangling the sleeves of his new tunic around his throat. He set her down and her cheeks were flushed with color. Aenor was glaring at him in a perfectly scandalized manner and he imagined she would give him a rare scold as soon as they were out of earshot. He did not care.

They dressed in the new garments, and Brenna presented Dylan with fresh hose, stolen from the blacksmith, she said, and a pair of worn but serviceable boots as well. They pinched his toes a little, but he was willing to suffer the discomfort. The cats interfered constantly, until Dylan commanded them to behave, and the chatelaine laughed at their outraged expressions as they obeyed.

''I have one small, final gift for you, Dylan. It is no more than a token.'' She held out a tiny figure of an orange cat, cunningly made so as to appear almost alive, small green stones gleaming in its eye sockets, and the pink enamelled tongue curling in a yawn. ''Any man who can make my cats behave ought to have it.''

''Thank you. It is a marvel, and so are you.'' He bent and kissed her hands.

They returned to the great hall, dim and gloomy with its great hangings. Brenna took them to the huge door, and they stood awkwardly, eager to be gone and reluctant to leave.

''Off with you now. I cannot bear long farewells.'' Brenna's voice was falsely cheerful. They each kissed her again and walked outside into a golden glade full of the afternoon sun. Several birds chattered in the trees, and a squirrel ran up to Dylan.

"I suppose she could not manage the horses," Aenor said quietly.

"Or the donkeys," Dylan added, as they began to walk across the soft grass, the squirrel darting in and out over Dylan's boots.

"Why did you kiss her like that?"

"Because I found that to love and be alone was a terrible thing. She hurt my heart." He struggled to find words and turned back to look at the door through which they had just passed. "What?"

Aenor followed his look and they both stared at a tiny cottage, a thatch-roofed stone building not much higher than Dylan's head, dilapidated and deserted looking except for a small curl of smoke above the single chimney. It could not have held a hall or tapestries, and of the tower there was not a glimmer. He remembered that he had not seen a window in Brenna's home, and thought this was important but could not decide why.

"Now, *that* is magic," Aenor offered, clearly impressed. "If she had been ambitious, she could have been a Queen."

"Unfortunately, all she ever wanted was Morel, who is not fit to kiss the hem of her gown."

Aenor looked at him, touched his face with a soft hand. "Love is not always wise."

"Do you regret your choice?"

"No. I only regret that I will not see you astride a donkey," she said, and smiled so adoringly Dylan was certain his heart would leap from his chest.

Aenor walked beside him, quiet, pausing from time to time to look at a tree, to listen to a bird or frown at the sky. Finally she asked, "Was it always so grey? The sky? Or is it the season? I thought to see the sun blazing in an azure sky."

" 'Tis . . . August," Dylan answered, after counting the weeks on his fingers, "and if we were in Albion, the sky would be as blue as your eyes. But Franconia still lies in Shadow, though Louis is beginning to change that, and the sky reflects that.''

''I see. The Darkness had come into Iberia when I was . . . younger, but not here, not like this. How shall I count my years of captivity? As nothing, because my body has not aged, or an eternity, because I have learned things not meant for mortals?''

Dylan was disturbed by her tone, as well as by the question. Aenor, like her brother, had spent a season out of time as he knew it, and the world she remembered was probably quite different. It was, he decided, quite confusing, because there appeared to be several sorts of ''time'' involved, not just the years on the calendar and God's time, which various priests had assured him were vastly different, but the timeless time of the White Folk, and the halted time of enchantment. His mother would no doubt have an answer or a story or a tale about it.

Dylan took Aenor's hand and patted it abstractedly while he tried to remember some tale which might illuminate the puzzle, and realized that whenever he thought of his mother, he thought of her stories and little else. *I do not know her at all,* he thought, and felt a sort of dumb agony that he could have lived two decades with this remarkable woman and have so little of her. Perhaps she had hidden herself in her stories, like some towered scholar, or perhaps he had never tried to get beyond them. She was, he knew, a passionate woman, full of terrors and angers, as was the woman beside him. But he had always ignored those things, and even felt outraged at their emergences. Did his father know Eleanor, he wondered, or had she hidden from him as well? *And will Aenor always be somehow remote from me?*

He found the thought intolerable, and he wanted to wrap his huge hands around Aenor's lovely throat and demand her secrets, her very soul. Dylan glanced at her profile, at the unmarred flesh above the bones, the dark line of eye lash against her skin, and knew that if he lived to be a thousand, he would never know more of his beloved than he did at that moment. It was both terribly, heartbreakingly sad, and completely right.

"In the end, Aenor, there is only now."

She gave him a sparkling look, a smile that cheered and frightened him, and nodded. "True. But how did you get so wise in so few years?"

"Wise! Hardly that. But even when men create machines to command time, they will still have only now."

"Machines?" Aenor was wide-eyed.

Dylan frowned, unsure if his mother's stories were history or fable, the ones about that future of flying ships and boxes that kept food fresh for years, then shrugged. It was all the same for him. So he told her a tale as they moved through the woods, and another as they passed a little hamlet where the cottage doors slammed as they went by.

The grey day was fading into twilight when they decided to stop. Dylan's feet ached from the narrow boots, and he longed for a horse, or the great licorne he had left near the entrance to the realm of the White Folk. Aenor was quiet and she drooped with exhaustion. He cursed himself for not seeing it sooner, then realized it was she who had pressed forward without pause.

They spread out their cloaks—Dylan's well-worn but now clean one, and another somewhat moth-eaten but serviceable that Brenna had given Aenor—in a pine-needled clearing. She stretched out, pillowed her head on a bent arm, and stared at the sky. Tears trickled out of the corners of her eyes.

Dylan viewed this phenomenon with dismay. Women, in his experience, cried for such a remarkable variety of reasons—for anger, joy, or sadness—that he could not fathom the cause, though he searched himself for some error or misdeed. After a moment he could not bear it, and reached out his silvery hand to brush the offending moisture from her cheeks.

Aenor smiled. "The world is so beautiful, even grey it

is more beautiful than I remembered. What an agony to never look upon the sky, the sun, to never hear the birds. My song seems quite pitiful by comparison.''

Relieved that these were tears of happiness, Dylan patted her hand and watched several forest creatures come out to pay him homage. It was still a strange sensation to find rabbits and foxes tamed by his very presence. Aenor might have been invisible or nonexistent for all the notice they gave her as they frolicked across his legs, the natural enmities between their kinds forgotten. Weary from the walking, he stretched out beside Aenor and fell asleep.

A howl echoed across the woods, a bloodcurdling sound in the stillness. He snapped awake into complete night and sat up abruptly. The small animals which had blanketed his body—hares, squirrels, foxes, and a solitary badger—scattered and scurried off into the darkness as the fearful cry was repeated by several voices. Aenor was on her feet, hand on sword hilt, quivering with alertness, before the last of them had vanished. Dylan stood beside her.

There were hoofbeats and the snort of horses, the jingle of bridle rings, and the savage growling of large animals. Wolves by their voices, he thought, puzzled. Dylan glanced toward the sky, but the starry track of the Milky Way was just a faint gleam, not the vivid river which had brought the hell hounds upon him before.

A dozen figures rode forward, cloaked and muffled, their auras nearly invisible, their faces shadowed by their hoods. Behind them a restless collection of large beasts moved—wolves, bears and red-eyed wild boars—all roaring or growling. The leading man lifted a hand, and silence descended.

He brushed away the hood and looked at Dylan. Pers Morel's long, elegant face seemed worn and weary. ''I believed you dead, Chevalier Sable.''

''No.''

''And you, Aenor. Must I drag you back down to the caverns a second time?''

"So it *was* you who stole me from my bed. Husband, I believe my grievance preceeds yours by some decades, and I demand the right to slay this mongrel."

Dylan was caught between his fear for her safety and his fair assurance of her ability to survive. "My lady, I wish you will not sully your noble blade with this creature's foul blood," he answered.

Morel laughed. "You foolish children, to believe you can stand against me." He raised his hands and made a swirling gesture.

For a second Dylan felt dizzy. Then his wild self woke with a suddenness that cramped his guts like a flux. His brow ached with the energy of the stag and the sacred cross as well, and the two warred for a long, almost unendurable moment. He gritted his teeth and bound them together with his will, although it felt like an iron stake being driven into his skull. No damn hedge wizard was going to push him around.

Beside him, Aenor gasped for air, as if she was being strangled. Her hand clutched at her throat and her eyes were wide with terror. Morel laughed like a madman. Dylan plucked one of Beth's leaves from his pouch and pressed it against the slender column of her throat as Morel shouted a command.

The pack of beasts surged forward around the mounted Guardians of the Way, baying, howling, and grunting their challenges. Aenor took a normal breath and he turned to face the attack, pulling his sword to battle them as a man. For a second he forgot the power of his beast-self.

As the lead wolf, a huge grey animal, a very king of wolves, prepared to spring at him, Dylan paused, drew air into his lungs, and lifted his empty hand. The wolf froze and howled, and the rest of the pack stiffened in mid motion. The howl became a whimper, a piteous sound in so noble a creature, and it fawned at Dylan's feet like a puppy.

Morel gestured frantically, but the pack did not obey

him. He turned towards his companions and they urged their horses forward to attack. The animals reared and tossed their heads as if reluctant to enter the fray, and one rider was unseated before the rest dismounted, leaving Morel alone upon his horse. It stood statuelike, deaf to his orders and unmoved by quirt or spurs applied with fiendish energy.

Dylan commanded. He used neither word nor gesture. His beast-will simply turned the pack, and with a horrendous communal bellow, they swarmed back the way they had come, ravaging the approaching men with great claws, sharp fangs, and deadly tusks. The riderless horses went mad, some dashing off into the forest, the rest lashing out at the maddened animals which were attacking without discrimination. In a minute the glade was a charnel house of rended men and bleeding horses. The pack scattered into the woods, their fury spent, fleeing Dylan's mastery as much as anything else.

Morel remained untouched upon his horse somehow, an expression of rage and confusion on his features. He gave a glance at his dead or dying companions, and bent his head forward for a moment. Then he dismounted and pushed his cloak back. He pulled his sword in a confident gesture, every inch a fearsome fighter, easy and graceful in his movements.

"Before I kill you, you really must tell me what sort of misbegotten creature you are," he almost purred.

Dylan looked at him and felt a curious sadness. He was not angry at Morel any longer, for what the man had worked to preserve was already in ruins below the very earth they stood on. The White Folk were dying; Brenna de Chanterelle would never have her vengeance or the love she longed for. He had Aenor, but at a great price which he knew would haunt him until he was laid to rest in the bosom of his grandmother. It seemed such a horrible waste.

The leather pouch on his belt was suddenly very heavy

and wriggled as if it was alive. Suspecting some further magic, he glanced down at it. A tawny triangular head popped out of the opening followed by a soft paw. At the same moment he recalled the ending of one of his mother's tales.

"Why, I am King of the Cats," he said, as the animal leapt from his pouch, fell to the ground in a graceful bound, and grew to an astonishing size in a moment. It attacked Pers Morel with huge claws and sharp teeth, and the man screamed and brought the edge of his sword against its torso. The two figures wrestled desperately for a moment, and Dylan found Aenor clutching his arm in horror.

Morel struggled, then pulled a small knife from his belt and stabbed at the great cat until it bled in several places. Finally he shoved the knife under the heavy torso and stabbed the beast in the heart as it sank its teeth into his throat and tore the flesh apart. The two fell as one and the cat vanished.

Brenna du Chanterelle lay upon the bloody breast of Pers Morel, her arms around his shoulders in a lover's embrace, her red-smeared mouth curved in a terrible smile. Her dishevelled black hair spread out softly, and they might have been asleep except for the gaping tear in Morel's throat and the many wounds on the woman's body.

Aenor sobbed against Dylan's shoulder and he almost felt like joining her. Instead he held her close and comforted her with clumsy pats and meaningless words. Finally she calmed.

"Oh, Dylan, he . . . he stole my voice. It was horrible, as if he had taken my very soul, and I hated him."

"There, there. It is over now," he said inadequately. He remembered the instant when Morel's magic had rendered him powerless and understood how she felt.

"But *that*," she said pointing a shaking hand at the corpses, "that is worse." She shivered all over and took

her cloak up from the ground, pulling it around her.
"Vengeance is horrible. Let us leave here quickly."

"Surely." Dylan recovered his cloak and felt a soft
nose butt him in the back as he stood up. Morel's horse
nickered softly, and bent its head reverently. Three of the
other horses crowded around them, their flanks slashed
here and there, but less hurt than he would have expected.
They ignored Aenor and blew warm, horsey kisses into his
face.

Dylan gathered their reins and turned them aside. He
helped the woman mount and grinned at the lovely sight
her long legs exposed as the skirt rode up over the saddle.
He got on Morel's big black animal and felt something he
had never experienced before, a sense of oneness with the
beast which was quite uncanny. It was not the wild part of
Dylan which responded, but his very human self. This was
simply the best horse he had ever ridden, and he loved it
with a passion approaching that he held for Aenor. They
rose slowly into the west towards Angers and another day.

XX

Morning came with a thick pall of mist which rose off the river like an Albionese fog. The air was still and breathless, and Dylan looked towards the west for some sign of an approaching storm. There was nothing but sickly greyness, and the rising sun behind them was an amber orb.

Aenor stood in her stirrups and leaned forward, sniffing. "Do you smell smoke?"

Dylan scented the air and caught the rank odor of rotting vegetation, sewage, and just a whiff of wood smoke. "A little, yes. Why?"

"I smell a great deal of it."

"Your lovely nose is clearly a finer organ than my own."

"Is it? Dylan, I fear Angers is burning."

"Perhaps Louis has come to the city already and departed for somewhere else." He hoped that he would somehow avoid another meeting with the King, despite his promise to return and fight the Shadow.

"Is he not your friend? When you told us your tale you spoke well of him."

"He is a great man, and his soul is as pure as any, but he is still a King. Worse, he is a King who serves God, so he can make the pretense that what he chooses is not his own will, but that of the Lord. A King, a priest, and a mage. That is a dangerous combination, I think, and I sense too that more draws him to Angers than the force of Shadow. Brenna du Chanterelle is not the only one who seeks the future in dark crystals.''

''Are you afraid of him, my love?''

''I am afraid of any man who wields great powers and who answers only to God. And I do not care for magic.''

Aenor nodded and reached across and touched his hand. ''Shall I abjure the power of the song within me?''

''No! I am not so mean spirited that I would ask you to deny a part of yourself. Louis is an honorable man, but he is only a man. That is what disturbs me. He will see you as a prize, a pawn to use in his plans, and I may face the choice of regicide or submission.''

''I have no say in this?'' Aenor's voice had a slight edge to it.

Dylan felt trapped. She was his to protect, to care for, because she was a woman. That was the way of the world. But she had proved repeatedly that she could, in many ways, look out for herself. True, if he had not come to the caverns of the White Folk, she might have languished there ageless for several aeons. Or she might have escaped on her own. He wished he might consult his father, for surely Doyle had faced the same problems with Eleanor. How could he be manly in the presence of her undeniable power? He was unnecessary in the fulfillment of her destiny.

''No. You have the same choices I do. And your temper is much quicker than mine. You might rob Franconia of her King in a moment of anger, as you sung the roof down upon the hapless Margold.''

''She deserved it.''

''Perhaps. But do not be too quick to seize death as a solution to any conflict.''

''They took my will, Dylan, and locked it away from me, and something within me screams that I must never permit any force to do that again. I cannot submit.''

Dylan heard the pain in those words and realized this

was a wound too fresh to have healed, and that it might never become so. It was like his own horror of death and destruction. The cleansing of Paris would forever weigh upon him. Perhaps that was the real mystery of the world; that a man might do deeds too terrible to speak of and yet eat and drink and love.

"Then we must seek a compromise, *macushla*."

Aenor made a face at him. "Gah! I have no talent for such, so I must be glad that you seem to."

Dylan saw for the first time the power of the peacemaker and wanted to possess it. "We will just point out to Louis—or to your brother—the peril of bestowing you as they might think fit."

"Would you not fight to keep me?"

"Yes. And that terrifies me."

"Why?" She sounded genuinely puzzled.

"Because I am a beast, and any man who does not fear the beast within him is a fool."

"Dylan, beloved, what is it like to change?"

"I am very new to it," he began, enchanted by the way his name sounded on her lips, "and I wish my father were here, for he knows it very well. I wonder why he never told me about it?" He was fairly certain his mother had forbidden it, for she always got an expression of faint distaste on her face when her own transformations were mentioned. "I have no mastery over it, though perhaps that will come with time. It is as if there was a tiny imp inside me who appears when certain kinds of danger come. It wrenches me out of my self, and it is both terrible and wonderful. It is a wild thing, and once I almost chose to remain a beast." He remembered the heady scent of the hellhound bitch, the warm, musky smell of her flesh, and the temptation of untrammelled bestiality. He was not sure he would ever be free of a faint yearning for the freedom of the woods of the world. It seemed almost shameful to be beside this splendid woman, lover and friend, and long for the quietude of ancient forests. Beth had told him he must find the god within himself, and he thought perhaps it was one of those strange deities of old Egypt, part man, part animal, ass-eared Set or dog-headed Anubis, his mother had told him of. It was not a comfortable idea, he decided.

"Does it almost sweep you away, like a rushing river?"

"Yes, almost."

"My song is like that too. Greater than myself, as if I were only a course the music runs through. It almost frightens me that I will be washed away into oblivion—not Aenor, nor Alianora, not anyone. I was mindless so long." She touched the jewel at her hip. "And, too, I only borrow the song, I think. I wonder why my grandmother gave it to me and not to one of her daughters."

"Who knows? Perhaps some goddess guided her, or she looked in a crystal and saw the future."

Aenor giggled. "My grandmother never took counsel but from herself. She was born to rule."

The mist began to darken and the smell of fire intensified. They followed the river and passed small hamlets which might have been deserted except for the curls of smoke from chimneys and the occasional brave soul who stuck a head out to look at them. They heard the homey sounds of screaming infants and lowing cattle and though they were both hungry, they did not stop to ask for food. They both felt the sense of urgency, the bristling tension in the air, and spurred the horses into a bone-rattling trot.

Smuts began to rain from the air, fouling lungs and nostrils. The surface of the river, barely visible under the fog, was dull and leaden. Aenor's golden hair acquired a grey covering, and she coughed from time to time. Bits of ash collected on her skin, rubbed in as she brushed them away, until she was a pair of bright blue eyes startling out of a nearly black face.

"You look like one of the forge folk," she told Dylan, informing him that he presented no better appearance than herself.

"Probably. I would suggest a quick wash in the river, but I think it is dirtier than we are."

Perhaps a minute later a howling pack of lightless Shadow Folk darted towards them from a small copse, waving pitchforks and cudgels. Aenor wheeled her horse into their midst, using her sword effectively, and Dylan followed her, his horse lashing out viciously at the attackers. The two riderless horses behind him joined in the fray, and the Shadow people fell or fled.

Dylan bit back several sharp criticisms for his head-strong beloved, and she glanced at him. "I know," she said. "Be careful. Look before I leap."

"Well, do try not to get yourself killed, dear one," he responded, more mildly than he felt. His heart was almost cramped with fear for her safety.

Aenor hung her lead a little. "I deserved that. Very well. I shall try to school myself to caution, but you must admit it is very difficult." She wiped her blade clean on her cloak and sheathed it calmly.

Dylan reminded himself that she was competent with her weapon and that he could not protect her from everything. "I shall be pleased when I can get you a helm and some mail and a shield."

"And more pleased if I would sit quietly over a 'broidery frame while you ride off to slay dragons."

Dylan laughed. "True, but I know that is not possible."

"I was always dreadful at needlework."

"That I believe. Now, let us ride as swiftly as possible, and hope we do not meet any more Darklings."

"Ride where?" she asked practically.

"North, for now."

They rode away from the river a little way, then struck northward, encountering small bands of Shadowlings who scattered before them without much trouble. The air was so choked with ash that they could barely breathe, and the horses snorted and wheezed, so they could not travel as fast as they would have liked. The sun had climbed to

midday before they encountered the first evidence of Louis'
presence, a dead man-at-arms in a blood-smeared blue
tabard with the fleur-de-lys upon it. His chest was spiked
on a spear, and his young face seemed surprised under the
helm. Beyond him lay another even younger and just as
dead, his slender neck almost hacked through by some axe
or sword.

Dylan, hardened as he was after Paris, still experienced
a tremor of disgust, a sense of sickness and futility, of
waste. Aenor sat her horse like a statue, showing no
expression whatever except a slight narrowing of her eyes
that might bode ill for someone. He would have preferred
a few womanly tears or at least some quivering lips, the
way Rowena, his sister, did when she did not quite cry.
This stony female saddened him, but he said nothing. He
urged his horse forward, and she followed.

After a few minutes they could hear the roar of a battle.
It was like some odd brazen beast howling in the distance
at first, until it became the distinct sounds of men screaming and shouting, of weapons clashing, of horses mad with
fear. The air was so thick with ash it might as well have
been night, and they blundered forward towards the sounds,
their horses picking their way over the fallen corpses of
friend and foe alike. They were upon the battlefield before
they were fully aware of it, when a group of squatty
fellows with looted short-swords swarmed towards them
fròm the shadows.

Dylan wheeled his horse around as he unsheathed his
sword and felt the beast under him respond as if it had not
already had a day's hard travel. Its elegant hooves lashed
out behind and caught one attacker in the chest while
Dylan slashed another from the shoulder to belly. Aenor
charged into the fray swinging the odd-shaped sword across
the up-lifted arm of a Shadowling. The green gem in the
hilt glinted evilly against the ashy darkness, then raised a
shaft of clear but verdant light. The ashes swirled away as
if repelled by the light itself, and she cut down another

man. Dylan dispatched three more, and the spare horses accounted for a couple before the rest of the troop retreated into the murk.

Aenor seemed enveloped by the green light of her beryl and it cast strange shadows under her eyes and below her chin. Unsmiling, dry-eyed, and grim, she appeared to him the embodiment of some fearsome goddess of death. He could not believe this was the same woman who had clutched him between lubricious loins and howled with pleasure beneath him only hours before. That seemed a sweet dream, and he had woken into nightmare.

"Do you know any songs for clearing the air?" he asked as if nothing had changed.

She gave him a look as if he was a stranger, then sighed and smiled a bit, banishing the crone into nothingness. "I think I can do something about it."

Aenor held the sword by its short quillons, so a crosslike shadow fell upon her breast. The beryl reflected onto her wide brow and she sang a long, deep note that seemed to rattle his bones. It went on until it was almost painful, the area where they sat on their horses almost pulsing with a green light that became yellower and yellower, until is was a miniature sun. A wind screamed at them from their backs, a howling, rainless storm that tore the song from her lips as it ripped the ashy overcast to tatters, revealing the hard-pressed forces of the King and the startled faces of masses of Shadowlings.

Franconian banners bowed in the howling gale and their poles snapped and broke, the cloth billowing away like strange birds. Lines of men-at-arms wavered and shielded themselves from stinging swirls of dust for perhaps three breaths and then returned to the grim task of slaughter, the ragged but numerous Shadowlings pressed forward like a silent tide.

The sudden illumination seemed to hearten the Franconian forces and they regrouped and began to strike at their foes. It was like holding back the sea, because the Shadowlings did not care if they died. Dylan took this in and urged his steed forward. A bolt of lightning almost blinded him for several seconds, and then he was surrounded by the mindless faces of the Shadow Folk. He cut them down.

Aenor's horse reared and lashed out at a pair of men. She grasped the sword by its hilt and slashed at another foe as she clung to her reins. Another crack of lightning rent the gloom, and Dylan realized it was no sudden storm, but some great magic conjured by King Louis. Then he was too busy staying alive to think of anything. He could see Aenor whirling on horseback, hacking down Shadowlings like sheaves of grain, and once she paused for a second and shouted a strange word, but for the most part he barely knew what he did, except to kill the twisted faces that swirled around him. Once he nearly ran down a little bunch of Franconian men-at-arms before he distinguished friend from foe.

Aenor kept abreast of him, shining like a beacon, the blade of her sword red with blood and her smut-smeared face spattered with it. Her blue eyes were enormous and somehow deadly, and he glimpsed again the fearful crone. Dylan heard a sound like distant thunder behind him and turned to look. The ground shook and a herd of licornes raced into the fray, stabbing with their horns and slashing with their bright hooves.

His horse stumbled and a quarterstaff rammed him in the chest at the same instant, and Dylan flew out of his saddle as his sword arced away. He rolled to his feet and ducked as a stave whistled past his head. He lunged under the stick and caught the Shadowling in the chest, wrested the weapon away, and laid about him. He tried to reclaim his horse, but the press of Shadowlings was too great.

Aenor wheeled her horse around and urged it towards him. The air was again thick with smoke, the acrid stench of lightning and blood, and flying debris. Time seemed to pause for a moment as a fist-sized rock sailed through the murk and struck her wide brow. She looked surprised for an instant, then sagged across her horse's neck and slid off onto the ground.

Time paused. *She could not be dead. The gods could not be so cruel.* He would destroy the world if she was gone.

Dylan leapt across the space between them, smashing aside a Shadowling or two, and snatched the Crystal Sword from her limp hand as he straddled her fallen body. A jolt nearly numbed his arm as his hand closed around the hilt. He bellowed in rage and pain and felt the surge of change race across his muscles. The beast roared, and he was both man and animal. He barely noticed a soft nose butting him in the back as Aenor's horse pushed him aside and stood over her still form.

The sword was alive in his hand as he sprang forward to meet a fresh wave of Shadow Folk. The licornes thundered towards him, and he saw the unnamed beast which had carried him so many leagues across the land, trumpeting his challenge. Dylan leapt up onto the bony back and grasped the rough mane, snarling from slavering chops. His hands were still human enough to grasp the sword, but they were darkly furred and silver clawed.

Dylan swept down upon the hordes of mindless Shadowlings, the licornes behind him and beside him, belling their challenge and striking out with hooves and horns. Across the field the Franconians took new heart under the bolt-rocked sky and surged forward, catching the Shadow Folk between the two forces.

It was a screaming nightmare of blood and slaughter, and Dylan thought of nothing but hacking away at anything that stood in his path. His arm ached but the sword pulsed with killing. The great beast beneath him lunged and feinted as if trained to the task as they struggled through the howling horde.

A clear note rang across the clamor and Dylan dimly wondered if Gabriel the archangel had chosen this moment to blow the last trump. Then a dozen mounted knights charged towards him, their faces hidden under their helms. But the blazing aura of the King was unmistakable, the nearly blinding light of a godful man who handled his sword with more vigor than skill. The two groups met, joined, melted, and turned as one to ride down the remainder of the Shadow Folk.

It was over with a sort of shudder, a stumbling halt as the Franconians found there was no one left to kill but a few stragglers. Bodies lay in heaps across the field, and there was a kind of stillness broken only by the groans of the wounded and the soft moan of the dying wind. The knights paused as if bewildered, sheathed their swords, and drooped their shoulders in exhaustion.

King Louis raised his helm and looked at Dylan, shadow-rimmed eyes bright with weariness and relief. Still more beast than man, Dylan could only growl a greeting before he turned the licorne aside and went in search of Aenor.

The horses marked where she lay, the three mares and the stallion standing in a square around her, the corpses of broken-headed Shadowlings a mute testimony to their part in the battle. Dylan slid off the licorne, patted its flank with a silver claw-hand and bent over Aenor. She seemed so still, her golden hair unplaited into a froth around her head. There was a gash on her forehead and it bled sluggishly.

Dylan scooped her up, his claws tearing her garments a little, and howled. The sound rolled across the field and he saw that Louis had followed him. The slender king dismounted and reached out a hand to Aenor's long throat. His body's light coruscated like a rainbow, and the air smelled sweet—the clean, green smell of springtide.

Aenor lay so still in his arms, as if she slept, and Dylan felt his heart clench. He hugged her awkwardly against his chest, and stared with beast eyes at the baleful green beryl in the leaf-shaped sword he had dropped beside him. He remembered the power of it, the mindless killing, and he wished it had never been made. He heard the groans of the dying and smelled the blood and bowels of the fallen, and wondered how any man could take pleasure in it. He gave a bellow of anguish and rage, a dumb animal voice of his hatred and senseless death, and drew Aenor closer against him.

Morel's big black stallion nickered, pawed the ground, and blew warmly against the nape of Dylan's neck while the licornes stood in ranks around them, encircling the three of them. Aenor stirred and moaned faintly.

"She lives," Louis said, his voice ragged from smoke and shouting. The King glanced uncomfortably from Dylan to the woman and back again, and he looked very sad. "It might have been kinder if she had not," he added softly.

The woman's eyes fluttered as she lifted a hand to her brow. She opened her eyes and for a moment Dylan glimpsed again the fierce, unforgiving face of the hag. Then she smiled a little and stroked his ugly snout. Dylan felt the beast retreat at her touch, and his features re-formed.

"Did we win?" she asked simply.

XXI

King Louis, Dylan decided later, was a good man, but he did not have a great heart and he did not understand how to deal with the Plantagenet personality. His first mistake was to ignore Aenor's insistence that she would have no other man but Dylan, and his second was to exclude her from the council where a decision about her would be made. Dylan was allowed in as the only available Albionese, so that King Arthur's interests might be at least nominally upheld.

They were in a council chamber in the fortress at Paris a week after the Battle of Angers: the eight nobles Louis considered sufficiently loyal and trustworthy to listen to, the Bishop of Paris, Dylan, and a sweaty cleric to record the events. The room had been scrubbed and new tapestries hung upon the walls, fresh reeds scattered on the floor, but it still had an unused, musty feeling. Dylan tried not to squirm in his high-backed uncomfortable chair, and he tried not to smile at the singular lack of enthusiasm expressed by the assembled noblemen at the idea of welcoming the daughter of Geoffrey Plantagenet into their families. Two had begged off—quite legitimately—on the grounds of consanguinity, being sons or grandsons of her mother's siblings. The real issue was the taint of bewitchment, but no one, not even the Bishop, spoke of that. Dylan would have found the situation highly amusing if the circumstances had been otherwise. As it was, he had to curb the urge to turn into a bear and rend the lot of them to pieces.

There was a startled shout outside the closed doors, then a sweet, flutelike tone Dylan would have known anywhere, and the doors splintered into a million pieces. Aenor stepped across the rubble without lifting her skirts, dragging debris and two frantic guards who were loathe to lay hands on her in her wake. She wore a plain white gown of fine Flemish linen, embroidered round the throat and sleeves in bold blue, her hair unbraided in a golden waterfall; and the gaudy scabbard of the Crystal Sword made a barbaric splash of color against her garb. A blueish bruise on her temple was all that remained to remind him of Angers. The sight of it still gave him chills. She might have died, despite the plans and plots of Sal and Beth, and he could not bear the thought.

Aenor marched up to the long table and glared at everyone. "Which one of you has had the audacity to agree to marry me against my will?"

His Grace, the Duke of Burgundy, rose to his feet and smiled. "None, my lady."

"And you, you little pipsqueak, did you really believe you could dispose of me like some extra cows?" Aenor addressed the King, blue eyes blazing and with no respect whatever for the dignity of his office. It brought a fine rosy flush to her cheeks and made her even more beautiful. Most of those present had not seen her before, and Dylan could tell they were trying to weigh her appearance against their knowledge that she was in her mid sixties as the world counted years.

Louis shrugged. "We do not marry to please ourselves."

Aenor pushed her hair off her shoulders in an impatient gesture that lifted her breasts against the fabric of her gown provocatively. Then she put both hands on the end of the table and looked directly at the King. "Just because yours is dreadful is no reason to try to disrupt my life. I pity your wife and her joyless beddings—done from duty and not affection.''

''Silence!'' snapped the Bishop. ''This council is no affair of yours. Return to your quarters at once.''

''Go suck an egg,'' she replied. ''Or an orange. It might sweeten your disposition. I shall wed none but Dylan d'Avebury—and I would get about it, if I were you, since I have no desire to produce a bastard.''

Dylan was stunned. It was possible, of course, and women somehow knew these things, mysterious creatures that they were. He found himself blushing under the curious glances of several eyes, as if he had done something shameful. At the same time he knew Aenor was perfectly capable of pretending a pregnancy which did not yet exist, since the loss of her maidenhood might make her a less desirable marriage prize.

Louis looked hurt and disappointed. ''I thought better of you, Dylan. Still, it is no impediment.''

Dylan trembled with rage, the beast-wolf within him baying silently for release. He swallowed the bitter bile that rose in his throat and took a deep breath. ''What do you see when you look at her, *mon roi?* Do you see a woman of flesh and blood who has suffered an imprisonment of mind and body such as would have broken the spirit of any man amongst us? No, you see nothing but an heiress, a pawn to be played in the game of power and dominion. Do you consult with her noble brother, the King of Albion? No, you labor in haste to bind her estates to the Crown. I came to Franconia to find Aenor, and if my task were naught but rescue, I would not presume to my claim. But she is the song of my heart, and while I may be unfit to kiss the hem of her gown, at least she is more to me than land and power. If anyone is unworthy in this, it is you, my lord.''

''So you care nothing for great estates, but you did not

hesitate to ravish the poor girl at the first opportunity. Of course she fancies herself in love with you, her savior and rescuer. Women lack the wit to—''

"Enough, you whey-faced excuse for a King!" Aenor shouted, cutting Louis off. "The land must weep to bear your tread. It is your wits which are addled. I will sing the roof down on your fat head!''

"What does she mean?" asked the Count of Poitou anxiously.

"She has a lovely voice," Dylan said more calmly than he felt, "but I have seen her bring down a cave with it."

"She will not do any of that," Louis said, and lifted his hands to perform some magical gesture. Then he screamed and pressed his fingers to his brow where once a silvery birch leaf had rested for a moment.

The air shimmered and a smell like spring invaded the stuffy chamber. Beth, the Lady of the Birches, hovered about the shining surface of the table as the nobles gaped and the Bishop and the young priest crossed themselves and muttered Latin phrases. Louis looked ill, as if the vision of the goddess ate at his vitals.

"Mortals waste such time in bickering," she told Dylan, "I wonder they have any left for living." Then she looked at him. "You *still* have not learned to ask for aid, dear one, and I grew tired of waiting." She turned her lambent gaze on the King.

Louis bowed his head, looking older than his years, and rested his hands on the table. His lips moved silently in some prayer. Beth smiled benignly, her exquisite beauty well revealed by the scantiness of her leafy gown.

"Begone, foul creature," he said aloud.

The goddess laughed. It was a sound like all the freshets of springtide gushing past the last ice of winter, like the murmur of wind in young green leaves. "Alas, poor Louis, I am not so easily banished. Your young God has no power over me—poor crippled thing that you have made him." She turned and twirled, sending her draperies out in a leafy flutter. "No god has dominion over me, for I am life itself. *I* am the rebirth and the resurrection, and when you perish, you will come to me, to lie in my dark bosom, until you are called to rise again."

"Blasphemy!" bellowed the Bishop.

"Poor little man," Beth cooed. "Did you really believe you could escape me? Did you know that all your prayers and sweet smokes came to me? Pitiful Mary was but a face I wore for a time. I am Maiden, Mother, the Hag, and my will brings you forth and calls you back."

The Bishop leapt to his feet and held his scapular cross out from his chest. "By the sign of the holy cross, I send you back to the Hell from which you rose!"

Beth bent down and touched the thing, and the bishop stared at the garland of leaves which now hung around his neck. Then he tore them off in a fury and raced out of the room, screaming. Aenor and one of the dukes both burst into laughter, and Dylan grinned in spite of himself.

"Females!" shouted the King, in the voice of one tried to the end of his patience. He pounded a fist on the table in frustration. "I wish that God had never made you!"

"But he didn't," Beth answered. "Not the God you think you worship. It was quite different from what you might imagine—but that is not a tale for this occasion.

"You have done well, young Dylan, and you have pleased me in your labors. I count myself fortunate to have a place in your great heart which grieves so in the death of even the White Folk. You are such a gently-made knight, so caring in your ways. Were the Grail still achievable, you might seek it with a good will. But that ship has sailed out of the reach of man for now."

"I thank you for your words, gracious lady, and for your aid in my quest. The tokens of your presence have saved my life many times." He touched the green tunic he wore and made a reverent half bow. "I shall wear the birches with honor until I come, at last, to you."

"That," she replied briskly, "is a matter for heralds. My servant, Louis, look at me!" The King lifted his head unwillingly and stared at the goddess. "It is my plan that these two shall wed and bear the children I have foreseen. Their son will battle the Shadow, and their daughter will suffer greatly to accomplish the ends which are needful for the world. Aenor, child, give him the sword you bear. It will be a small consolation, and he will use it for his God's ends, which are also mine."

Aenor hesitated, fondled the great beryl stone for a long moment, and looked at Dylan. He turned his palms up with a shrug. "I wished to make it my dower gift," she said quietly.

"Dylan wishes no sword to lie between you. What did your grandmother tell you do do with the jewel?"

"If I could not give it to the man I love, then give it to God. So be it." Aenor reached down and unbuckled the wide belt that graced her slender hips, removed the Crystal Sword in its scabbard, and slid it down the table with an expression almost like relief on her face. "It was a heavy burden, though I did not know it." She slipped around the table and reached for Dylan's hand.

The sword lay in front of Louis, the gems in the scabbard gleaming faintly in the light coming in from the high, narrow windows. The beryl glowed like a great green eye. He frowned a moment, then reached out a hand to touch the hilt. He gasped. "Such power! I am unfit to wield such power."

"True," said Beth, "but you are the best Franconia has at the moment. Carry it against the Darkness and all will be well. Raise it against the Light, and it will slay you." She was gone, leaving behind only a clean smell and a memory.

There was an enormous uproar in the corridor beyond the broken door. Dylan half expected to see the Bishop returning with a troop of incense-armed priests or at least some guardsmen. Instead, he saw his mother, and behind her, King Arthur and Doyle, plus shouting Franconian and Albionese knights and milling men-at-arms.

"Who have you the right to sign treaties in my name?" roared Arthur good-humoredly. Then he stopped and stared at Aenor. "Sister?" he whispered. "But surely this cannot be."

Aenor regarded her younger brother critically, taking in the ruddy hair and a beard a little tinged with grey, the strong white teeth, and the air of easy authority which covered his travel-stained garments. The Fire Sword hung easily from his hip, the ruby in its hilt flashing wickedly.

"You have grown up quite handsome," she replied, "which I never imagined you would. You were such a scrawny boy."

"Sweet-tongued as ever, I see. Though it is some miracle, you are most assuredly my sister, untouched by time. No one else ever had those eyes." Arthur glanced from Aenor to Dylan and back again, taking in their clasped hands. Then he gave Eleanor d'Avebury a curious look. "It seems I will have you in the family after all, doesn't it." Then he pushed forward and bowed to Louis. "I hope you will forgive my bursting in this way, but when that damned treaty arrived I could hardly sit around Westminster and twiddle my thumbs, could I? My Queen has often chided me for my lack of manners."

Eleanor d'Avebury walked over to Dylan as he rose. She raked him with grey eyes, and he could see the lines of strain around them. A few weeks had aged her terribly, and while the love shone in her eyes, the fear for his safety did as well. *Would Aenor clutch at their firstborn this way?* he wondered. Then he embraced his mother and muffled her sobs against his shoulder. He patted her shoulder futilely and felt like a beast for making her suffer. With a kind of chill he remembered Beth's words, that his and Aenor's son would someday battle the Shadow and the

Darkness, and he cursed silently that he was no more than a pawn in the game of the deities. Mortal suffering was nothing to them.

Untrue, young Dylan. We share your pain and we do these acts that the world might not gutter out like a candle in the wind of Darkness. Your task is done. Go now and live in such peace as you can persuade your contentious bride into. Go to the south, into the sunlight, and raise horses and babies. It was Sal's voice he heard, stern and acerbic, the whisper of the willows.

And my children?

We are all hostages to fortune, my son.

Eleanor raised her head and brushed tears off her face, smearing dirt under red-rimmed eyes. "Do not argue with her, Dylan. She always has the last word. Now, introduce me to my daughter-to-be. I promise I will not cry again until the wedding." She gripped his hand almost painfully, and Dylan knew what her words cost her. She gazed at his strange silvery hand. "Besides, you must have quite a tale to add to my collection. Perhaps it will inspire the king again. *The Lay of Dylan Silver-Hand and . . .*"

"Aenor Golden-Throat," he said, and joined the hands of the two mortal women who rivaled any goddesses in his heart. He was glad he could not see into the future, that he was spared foreknowledge, that he would be surprised at his inevitable death, and that he would not know the moment when Aenor would slip from his hands and when his mother would return to Sal's final bitter embrace. Dylan clung to the promise of children, sunlight, horses, time. He clasped Aenor's shoulders and knew eternity would not suffice. She turned her face upwards, smiling, glowing, and he was almost content.

LOOK FOR THE THIRD BOOK
IN THE CHRONIQUE D'AVEBURY,
THE RAINBOW SWORD,
BY ADRIENNE MARTINE-BARNES,
COMING SOON FROM AVON BOOKS!